EVENING INTRIGUE

A Clay Arnold Thriller

STUART FABE

Author's Note

THE NATURE OF LIGHT is a source of enduring fascination for me. We all recognize what light looks like in its various forms, natural and artificial, but to articulate the essence of light to someone is a challenge. And yet, since the dawn of life on Earth, light has been an indispensable source of energy for most species of flora and fauna.

In preparing to write *Evening Intrigue* I saw an opportunity to explore the concepts of light from Clay Arnold's perspective as a world-renowned photographer, and from his friend Tori Rawlins's point of view as a person who only began seeing the visual world in her later forties. Interesting juxtaposition, I think. Certainly for Clay, managing light is essential to his work as a photographer. For Tori, light presents a rebirth into a world that she had previously known only by sound, touch, smell, and taste.

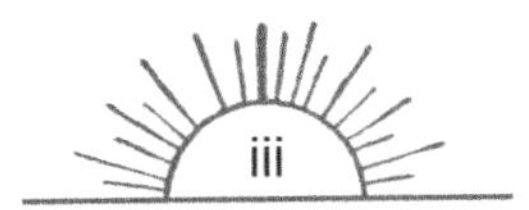

As with all of my novels, I wrote *Evening Intrigue* purely for entertainment. Much of the story is rooted in the conjurings of my fertile imagination. I'm a storyteller, after all. This is the sixth suspense story in my Clay Arnold series. As for my hero/alter ego, Clay Arnold, well let's just say that he keeps evolving as a man who no longer feels the visceral urges to be an avenging vigilante. Instead, he's found happiness as a devoted husband, father, and friend. Alas, Clay has an uncanny knack for getting drawn into serious conflicts from which he has to extricate himself and others.

Writing suspense fiction has become a great source of intrigue and satisfaction for me. I enjoy researching various topics and try to craft exciting, page-turning plots; but my true enjoyment comes from creating believable, unique, and diverse characters. Ultimately, I feel that I write most fluidly when I just relax and leave myself open to unforeseen possibilities. I basically just open the mental tap and watch what flows out. I sincerely hope you enjoy reading *Evening Intrigue* as much as I enjoyed bringing the story into the light of day.

Stuart Fabe

Dedication

*In Loving Memory of
Alan and Donnabelle Stanley
No Finer Couple Ever Walked the Earth*

And To

*The Three Stanley Sisters
Marla Helton, Brenda Rabold, and Linda Wall
Who Have Endured Great Heartache and
Continue to Shine*

Chapter 1

"I CAN SEE!" WHEN MY lifelong friend, Tori Rawlins, cried out those three stunning words a year ago, it changed the dynamics of our family forever! Where do I even begin? How can I explain the inexplicable? How can I or anyone in our family ever adequately express the profound gratitude we feel for Tori's emergence from an existence in total darkness to the wondrous light of our visual world?

Ever since her birth some forty-plus years ago, Tori had been blind. She was born with a

congenital defect with no hope of medical correction. Then last year, Robert Midew, the president of the Keweenaw Bay Indian Council in the Upper Peninsula of Michigan, miraculously gave Tori the gift of sight. I know, that sounds like an outlandish exaggeration, but trust me when I say that Robert has very special mystical powers. In appreciation for what my son, Rennie, and I did to help safeguard a sacred Chippewa artifact, and for fighting to defeat an ancient enemy, Robert gave me gifts beyond measure.

Among those benefactions, Tori was given the gift of sight. I still can't believe it. No one can. Watching her explore her newly sighted world day by day, moment by moment is indescribable. Nearly a full year has come and gone since Robert's incredible sorcery brought sight to Tori's eyes, and yet I still notice vestiges of her blind life. Little things like still putting her toe out to check for physical obstructions or extending a hand to help judge distance. In some ways watching Tori navigate her recently bestowed visual world is like watching a child explore and grow and become evermore aware and curious about the life around her. It's truly a life-altering experience for each of us in our family of friends.

In addition to Tori now being able to see, our aged friend, Mace Davis, was imbued with a life-prolonging infusion of inner strength by Robert Midew that should enable him to enjoy life and look after the brewery complex for a few more years yet. Mace is an inspiration to me. We've experienced and survived a lot together, and I'm thrilled beyond the moon that he should be with us for a few more good years. Robert intuited how very important Mace is to me, and I'll never be able to thank him enough for his insight and caring.

And my darling wife, Maggie, received a flawless diamond from Robert the size of a large hen's egg. On a lark Maggie and I had it appraised a couple of months ago by a reputable gemologist, and I don't even want to say how much he said it's worth. For now, we're perfectly happy to let it nest in the deerskin pouch Robert had wrapped it in, and we keep it stored in its original wooden box on the fireplace mantel in our bedroom.

And I would be remiss if I didn't mention another important gift Robert has given my family. Our adopted son, Rennie, played a major role in helping Robert and the Chippewa people protect a precious tribal relic, the sacred Megis shell. In so doing Rennie and his National Park Service supervisor, Ranger Kelli Katterman, earned Robert's deep respect, and in turn, Robert offered to work closely with them in presenting the magnificent Paleo-Indian cave art that they found under Brockway

Mountain to the outside world. Robert's guidance should prove instrumental in ensuring Rennie's doctoral candidacy in Sociology at Northwestern University and in launching his professional career. As Rennie's dad, I couldn't be prouder.

Robert's gift to me was his gifts to all of them, and I never could've received anything more meaningful. Honestly, I've never been a devout man of God, but I swear the events of the last year, surviving the terrifying lows and soaring with the stunning highs, have brought me closer to finally acknowledging that Homo sapiens ain't exactly calling all of the shots. I don't know who is, but I know it definitely isn't us.

As for me, well, my name's Clay Arnold, and I live here at our home in the old beer brewery complex along with the aforementioned folks. I'm a photographer by trade, and I'm proud of the body of photographic work I've done over the past thirty-plus years and also grateful for the recognition and remuneration I've continued to receive for my efforts. But at my core these days, I am a devoted husband, father, and friend. Yes, I admit to having exorcised my angry demons in years gone by as an avenging vigilante, exacting my personal form of justice and executing racists, right-wing extremists, and yes, a few sons of bitches who out and out deserved a good ass frying with my Demon Camera. Yeah,

I admit to not having been, uh, very tolerant of people who prey on vulnerable folks, but being a husband and father has fortunately distracted me in kinder directions. In fact, anymore I sometimes give people more credit than they deserve, but that's a redeeming fault I'm learning to live with. As I enter my late forties, I try not to think about the many conflicts I've endured, several of which I initiated with malice in my heart. Despite those episodes, I now prefer to meet people at least halfway with a live-and-let-live attitude. I say "prefer" because I've come to know how rudely life's journey can throw me a nasty curve that threatens the safety of people I care about.

Right now as I contemplate these mind-blowing thoughts, I'm standing on our rooftop deck overlooking the renovated nineteenth-century beer brewery complex that I own. Maggie, along with our younger son, Bodie, and I live in the original bottling building which we've totally redesigned over the years with ultra-modern amenities. We've blended the old architecture with a fresh contemporary interior and updated lighting and utilities. It's also the site of my antique camera museum which Mace curates and looks after when I'm away on photography assignments.

As I look across the cobblestone courtyard, I see the old power plant where Mace lives. At age eighty-something he still dutifully takes care of the maintenance of this large property. He's an amazing man, and I couldn't ask for a better friend. We've literally saved each other's butt on more than one occasion, and he's privy to secrets that I've never even shared with Maggie.

And now I see Tori step out onto the porch of the old original farmhouse that the Block brothers built when they emigrated from Bavaria in 1856. It's here that they opened their beer brewery along the White River just a few miles above Indianapolis, Indiana. Tori has lived alone in the farmhouse ever since her brother and my oldest friend, Weed Rawlins, was killed by a henchman's bullet several years ago now. A deep sense of sadness wells up inside me as I think about how Weed died in my arms when we were searching for Samuel Morse's hidden art treasure. The sadness grows even deeper when I consider that Weed never had a chance to witness his sister's ability to see.

Maggie steps out onto the deck to join me, and we enjoy the warm glow that the early afternoon sun is casting on us. We both look down at Tori's position on the farmhouse's porch and watch as she turns to face the sun and absorb its bright energy. For years the sun was a source of warmth for Tori, but she never experienced its brightness until Robert Midew endowed her with the gift of sight.

"Well, what do you think, Maggie? If you'd known in advance everything we've been through since we got together, do you think you would've hooked up with an aging juvenile delinquent like me?"

"Well, Clay honey, you know that's something I think I'll just have to ponder a little." A few moments go by without her saying anything else, and I turn to see if she's serious or not when I get a playful elbow to my ribs. "Well, Mr. Arnold, it is a very valid question, but you know I'm in this marriage for the long haul. Now having said that, please … for the love of everything sacred to us … can we please put all of the death, carnage, and heartache behind us?!"

"I say that's a great idea, darling, actually both things: Our staying married for the long haul, and our never getting involved in any more turmoil. You know me, I'm as easygoing as a little lamb anymore. I mean seriously, Maggie, what could go wrong?" I regret those words the instant they leave my mouth, and my antiperspirant fails a little when I glance into my beloved wife's eyes and see a look that could freeze molten lava. "Uh oh," I manage to mumble as I prepare myself for a little "Maggie education."

"What could go wrong you ask, Sir Husband? Gee, where should I begin? How about the time my niece got kidnapped by that wacko astronomy professor at Kissinger College in Greencastle?"

"Yeah, but we got her back safely, though!" I feebly try to reply.

"Silence!" Maggie asserts. "Or, darling, how about the time Rennie almost went over a thousand-foot cliff at Dead Horse Point in Utah?" Maggie softens her voice a little, and continues, "And I know you haven't forgotten Weed getting murdered in Washington when you guys were searching for clues to Samuel Morse's art treasure, or when Bodie and the president of the United States got abducted by Russian thugs on the Brule River in Northern Wisconsin. And, those are just the things that I know about!"

"No, I haven't forgotten," I say softly as I pull her close to me, and her tears fall onto my neck. "I'm so sorry, Maggie, I never wanted any of that for any of us. You know that. You're the best part of my life, and you and the boys and Tori and Mace are the only things I really care about. Whatever fame I've achieved and whatever assets I've acquired, it all pales in comparison. You know that."

"I know, Clay. I know that, but I swear when you told me about how you and Rennie were nearly buried under Brockway Mountain, and that none of us would've ever known what happened to you, it's just more than I can bear."

I stroke Maggie's hair lightly and hold her close. "I'm sorry," I say again, "I shouldn't have told you about that." We just lean into each other for long healing moments with our arms wrapped around the other, feeling as one. It's the most peaceful feeling that I know. That is, until the mood is broken.

"Hey, what are you guys doing up there?" we hear Tori holler from down below on her porch. "You're too darn old to be making out!" she jests. "Or maybe ol' Clay is feeling tuckered and needs a woman to lean on. How's he holding up, Maggie?"

Maggie looks down at my bulging dungarees and hollers back to Tori as only close, sisterly friends can, "Oh, he appears to be holding up pretty well on his own. Just me, Clay, and Mr. Happy up here!"

"Darn it, Maggie, is nothing sacred?!" I hoarsely chide.

"Well," Tori replies, "I'm making some great soup and salads down here if you want to have some lunch instead of nibbling on each other. Should be ready in about twenty minutes."

"Sounds great, Tori," Maggie shouts back. "We'll be down in a bit, but first my darling husband and I need to, uh, consummate our earlier communication."

"Wattaya say, Mr. Former Avenging Vigilante, care to help a damsel in distress undress?" she suggestively offers my way.

"Maggie, seriously though, it's important that you know that I heard everything you said earlier about being scared, and all of the bad stuff that's happened to our family. It scares me too, honey. All I want is for us all to be safe and happy."

She looks in my eyes. "I know that, Clay, and I'm sure we'll talk about it again in the future. It's part of the healing process, but for now let's put that heartache behind us and go burn some calories and relieve some stress before we sit down for lunch." And at that we step inside, and Maggie lowers the blinds, gives me her come-hither look, and pulls me close.

"But where's Bodie?" I try to ask maturely. "We don't want him walking in on us." I stammer.

"Not a problem, darling. He and Mace went to Indianapolis to pick up some things Bodie wants to take with him this summer to Camp Voyageur. They'll be gone for a while yet."

I look into Maggie's glowing green eyes and slowly begin to enjoy the trim form of her welcoming body. Being the spiritual cuss that I am, I stare heavenward and ardently proclaim the first words that come into my naughty brain, "Oh Lordy, there is a God!"

Chapter 2

TORI STIRS THE LARGE POT of hearty soup on her stovetop and marvels at how the aromatic ingredients simmer and swirl. Corn, black beans, tomatoes, little chunks of chicken, garlic, and basil all coalesce into miniature whirlpools with each stroke from her wooden spoon. She adds a bay leaf that floats along the surface like a small boat riding on the eddies of a frothy waterway. Her eyes widen in pensive wonder when she considers that such a scene is mundane and meaningless to any normally sighted person, but for her, even though she's been

able to see for nearly a year now, the motion of the soup's ingredients is like a small spiral universe that still needs to be explored and comprehended. "I can see!" Tori says aloud to herself, and a small reflective tear falls into the soup, adding a drop of human salt to the recipe.

She quickly puts the finishing touches on the three salads, sets the table, fills water glasses, places a lid on the bubbling soup pot, lowers the heat to simmer, and heads off to her bedroom to finish getting dressed. She slides effortlessly into her skinny jeans and puts on a lavender-colored sweater that nicely accentuates her curves. Her long, naturally blond hair cascades over her shoulders nestling her shapely torso.

"Hmmm, not bad for a gal in her late forties!" She muses to herself. "So, some people say that I'm pretty. I'm still trying to figure out exactly what that means, but I'll take it as a compliment."

She hears the front screen door open and close, followed by Maggie's voice, "Tori, Clay and I are here. Where are you?"

"C'mon back to the bedroom, Maggie. I'm just finishing getting dressed. Clay, would you please stir the soup for us a little? It's almost ready."

"There you are!" Maggie says as she enters the bedroom and sees Tori standing in front of the floor-length mirror, shifting from side to side inspecting her appearance. "How do I look, Maggs?" she asks her best friend.

"You look mahvelous, dahling!" Maggie croons. "Simply mahvelous!"

"Cool! Hurray for me!" Tori chirps. "You know, Maggie, I'm still getting used to the concepts of what people find attractive and what they don't. I was thinking a minute ago that some people tell me I'm pretty, but I'm not so sure what that means. I mean, I'm just Tori! What do you think, Maggie?"

"Well, you and I are best buds so I'm a little biased, but objectively I think you're a very beautiful woman!"

"Really, Maggie?! But I'm in my forties, and my face and body are showing some age. Do you really think I'm attractive?"

"Well, let me put it to you this way. Do you have any idea how many men and some women turn their heads to look at you when you walk down the street or enter a room?"

"No, not really," Tori admits. "I mean maybe a little, but I think they're looking at my clothes or maybe a speck of spinach that's stuck to my teeth or something."

They both laugh at that image. "Why don't you ask Clay what he thinks about your physical appearance. He's photographed some of the most gorgeous women in the world."

"Well, Clay and I have known each other since we were about three years old so he might be a bit biased too."

"Yeah, well he's still a guy and a bit of a horn-dog at that. I'd be curious to hear what he says, but I honestly do think you're a very attractive woman."

Tori shifts herself from side to side again as she takes a final look in the mirror. "Well, I am who I am! C'mon Maggs, let's go eat some soup before Clay scarfs it all down!"

The two friends sashay into the kitchen and find me with the wooden stirring spoon in my mouth. "Hot!" I manage to exhale. "Really good but really hot!"

"Does it need anything else?" Tori asks.

"No, it's perfect with just the right amount of salt!"

Tori smiles to herself thinking about how her tear had dropped into the soup a few minutes ago. "Great! Well, bon appétit! Let's eat, guys!"

We sit at the kitchen table and begin to enjoy Tori's soup and salad. I look around and see many objects that I'm familiar with, including Weed's harmonicas, a cherry side table that Mace made, and some of my favorite photographs. Tori sees me looking at a photo that I snapped several years ago of her and her late brother, Weed. As they often did, they were performing at Stella's Diner, a great local restaurant by day and a popular night club by night that draws patrons from miles away. Mace and I had gone to Stella's for a night of great grub and spirited entertainment which is always the case when Stella's around. It was a hoot, that is until Newt and Twit Hacker started running over folks in the parking lot with their pickup truck sporting a Confederate battle flag. Yes, that's right, the same Hacker brothers that attacked Tori, Rennie, and our dog, Lex, several years ago along the White River and later blew up the Hoosier Homestead Insurance Company and damn-near demolished Conner Prairie Hospital. Weed, Mace, and I were finally able to kill them and their crazed father, Clement, saving many other lives. Okay, we had some help, too, from our lifelong friend, Trent Reynolds, and the entire Indiana State Police Department. We all stuck together and survived a series of very ugly encounters. Seems like a long time ago now.

"It's almost like a dream when I think of Weed," Tori says softly. "I'm so grateful that you took pictures of us, Clay. I still miss him so much and will always remember how devoted he was to me; how much he never wanted my blindness to stand in the way of my living as normal a life as possible." She gently squeezes my hand, and I respectfully nod my understanding.

"He was the best!" I reply. "When you guys performed together at Stella's, everyone stopped what they were doing and listened. No clatter of dishes. No loud laughter and side conversations. You guys owned the place!"

A few moments pass and Maggie interjects to lighten the mood, "So, Clay, Tori asked earlier me if I think she's attractive, which I definitely do, but I suggested that she ask your opinion given the number of beautiful women you've photographed."

"Uh, yeah, sure." I reply. "You're attractive, Tori." I take another spoonful of soup and look up to see both Maggie and Tori staring at me with expressions that imply, *'That's it?!'* "What?!" I ask. "Did I say something wrong?"

"No, Clay," Maggie replies, "but I thought you might elaborate a little more. Tori says she's still trying to understand the concept of what beauty is."

"Well, seriously, as the old adage goes, *'beauty is in the eye of the beholder.'* What do you think, Tori?"

"Intellectually, I understand that, Clay, but I'm still getting used to how we culturally define what's beautiful and what isn't."

"You know, Tori, as I think of it you were probably more tuned into real beauty when you were blind than most of us because you took people as they came without factoring in their physical attributes. Now, having said that, I objectively find you to be a very attractive woman. Surely, you've seen people stare at you."

"She has," Maggie intercedes, "but she thinks it's because people like her clothes or see spinach stuck to her teeth." That comment certainly lightens the mood.

"I suppose," Tori replies softly. "It's all a little bewildering sometimes, you know, having lived my life without sight for so many years, and now, well, you know, life's a bit of a mystery sometimes."

Both Maggie and I nod our understanding, and Maggie asks, "Have your therapy sessions with Dr. Dale been helpful to your dealing with the bewilderment or have they opened up even more questions?"

"Well, both actually. Adrian, I mean Dr. Dale, has been very helpful, especially in my early sighted days. He believes I've been learning to deal with a serious degree of sensory overload as my brain and emotions have struggled to process the constant barrage of images that my vision presents. Everywhere I turn I see something new. It's quite startling at times, and Adrian has helped me calm the stress I feel and process visual stimulation in a more compartmentalized way. But, yeah, Maggie, the therapy sessions have been helpful in quelling the mysteries of living in a sighted world. And, Clay's photography has been very helpful too. As a wise man once said, *'a picture is worth a thousand words.'* Regardless, life is filled with mysteries, yes?"

"And, if you want to witness even more mystery," I add, "just wait until you meet Robert Midew and learn more about the ancient Chippewa Indian legends and the teachings of their Midewin medicine men. There are legends that are based in far more fact than we know."

"I can't wait to meet him and thank him for giving me a whole new way of visually seeing the world."

"Me too!" Maggie adds enthusiastically. "For a lot of reasons, not the least of which is for saving my husband and Rennie from fates worse than death under Brockway Mountain. Have you spoken with him recently, Clay?"

"I have," I reply.

"And?!" Maggie prompts.

"Well first, you haven't met Robert yet so it'll be hard for you to appreciate his, uh, unique talents until you do. He actually called me this morning to tell me about the curating he's doing with Rennie and Ranger Kelli Katterman to help prepare the magnificent Paleo-Indian art under the mountain for presentation to the world. They're getting closer. Robert is very excited and proud that the Keweenaw Bay Indian Community, in concert with the National Park Service, will be making a major announcement about the ancient Chippewa cave paintings. He asked me if I could recommend a trustworthy art organization that would be a great match for exhibiting images of the cave art throughout the world. I immediately thought of our great friend, Lucretia Land, and the Land Foundation. I encouraged Robert to do his own research about the Land Foundation so he's comfortable, but I told him that Lucretia would be the best person for him to work with. I gave him Lucretia's telephone number and sent her an email stating that she could expect a call from Robert Midew about a historically important American art project. I didn't go into many details because I want her to hear about the significance of the artwork from Robert. I told her I'd seen the cave art firsthand and assured her that Robert is the real deal. I asked both of them to call me after they spoke."

"Very cool!" Tori evokes. "Very cool, indeed!" Maggie adds.

"Yeah, it's far cooler than you really know," I say. "Robert also said that he's been sensing some troubling energy coming from under the mountain although he chose not to elaborate when I pressed him for what that meant. Like I said, Robert's a huge mystery in his own way."

"Did Robert say anything else?" Maggie asks.

"Well, we talked about the ancient cave paintings and how pleased he was with Rennie and

Kelli's work, and then he said something that surprised me."

"What!?" both Tori and Maggie ask in unison.

"He said that the three of us would be taking a trip very soon and that challenges and opportunities await."

"Uh oh, I wonder what he meant," Maggie offers. "I mean, I like the opportunities part; the challenges part not-so-much. I wonder if he's right, and if so, where we'll be going."

"I've learned to take whatever Robert says as gospel. Let's just say that information has a way of flowing to him. I suspect we'll know soon enough."

We finish eating our lunch, and the three of us make quick order of putting food and condiments in the refrigerator and washing the dishes. Just as we finish, I feel my phone vibrate in my pants pocket and pull it out and see that it's Lucretia calling from the Land Foundation in Chicago.

"Hi there!" I say as I walk outside onto the front porch. "I take it you received my vague email and have spoken with my friend, Robert Midew."

"Hi there, Clay, it's great hearing your voice, and yes, indeed, I have spoken with Mr. Midew. Quite an interesting chap. Is he as intriguing in person as he is on the phone? I couldn't believe what he told me, Clay. He subsequently emailed me a few images of the vast ancient Chippewa cave art, and

I think I can safely say that what they have will totally rewrite the history books about indigenous Indian life and artwork around the Great Lakes. Seriously, the cave paintings are really quite stunning and exhibiting them would be right in the Land Foundation's wheelhouse."

"That's exactly what I told Robert."

"But first, Clay, how are you and Maggie and your close family of friends?"

"We're all doing fine, Lucretia. I'm still running around the globe taking on photographic assignments that excite me. Maggie is working less with her public relations business but still keeping quite busy with a couple of great, long-time clients that would be lost without her. Mace is thriving and doing a masterful job keeping our brewery complex running like a fine watch and loving his work curating our antique camera collection for visiting groups. The Samuel Morse daguerreotype camera that your jerk brother, Malcolm, surreptitiously put up for auction is the star of the collection, and Mace and I beam whenever we look at it. Right now Mace and Bodie are in Indy picking up supplies for Bodie's return to Camp Voyager in a few days. I know Mace will be very sorry that he missed your call."

"Well, please give Mace my very best. I'm delighted that the camera Monsieur Daguerre gave Samuel Morse is in your collection, Clay. You guys certainly earned it. And Tori? How's she getting along these days?"

"Tori is doing remarkably well. She sees a therapist who is helping her deal with the stress of visual overload, but she's doing very well. In fact, she's been singing with a great backup band at Stella's Diner fairly regularly. She and Weed used to perform at the diner together, and Stella's is sorta like home for her. But hey, instead of my telling you about Tori and Maggie, let me put them on the phone. I know they'll both want to talk with you."

"Great!" Lucretia replies. "I have an idea I'd like to share with them."

I walk inside and hand the phone to Maggie and Tori and then return to the front porch to give them some privacy. I sit in the old wooden chair that used to be Weed's favorite. I lean back and put my feet on the handrail just like Weed used to do with his harmonica and a tumbler filled with Four Roses bourbon. A moment later there's a flash of fur and whiskers as my old buddy, Satchmo, leaps up onto my lap purring loudly.

Satchmo is by far the largest darn Maine Coon cat that you ever saw, and we've been hanging out here together at the brewery complex for going on nearly twenty years. I adore the old cat, and he's probably privy to more of my secrets than even Maggie and Mace.

"Hey there, buddy, where've you been?" I ask. "Are keeping our home free of pesky rodents and safe for democracy?" Satchmo replies by rubbing his muzzle against my nose and chin, a display of affection that we've repeated dozens of times over the years. I lightly stroke his throat, and he purrs even louder. A moment later he sees a flying insect and goes bounding after it. Gone. So much for nuzzling.

I put my feet back down on the porch floor, close my eyes, and let the warmth from the sun and a full belly gradually lull me into a deep sleep … and then I dream. In my dream I'm walking in a dark foreboding cavern with Robert Midew at my side. We're under Brockway Mountain in the Keweenaw Peninsula of the Upper Peninsula of Michigan. We're searching for my son, Rennie, and Ranger Kelli Katterman who is his supervisor for his summer internship with the National Park Service. Both Robert and I are deeply concerned because there's also a menacing adversary lurking somewhere under the mountain. The Windigo is an ancient, evil, man-eating spirit that has lived for centuries in this deep, dark world feasting on the flesh of any being that makes the mistake of entering its realm. Robert knows most of the terrain under the mountain, but it has been many years since he's ventured here. I see dread etched on his face. In my dream we enter a great room under the mountain whose walls are studded with diamonds and precious gems and broad veins of copper, gold, and silver. We come to another chamber and see magnificent cave paintings showing various scenes of ancient Indians living peacefully above ground. Their tribal home is nestled along the shores of Lake Superior, known to their Chippewa tribe as Gitche Gumee. One stretch of cave paintings is deeply disturbing though, as it shows the ancient Indians fighting a huge adversary, the Windigo. Many Indians lie dead and Robert evokes an ancient incantation for his fallen ancestors. As we prepare to leave the chamber, Robert halts our steps, and we see the Windigo some fifty yards ahead of us blocking our path. It is the most menacing creature I've ever known. It bellows savagely and begins to charge us. I cry out frightfully and try to run, but my feet are frozen with fear. I then sense a hand on my shoulder. I try to push it away and awaken to see Maggie and Tori standing on the porch with me.

"Clay! Clay, Honey, are you okay? We finished our conversation with Lucretia and heard you moaning out here."

"Hunh?!" I say in confusion as I return to consciousness and realize I'd been experiencing a nightmare. "Oh, yeah, no, I mean I'm okay. Wow, I just had one terrifying dream though. Give me a minute, okay?!" I stand up and try to shed the vestiges of my sleep, but the nightmare hangs on me like a death shroud.

"Are you sure you're okay, Clay?" Tori asks. "You still look a little addled."

"Uh, yeah, I'm okay," I lie. "I just need to get my equilibrium back. Did you guys have a good conversation with Lucretia?"

"Yeah, we sure did," Maggie replies, "and your friend, Robert Midew, was correct about our taking a trip. Lucretia has invited us to visit her in Chicago next week. She wants to show us around the Magnificent Mile and share several of the Land Foundation's fabulous paintings as a way to introduce Tori to their panoply of American art. Isn't that great?!"

"That sounds wonderful," I reply brightly although I still feel like I'm reeling from the horror of my nightmare. "Bodie leaves for Camp Voyager in a couple of days, and Mace and I can take care of everything around here."

"I told Lucretia that I have a performance this weekend at Stella's Diner, but that next week would be perfect," Tori adds. "Wanna come to Chicago, too, Clay? It'll be fun!"

"Uh sure, I love Chicago, and it would be great to see Lucretia, but let me confirm this with Mace when he and Bodie return from Indianapolis, okay?" As if on cue, we hear my old truck's tires on the courtyard's cobblestones and see Bodie and Mace pull up close to where we're standing on the farmhouse porch. Maggie and Tori step off the porch to welcome them home, and to help carry their bags of supplies. I happily watch my family of friends come together and walk off the porch to join them. For a quick second I flash back on the nightmare and picture Robert's face in my mind. He appears deep in thought, and I can't seem to totally shake a feeling of dread from the terrifying images of my dream.

Chapter 3

T HE WEEKEND FINALLY COMES, and Maggie and I are running around our home making sure Bodie has everything packed for his summer at Camp Voyageur. "Hey, let's get a move on, guys!" I holler to Bodie and Maggie. "Bodie's flight is scheduled to depart in two hours."

In truth, we've got plenty of time, but I'm excited about Bodie enjoying his third summer at the same boys' camp I attended when I was his age. Bodie has a direct flight from Indianapolis to Duluth, Minnesota, and then the camp will have a bus filled

with excited kids waiting for him at the airport. From Duluth they'll travel about forty-five minutes southeast back into Wisconsin to Camp Voyageur located on Lake Winneboujou at the edge of the Brule River Forest. Yes, this is the same Brule River where Bodie and President Jacob Horvath got abducted by nasty Russian agents three years ago. I shudder when I think about how close we came to losing both of them. Thankfully, our new friend, Banks, and I were able to rescue them at the last minute. Thankfully too, Bodie didn't seem to display any long-term negative affects from his near-death experience. Perhaps his saving the life of the president of the United States and becoming a national hero helped assuage any psychological damage. Ah, the resilience of youth!

So, the hour of Bodie's departure from home finally comes, and Maggie, Bodie, Mace, and I load up Bodie's gear in my faithful old Toyota Tacoma pickup truck that I've affectionately named "Pappy." I know there'll come a time when I need to "retire" Pappy from active duty, but when you've owned a vehicle for darn near eighteen years, it's hard to let go. Despite Maggie's suggestions that I get a new vehicle, I'm just not ready yet. "What for, runs great!" I generally reply whenever Maggie broaches the subject. "Maybe next year."

As planned, Tori chooses to stay home to practice for her performance tonight at Stella's Diner. She wraps Bodie in a warm hug and reminds him that he's promised to email pictures of camp life to her. They say their goodbyes, and I drive Pappy out of the courtyard and head south toward Indy.

I can't imagine the number of times I've made this drive to the Indianapolis airport over the years. The good news is that highway traffic is reasonably light this time of day, and we get to the airport on time. Finally, Bodie's flight is called, and he grabs his carry-on gear and trots toward his gate. He's so excited about going to Voyageur that he darn near forgets to say goodbye to us. All goes well, though, with the only casualty being Maggie's mascara which runs as she tearfully says goodbye to her "baby." Okay, I admit to being a little choked up too. An hour later, Maggie, Mace, and I arrive back at the brewery complex feeling a little sad that we won't have the excitement that an energetic kid creates for eight weeks.

When we return home Maggie walks over to the farmhouse to check on Tori and offer her any help in preparing for tonight's performance. Mace asks me to join him in the subbasement. He says he has something new to show me.

Now, the subbasement is two floors beneath our living quarters and my antique camera museum in the renovated bottling building and one floor under my photographic darkroom. Originally, the subbasement was used by the Block brothers for storing kegs of beer that they brewed. In recent years though it's served as a secret laboratory of sorts where Mace and Tori's brother, Weed, designed and made unique killing devices from pieces of antique detective-style cameras that I'd collected. That was back in the day when I was in full avenging vigilante mode. The weapons that they cleverly made for me included a gentleman's cane that doubled as a rifle, a modified watch camera that emitted a nasty electrical charge, and my very favorite, the Demon camera, which is small enough to hold in the palm of my hand and deadly enough to discharge a blue arc of electricity that can bring down a big man. I won't say how many times I've used these weapons to avenge right-wing racists and bad dudes that preyed on less fortunate folks. My active avenging days are in the past now that I'm a contented husband, father, and friend, but experience has taught me that I never know when I'm going to get dragged into some volatile situation where lethal defense is the only option. My Demon camera has proven its worth on many occasions, and when I travel, it always resides in my pocket, just in case …

"So, Mace, what do you have to show me?" I say as we enter the subbasement test lab.

"Well, Clay, the other day I was reviewing some of Weed's old notes from his student years at MIT, and it dawned on me that I could exponentially boost the electrical surge and battery strength of the Demon camera if I used this lithium-magnesium ion compound that Weed had discovered."

"Well, you're talking way over my pay grade, but how much more 'juice' do you figure you can get?"

"Probably by a factor of five, enough to stop a Cape Buffalo with only a 20 percent depletion of the battery life."

"Sounds impressive," I reply. "Does it add much more weight?"

"A little but not too much. You can still comfortably carry it in your pocket. Wanna give it a try?"

"Uh, sure, I may be in my late forties, but I still have enough juvenile delinquent tendencies residing inside me that I still like blowing stuff up."

"Great, but this new chemistry does more vaporizing than it does exploding. I have a feeling our military might like to get their hands on this, but for now let's just keep it as our dirty little secret."

"You are a wonder, my friend. Do you want to place a paper target on the wall, and I'll give it a go?"

"Paper's too easy, Clay, so I carted a stack of iron weights down here, probably weighing fifty pounds or more." He points in their direction against a far wall.

"Okay," I say dubiously as I point the new, improved Demon camera in their direction.

"Ready?!" I ask Mace and without waiting for his reply, I press the discharge button. Immediately an angry arc of blue electricity leaps from the Demon, but instead of exploding the stack of weights to smithereens, they just dissolve into a gooey puddle of slag and then begin to evaporate into nothingness. I look over at Mace with shock etched on my face and see him grinning like the Cheshire Cat.

"Holy shit!" I exclaim. "Where'd it all go?" I ask incredulously.

"Darned if I know. Now check the amount of battery you have left," Mace advises.

"Eighty percent," I reply. "So, do you figure I can get maybe three or four blasts with this thing before the battery is totally depleted?"

"I do," Mace proudly replies. "Not bad, huh?!"

"Not bad at all, mon ami! Very impressive, indeed, and Weed would be very proud of you! I like what you've done. I just pray that I don't have to use it, or that I don't vaporize myself if I do."

"Now, I have something else I want to show you, too, but I'm not sure if it'll be ready before you leave for Chicago. I got the idea reading more of Weed's science notes around the time when the Pentagon and CIA were trying in vain to recruit him to work for the government. I'm naming it the 'Weed Killer' after our buddy, Weed."

"Wanna give me a little hint of what you've come up with?" I ask.

"Well, just a little because I'm still working on it. I will tell you that its power is based on a combination of microwaves and harmonics. I've developed a weapon using Weed's old chromatic harmonica, but I'm still futzing around with the targeting mechanism so it doesn't wipe out the user. I think I'm getting closer to perfecting it."

"Uh huh," I reply. "I have faith in you, but again, you're talking way over my head, Mace."

I like that these devices look somewhat commonplace and are easy to conceal. Helps going through security at airports, or fooling adversaries about their real strength. I place the super-charged Demon camera in my pocket, and we straighten up the lab a little. Five minutes later Mace and I ride my home elevator two floors up to ground level and walk over to the farmhouse to join Tori and Maggie. We enter and see Maggie serving as an audience of one while Tori sings some new songs she's been working on with her band.

"Sounding good, Tori!" Mace exclaims. "Gonna have those folks at Stella's begging for more."

"Aw c'mon, you really think so, Mace?"

"He does and so do I," I chime in, "and apparently someone else, does too. Who sent you the flowers?" I point to a dozen yellow roses that were delivered while Mace and I were messing around with my favorite weapon in the subbasement.

"I really don't know. The florist delivered them a few minutes ago, and I noticed a card, but it was signed, *'An admirer who thinks you're beautiful.'* That's it. I called the florist shop to see if they have a record of the sender, like from a credit card, but apparently my 'admirer' prefers to remain anonymous. The flowers were paid for in cash. Curious, huh?"

I look at Maggie and both of us arch our eyebrows skeptically about the sender. "And earlier you were wondering if people find you attractive," Maggie reminds Tori. "I guess you can make that a resounding yes, right guys?!"

"Right as rain," Mace replies. "And without sounding too fatherly, Tori, just remember there are a lot of weirdos out there, so be aware of your surroundings, okay?"

"Yes, Father Mace, I'll be careful," she says playfully as she wraps the old guy in an affectionate hug. "I'm sure it's just some lonely guy who's too shy to step out of the shadows. It was nice, whoever it was, to send the flowers though."

I look over at Maggie again and our eyes meet. "I'm sure that's it, just some lonely guy wanting to express his affection," I offer neutrally, but Maggie looks at me again and senses from the expression on my face that my bullshit meter just got launched.

"What time should we leave for Stella's Diner?" I ask Tori.

"Well, my guys and I come on at eight o'clock, so maybe we should get there, say around seven, and you guys can grab a quick dinner before the fun begins. We probably ought to leave in about twenty minutes. How's that sound?"

"Well, we better get a move-on, Clay. Let's meet at Pappy in twenty minutes then."

Maggie and I scurry across the courtyard to our home and run up two flights of steps to our bedroom instead of waiting for the elevator. "What're you wearing tonight?" Maggie asks me as she begins peeling off her clothes and dashing for the bathroom.

I catch up with her and see that she's standing at the sink wearing her bra and panties, looking quite desirable I might add, and so I evade the question and wrap my arms around her from behind. "I'm wearing a smile," I say honestly, "and I think Mr. Happy is smiling too!"

Maggie turns around to face me with a winsome smile and says,"Not now, you beast. Possibly, maybe, probably later if you leave me alone for ten minutes. Now, go put on some nice clothes that don't smell like something that you and Mace just blew up!"

"Oh, you can smell that?"

"Yes! Bye! Go get dressed!"

Fifteen minutes later we step outside to the courtyard and see Mace and Tori already waiting beside Pappy. "Looking gorgeous!" Maggie lauds Tori. Her long blond hair lays softly over her shoulders with two lovely braids running along the sides of her head. She is wearing no makeup with the exception of a little iridescent eye shadow and mascara to highlight her already captivating silver-blue eyes. Her outfit is very sophisticated with a hint of big-city teaming up with country casual ... tight jeans, a stunning red top showing off her curvaceous shape, and white boots ... the All-American Girl.

"Holy cow, Tori, you look amazing! Hell, I'd send you flowers too, and I've known you since we were three, and I'm a married man!" That last remark earns me a sharp jab from Maggie's elbow.

"He's right, though, Tori, you are a vision!" Maggie adds. "Now let's go get some dinner and watch this 'vision' blow Stella's audience away!"

Chapter 4

F YOU'VE NEVER BEEN to Stella's Diner before, let me assure you it's a special experience. We drive Pappy up to the main parking lot in front of the diner, and it's already packed. The business model our friend, Stella, has put together wouldn't work for most restaurants, but the crafty owner has made a huge success story of her little ol' diner. Yes, by day Stella's is pretty much a "little ol' diner" which also happens to serve some of the best breakfasts and dinners for miles around. Over the years Stella's increased the size of the diner and then put

a massive amount of money into building a large professional kitchen and a darn fancy supper club with a full bar and live entertainment. I remember asking Stella one time why she didn't just close down the original diner and focus on the high-profit supper club. She said she could never do that because it was her roots and because she knows people just love diner food. I give her a lot of credit for making it all work.

Then, of course, there's Stella herself, and no more fascinating a lady ever strutted across a restaurant floor. I'd gauge her to be in her midfifties now and a widow ever since her late husband, Vern, fell into the deep fryer a few years back. But Stella is a can-do girl, and she's kept her dream alive and has been pushing hard ever since. To look at her, you just have to smile. For years now, she's been wearing really tight animal print yoga pants; you know, leopards and zebras, some fish and butterflies. Plus, she likes to wear colorful frilly tops that help accentuate "her girls," as she likes to call her breasts. But it's her teased-out hair and wild colors and sparkles that really catch your eye. If we think Tori is a "vision," which she is, then a dolled-up Stella is pure technicolor.

Mace, Maggie, Tori, and I get out of Pappy and enter the diner's front door. We pass through a softly-lit foyer into the spacious supper club, and there at the front desk training a new employee is Stella herself, looking pretty much like I just described. Pure technicolor! The moment she sees us enter, she rushes out from behind the desk to say hello. "Tori, honey, I think we've got a full house tonight. Everyone wants to hear that pretty lady sing and hear these great musicians backing you up."

"I love it, Stella, we can all have a fun time and make some dough in the process. I better go get ready and meet with the guys. I'll catch up with you later, okay?"

"And, Maggie, darling, is this famous husband of yours looking after you the way he should?"

"Yes, Stella, pretty much, but you know Clay well enough to know that he's sorta like a work in progress."

"Amen to that," she says as she sidles up and gives me a big kiss on the cheek.

And then Stella trains her eyes on Mace. "Mace Davis, where the hell have you been, sir? Come here and give Mama Stella a big hug so I can feel that manly body of yours against mine." Poor Mace never knows quite how to take Stella so he pretty much does whatever she asks. "Mace, honey, you know you're the only man on the planet I'd run away with," she coos at him. "You've gotta come around more often or you might give a girl a complex."

"Yes, ma'am," he replies and manages to muster a confused, sheepish smile as he gives Stella an awkward hug.

"C'mon guys," Stella says, "I've reserved a table for you right up front close to the stage. Samantha, here, is gonna take wonderful care of you, and I'll catch you later on" … and then she's gone.

"She makes me nervous," Mace whispers to me. "I never know how to take her." I look at him and just laugh. "You're such a stud, Mace Davis!"

Samantha takes our drink orders, and we settle into the comfortable room. The lights are lower now, and a few minutes later we hear a saxophonist blowing soulfully with a spotlight showcasing him at the corner of the stage. The three of us sit there soaking up the mood and drifting away with the muted, doleful brass. His name's Roscoe Ray Snyder, and he's been a blues musician longer than I've been alive. Tori met Roscoe Ray through her brother, Weed, many years ago, and when Weed was murdered, he told Tori that if she ever wanted him and his guys to perform with her, they'll be there. He once told Tori that when it came to the blues, Weed Rawlins was the blackest white dude that he ever knew which was very high praise coming from Roscoe Ray.

Next, we hear a light whisking sound on the drums, and another spotlight shines on a new musician, Dave "Sticks" Sapadin, or just Sticks as his friends call him. Sticks lets loose on his drums with almost superhuman virtuosity which has patrons standing on their chairs to get a better look. And, next comes the baddest brother of them all, Tad "Doctor Cool" Robinson on keyboard and harp, and the stage lights up as the three of them take turns doing solos and getting the audience wound up in a frenzy and begging for whatever's coming next.

And what comes next, of course, is our Tori Rawlins, and the crowd goes even wilder as she enters the stage and takes the microphone in her hands. Loud shouts, clapping, whistling … a whole lot of carrying-on going on. Maggie shocks me when she puts her fingers to her mouth and lets loose with a string of really loud wolf whistles. I look at her incredulously and say, "I never knew you could whistle like that!"

"Yeah, well, Clay, honey, it's just one of my special talents. You didn't think I was gonna share all of my secrets with you right away, did ya, big guy?" And she whistles some more.

"Well, I guess not, darlin', but considering we've been married for fifteen years, you'd think I'd know about your whistling skills by now, just sayin'."

Tori is in her element on stage, and I can't help but think how proud Weed would be of his sister. Over the next forty-five minutes, the band and

Tori perform a series of really lively songs, many of which are Tori's compositions. And then, Tori and the band slow the tempo down, and she sings a song she'd recently written about love lost and love regained. She closes her eyes because of the bright stage light and withdraws into her familiar world of darkness from when she was blind. The audience is mesmerized into silence as the band members approvingly look on and Tori sings a cappella. I look around the room and see all eyes trained on her. Her golden hair shimmers under the solitary light in the room, and the only sounds that can be heard are the beseeching, mellifluous words flowing from Tori's voice.

"She's amazing," Maggie whispers to me as she hugs my arm. A few tears flow down patrons' cheeks, and from the rear of the room some guy screams out, "I love you!" and makes a rush for the stage. Instinctively, I reach my hand in my pocket and feel the familiar shape of the Demon camera in case things get too far out of hand. Fortunately, Stella's beefy security staff, a.k.a. bouncers, intercept the overly-enthusiastic and inebriated patron and calmly lead him back to his seat. No harm, no foul, and Tori continues to sing like an angel until she finishes her set.

"We'll be back after a short break everyone. Don't go anywhere and order-up so Stella can make enough dough to pay us tonight!" The crowd loves her humor, and Stella and Tori spy each other and both give a hearty thumbs-up on tonight's show.

I relax and catch Mace's eyes looking at me, nodding that he knows what I was thinking. Fortunately, everything's cool, but I look around the room to see if there are other patrons to be concerned about. All seems well enough, but at the last moment I spot a lone guy standing near a side entrance wearing dark glasses, a full length coat, and a hat concealing most of his face and head. He spots me looking at him and slips back into the shadows. I can't help but wonder who he is and why he's trying to conceal himself. Again, I see Mace looking at me and in the direction I'd spotted the lone man. Mace saw him, too, and excuses himself from the table and walks toward the side entrance. A few minutes later he returns to the table shaking his head to indicate that the man's gone. Fortunately, Maggie hasn't been aware of our concern, and the three of us order another round of drinks from Samantha during the break.

Twenty minutes later there's the baleful wail of a saxophone as Roscoe Ray Snyder signals that the second half of the show is about to begin. Sticks Sapadin does a drum roll, and guests take their seats. Roscoe blows his sax again, and everyone quiets down for the next musical offerings from Tori and her guys.

I spend the rest of the performance enjoying the music with Maggie by my side but casually scanning the audience for the lone man we'd spotted earlier or any other inebriated person who might feel anointed to mess with the good karma. Fortunately, everyone behaves themselves, and the music ends with the audience giving a rousing standing ovation. Mace, Maggie, and I remain seated, waiting for Tori to catch her breath and settle up with Stella and the guys. We watch everyone saunter, strut, stagger, and sashay out of the supper club, and a few moments later Tori comes running up to us breathlessly.

"How'd we do, guys?!" she asks us clearly still luxuriating in the thrill of playing live to a packed house.

"You were terrific!" the three of say almost in unison. "Just look at the faces of everyone leaving here. Looks to me like everybody sure had a great time!" "And, what do you have there?" Maggie asks pointing to a bouquet of yellow roses that Tori's holding.

"Yeah, pretty, huh? Someone left them in the dressing room for me."

"Any note?" Mace inquires.

"Yes, but the giver didn't offer any name. The little card just read that I was, uh, delicious tonight."

"Delicious? That sounds a little creepy to me," I add. I choose not to say anything about the concealed figure that Mace and I saw earlier. No reason to spoil Tori's moment, especially since I have nothing to go on except my gut. Mace and I make brief eye contact though.

"Aw c'mon, Clay, someone was just being nice," Tori defends. "They're pretty!"

"They are pretty," I relent. "Are you ready to go home or do you want to have a late dinner here?"

"No, I think I'm ready now," Tori replies. "I'm a little tired and besides I've got more soup at home."

I leave a generous tip for Samantha, and the four of us say goodnight to Stella who seems to be running around the diner with the same verve she displayed hours ago.

"Now, Mace Davis, I'm serious about you not being a stranger around here! Big, handsome man like you makes a girl like me get all atwitter. Come here and give me another hug."

"Yes, ma'am," Mace replies sheepishly, and then we all say a final goodbye and step out into the night air.

"You're such a stud, Mace. No wonder Stella has the hots for you," I tease.

"Don't you dare start with that hooey, Clay. That woman makes me really nervous."

Both Maggie and Tori tightly hug Mace's arms. "Oh, Mace, sweetie, you're such a hottie! Are you really scared of some middle-aged woman wearing tight-ass yoga pants? Maybe it's the leopard print ... Meow!"

"You quit that! Now, you're all making me nervous!"

Chapter 5

As the weekend draws to a restful end, Mace and Tori join us at our place for Sunday dinner. Earlier Bodie texted us that he'd arrived safely at Camp Voyageur in Northern Wisconsin. He's excited to be back on what he now refers to as "hallowed ground" among friends, old and new, situated at the edge of the verdant expanse of the north woods.

I look at Tori and smile to myself recalling how she and her guys totally lit up the guests at Stella's Diner. She notices me smiling to myself and asks me what I'm laughing about.

"I'm not laughing about anything, Tori, I was simply thinking about your performance and what a great show it was!"

"Seriously, Clay?!"

"Dead serious, Tori, I think you guys are as good as anyone out there."

"Well, it sure helps to have the likes of Roscoe Ray, Sticks, and Dr. Cool behind you. I really appreciate the kind words. After the performance the guys told me they think it would be a good idea for us to play together more often in the future. I think I'd like to do that, so we'll see where this goes."

"Sounds good, Tori. Weed would be very proud of you. Oh, we're going to leave midmorning tomorrow. Do you need Maggie or me to help you with anything?"

"No, I'm fine, thanks. I left food and water for Satchmo, watered the plants, even did a fast load of laundry this morning. The only thing I nearly forgot to do was cancel and reschedule my therapy appointment with Dr. Dale. Strangely, he seemed a little off-put when I called to reschedule. Wanted to know where I was going and when I'd be back. I gave him several days notice. His reaction surprised me."

"Has he acted like that before?" I ask.

"No, not really, but I've begun to notice little chiding comments from him, but I write them off to his being a little full of himself and profession-ally aloof."

"You know, Tori, there are other good therapists out there," I say.

"I know. Adrian's alright. He just gets a little weird sometimes."

Maggie returns from the kitchen, and we're all seated now around our candlelit table. As a rule, we don't say grace in the traditional churchy way, but one of us will often take the lead and offer some brief comments of gratitude for something that's occurred. It's nice. Tonight, Maggie takes the lead and talks about how grateful she is that Bodie is safely nested at camp, and that we're all together and looking forward to a great visit with Lucretia in Chicago. She thanks Mace for looking after everything while we're gone, and I tease that he's probably got a hot date with Stella the moment we leave. I don't think he saw the humor in it. Oh well!

After Sunday dinner Mace and I take care of clearing the table and doing the dishes while Maggie and Tori sit down with a bottle of wine for some spirited games of cribbage; cursing and ugly name calling permitted. I smile as they pull the cribbage board out because it's a game that I learned when I was a camper at Camp Voyageur. I am 100 percent certain that Bodie will be playing a bunch with his cabinmates over the summer.

My cell phone vibrates, and I look and see that's it's our other son, Rennie, dutifully making his Sunday evening phone call. Mace walks into the living room to join the ladies, and I step out onto the deck to enjoy a private conversation with my son.

"S'up?!" I ask trying to sound all hip and everything. "How's your bad, beautiful self?!"

"Dad? Is this you trying to sound like you're straight outta Compton?"

"Of course, it's me. I take it you'd prefer that I talk like your normal dad instead."

"Uh, yeah!" he exclaims. "You aren't exactly black, Dad, or particularly hip either."

"Ouch!" I exclaim. So, the back story on our adopted son, Rennie Cotton, is a little lengthy, but suffice it to say that many years ago I did a photo-essay on life on the tough streets of inner-city Indianapolis. I shot a picture of a young black boy sitting alone in the shadow of an old tenement that was published and became an instant international sensation. With Mace's help we went looking for this young boy and found him living alone in squalor. Mace and I coaxed, actually bribed, him to come to work for us doing odd jobs at the brewery complex, and lo and behold, after a few rough patches he settled into our family of friends pretty well. He even saved Tori and our dog, Lex, when they were attacked by the nasty Hacker brothers on a path along the White River not far from home. That was some fifteen years ago and that terrifying episode certainly cemented his status as a bona fide member of our family.

Over the years Maggie and Tori took over the main responsibilities for Rennie's education and medical care, but his main tutor in the ways of the world was Mace. They bunked together in the power plant and forged a kinship that still runs very deep. After a couple of years Maggie encouraged us to legally adopt Rennie, and the rest is history. He graduated from high school with honors, got accepted into Northwestern University, and is now working on his doctorate in Sociology. It was during his summer internship last year with the National Park Service on the Keweenaw Peninsula of Michigan that Rennie and his supervisor, Ranger Kelli Katterman, discovered the ancient Chippewa Indian cave art, among other things, under Brockway Mountain.

"So," I begin again, "what're you up to? What's new with curating the cave art and artifacts?"

"Wow, Dad, it's like a constantly evolving project. Each time we interpret one of the scenes in the cave art, it opens up whole new topics to be studied and explored, like the structures that the paleo-Indians lived in, their tribal hierarchy, their diet, their clothing and hunting weapons, their relationship with plants and animals, and especially their supernatural belief systems. I think you recall one scene in particular where tribesmen are fighting a huge, fierce beast, the Windigo, and not many survived."

The very thought of the Windigo, the evil man-eating spirit, that had dwelled for centuries under Brockway Mountain, brought a chill down my spine. Last summer we learned all too closely that some mythical beings are, indeed, real. Robert Midew, Rennie, Kelli, and I had escaped the Windigo and survived, but just barely. In truth, if it hadn't been for Robert's grandmother, Nokomis, saving our butts and vaporizing the beast, we'd all be Windigo excrement by now. Both Rennie and I grow silent for a moment, each if us recalling in our own way, how close we came to death.

"Yeah, so Ranger Kelli and I have been working very closely with Robert, and we're finally ready for you to venture back up here to the Keweenaw to do your filming. I've got some dates we want to share with you to begin your work."

"Sounds good to me, Rennie. I'll make myself available, although the thought of going back into the bowels of Brockway Mountain doesn't make me feel all warm and fuzzy. I spoke with Robert recently, and he told me of the very good work you and Kelli are doing with him. I'm proud of you. Curiously, he mentioned that he had been sensing some unsettling energy coming from under the mountain. He didn't go into any real detail, but the fact that Robert mentioned it got my attention. Any idea what he might've been sensing?"

"Not really, Dad, but every now and then I see him staring into the distance as if he's divining something, but given Robert's mysticism, it could be anything. I just try to do my work and be as helpful as possible."

"Good strategy, Rennie! How's Kelli doing?"

"Oh, she's fine. We're spending a lot of time together and doing some pretty fascinating work. Plus, she's really pretty and has a quirky sense of humor."

"Good, I'm glad you guys are enjoying each other's company." I try not to read too much between the lines. I doubt that Rennie would give me a straight answer if I asked him if their relationship was anything more than professional, so I leave the subject alone. "Well, I know your mom, Mace, and Tori will shoot me if I don't hand the phone over to them. Text me the dates, and we'll talk soon. I'll text you back to confirm the dates once I've checked my calendar and talked with your mom, okay? Give my best to Kelli and Robert."

I walk back inside, say goodbye to Rennie, and hand the phone to Maggie. Ten minutes later they're all still yakking on the phone, and I walk back out to the deck with Satchmo to polish off the bottle of wine and fend off thoughts of the Windigo. Oddly, the remnants of the unsettling dream I had on Tori's porch a few days ago are still with me. I'm very surprised that I still remember the dream as clearly as I do, and I have an odd feeling that whatever Robert's sensing is also invading my thoughts. Another chill goes down my spine, and I loft Satchmo onto my lap for comfort. Another fifteen minutes later, everyone has had a chance to catch up with Rennie, and we all decide to call it a night. Maggie and I finish cleaning up the kitchen and then head upstairs and crawl into bed. I hold her close, praying for peaceful dreams.

"Are you okay, Clay?" she asks. "You seem unusually quiet and a little anxious."

"Oh, yeah, I'm okay," I lie. "I guess going to Chicago brings up some painful memories of Weed's death because of Lucretia's murderous brother, Malcolm. Rennie texted me when they want me to return to the Keweenaw to begin filming. Honestly, the last time we were all under Brockway Mountain together it was a pretty harrowing experience. Like I said, there are a lot of very painful memories."

Maggie kisses me lightly on the lips and draws me even closer. Thoughts of the Windigo and Malcolm soon drift away like smoke in the wind as Maggie mounts me and softly moans with pleasure. We make love like we've done so many times before. Our intimacy is a balm for my body, mind, and soul, and afterward, I drift off to sleep, free of demons, mythical and real.

The next morning arrives with a bright freshness, and after I improvise a sensible breakfast from last night's leftovers and talk to Mace about a few things, it's time to leave for our trip to Chicago. We're all excited to visit our friend, Lucretia Land, and see the priceless collection of American art owned by the Land Foundation. I'm particularly curious to see how Tori reacts to the variety of artistic styles represented in the collection.

"Are you sure you don't want to come, Mace?" I ask him as Maggie, Tori, and I pack our gear into Pappy for the three-hour drive north. "You know Lucretia will be disappointed if you don't come."

"I know, Clay, but I think I'll hang back this time. I've got to do some work on the sump pump in the subbasement, and I want to put some finishing touches on that project I showed you earlier. Please give Lucretia my very best though."

"All right, big guy, it's you and Satchmo holding down the fort then."

The three of us pile into Pappy and wave good-bye to Mace and Satchmo as we drive across the courtyard. I look in the rearview mirror and see Mace waving to us and can't help but wonder how much longer he'll be around, regardless of the life-boost that our friend, Robert, gave him last year. Robert warned me that his gift would only bring temporary physical enrichment to Mace; that no one lives forever. I feel Maggie squeeze my hand and look in her direction. Her expression says, *"Whatever you're thinking, Clay, it's okay. We're together, and I love you."*

I smile back at her and nod my understanding. Fifteen minutes later we take the entrance ramp to I-465 north to bypass Indianapolis, and another fifteen minutes after that we merge onto I-65 north toward Chicago where I know the traffic won't be nearly as accommodating.

I've driven this highway to Chicago more times than I can remember, but each time I notice things that grab my attention. As we approach the town of Rensselaer, I begin to see the looming shapes of huge windmills as far as I can see. They look like a bunch of Mercedes logos waving at unsuspecting motorists. Thankfully, their presence is a reminder of how our world is changing to reduce our dependence on fossil fuels. I figure that if rural, conservative Indiana has devoted thousands of acres to windmills, then a greener future is no longer a pipe dream.

I look in the rearview mirror and notice Tori idly gazing out the rear passenger window with her head resting on the door frame. She appears mesmerized by the twirling windmill blades, and I think back on when Bodie was a young boy whiling away the hours on a road trip vacantly staring at the passing landscape.

"Hey, Tori, what're thinking back there?" I ask to break the long quietness.

"I'm thinking about shadows, Clay."

"Shadows, huh? They're pretty cool, aren't they? I've often used them in my photography, especially when I'm shooting black-and-white images. They're great for composition."

"Yes, they are," she replies. "When I was blind I didn't have a clue what people meant when they talked about shadows. They're often huge and dramatic and yet have no real substance."

"Gee, reminds me of a few men I've known over the years," Maggie adds sarcastically.

We drive on with a new car game, trying to find the most interesting shadows. Two hours later we've pretty much exhausted our interest in windmills and shadows, and I take the exit for Merrillville to gas up Pappy and grab some lunch. As I'm gassing up my Tacoma, Tori and Maggie head off to use the bathroom in the station's convenience store but immediately come back outside.

"You definitely don't want to go in there, Clay. The bathroom is a smelly disaster and the man behind the counter is even creepier."

A moment later the station clerk comes outside and chides us for not buying anything.

"Uh, sir," I say. "We bought your gas. Isn't that enough?! Maybe if you cleaned up the place, people might be more willing customers."

"Are you calling my place dirty?" he parries.

"No, I'm not, but they are," I reply nodding at Maggie and Tori.

"Your place is a dump, mister!" Tori interjects.

The clerk grows even nastier and calls Tori a syphilitic whore.

"Jesus, pal, how about showing some manners?! C'mon girls, let's go!" We climb back into Pappy, and as I begin to pull away from the gas pump, I hear a loud sound of metal on metal and see that the station clerk has thrown a jack handle at the rear of my truck. I slam on the brakes and go outside to check for damage and see the clerk flip me the bird and grab an oil can.

"I don't know what your problem is mister, but you've dented the tailgate on my truck."

"Screw you!" he hollers back at me and hurls the can at me hitting me in the leg.

"C'mon, Clay!" Maggies yells through the open window. "He's not worth it!"

Now I'm pissed. "He may not be worth it, but Pappy is," I return.

"Screw you and your ugly wreck of a truck!" the jerk yells back at me standing his ground. Then, I see another guy come outside and stand beside his pal.

"Oh shit!" I mutter out loud as I begin to weigh my options. Since I have Maggie and Tori with me, I decide to cut my losses and begin to get back inside the truck and leave.

"That's right, you big pussy!" the new guy hollers. "You better get out of here before I whomp your skinny ass!"

From somewhere inside my pissed-off brain, I hear Maggie say, "Don't do it, Clay, they're not worth it, and we really need to pee!"

Despite my lovely wife's entreaty, I get out of the truck and notice that both of these jerks are now holding a hammer and wrench in their meaty hands.

"Are you sure you guys really want to do this?" I ask sternly. I hear Maggie call 911, but she's not sure exactly where to tell the operator to send the police. "It's an ugly independent gas station on the main drag," is all she can muster.

"You're going to pay for that damage to my truck," I say matter-of-factly.

"Drop dead, loser!" comes the first guy's uncreative reply, "Go get 'em Jerry!" and the second guy starts coming at me again. I reach my hand inside my jacket pocket and feel a familiar shape.

"All right, mister, that's close enough!" I advise. "Now, turn around and go back inside your greasy little hole in the wall."

He keeps coming, and I pull my Demon Camera out of my pocket and point it at him. I have it set for stun, but instead of frying his ass like I really want to do, I point it at another pump at the other side of the gas station. "Last chance," I offer.

"Get him, Jerry!" the first guy exhorts his pal, and I push the button on the Demon Camera. A nanosecond later an angry arc of blue electricity shoots out and engulfs the pump. From some twenty yards away I feel the heat as the pump explodes into an orange ball of liquid fire sending the two malcontents to the ground with singed hair and clothing.

"I warned you!" I say over my shoulder as I climb back into Pappy and start the engine. Maggie and Tori stare at me in stunned silence.

"So, who's ready for lunch?!" I ask them as if nothing has happened.

"I don't care about lunch," Tori blurts out, "but now I really do need to pee!"

From somewhere in the distance we hear the sounds of sirens.

"How about Panera?" I suggest as we exit the gas station onto the main drag again. "I love their Baja Grain Bowl."

Maggie looks at me in astonishment and then at the conflagration several yards away and rhetorically asks, "And, I had a child with you??!!"

Chapter 6

WE GET TO PANERA and each of us makes a mad dash to the restrooms. We come out and order our lunches, and while we're waiting for them to be delivered to our table, Tori asks, "What the hell just happened at that crappy gas station?"

Naturally they both look at me for an explanation. "Well," I begin contemplatively, "They insulted us as customers, they called you a syphilitic whore, they threw a jack handle and hit my truck, they hit me with a full oil can, they threatened us with bodily harm, they didn't back down when given

the opportunity; so I made them pay the price for their transgressions. I think that about sums it up."

"Okay," Maggie says calmly, "but what was that thing you used to blow up the gas pump? And how and where did you get it?"

"Oh, you mean my Demon Camera."

"Your Demon what?" Tori asks.

Fortunately, we have to pause for a moment while our food is delivered to the table, and we take a few bites.

"Seriously, Clay, how were you able to do that with that little Demon thing and have you ever used it before?" Tori asks.

"Uh, yeah," I say as I take another bite from my Baja Grain Bowl. "I've used it before, and it's saved lives, including vulnerable people, myself, and the president of the United States."

"You used it to save the president?" Maggie asks.

"Well, no, not exactly," I reply.

"So, if you didn't, then who used it to save the president?

"I don't think you want to know," I offer frankly.

"Who!?!" Maggie quietly demands.

"Uh, Bodie," I say evenly.

"You let our son use a lethal weapon on another person? He was only nine years old!"

"I didn't let him. He grabbed the Demon camera out of my jacket pocket and fried a nasty Russian agent who'd gotten the drop on us. It was either Vladimir Dumbfuck or President Horvath, Bodie, and me. Our son was a hero!"

I take another bite out of my Baja Grain Bowl and ask Tori and Maggie if they want a bite. "It's really good," I add. They just stare at me. After lunch we gas up Pappy at a station a little further down the road and listen to the clatter and clang of fire trucks as the firemen struggle to get the blazing inferno under control. By the time they do the convenience store has also been consumed destroying any visual record that a security camera might've captured. At this point in my life I've been involved in so many of these, uh, unfortunate incidents that I feel absolutely no remorse. After all, they started it.

We get back on I-65 north toward the interchange for Chicago, and as expected, Maggie and Tori take turns pummeling me with questions about my avenging ways.

First, Maggie asks me again where I got the Demon Camera.

"Uh, do you really want to know the answers to these questions?"

"No, I mean yes," she says.

"Weed and Mace made it for me from spare parts from my antique cameras."

"But how? Where?" Tori asks.

"Well, you know Weed was pretty darn talented when it came to making devices that blew shit up. Hell, the government wanted him to work for them. And Mace, well, you know he's pretty darn talented in his own right too," I say proudly.

Maggie and Tori are speechless for only a moment, and then they begin to pummel me again with more questions.

"Look!" I say. "You know that before Maggie and I got together, I was engaged to Dr. Jennifer Skyler. The Hacker men killed her when they blew up the Planned Parenthood Center in Broadripple where she was the medical director, and I went on a rampage for a couple of years wiping out asshole racists and right-wing pricks. I've told you this, Maggie. Weed and Mace were the guys who supplied me with clandestine weapons, and they were really good at it. We converted the subbasement at home into a laboratory of sorts where we fabricated and tested the weapons. After Maggie and I got together, and especially after Bodie was born, I stopped my ways as an avenging vigilante, but I know that there are still a lot of bad people out there, and I've decided to stay prepared. Some people carry firearms. I carry the Demon camera."

"So, who else knows about these weapons that you use?" Maggie asks. "Does Rennie know too?"

"Of course! I think everyone knew except you guys."

"Swell, Clay. That's just swell," Maggie replies.

We continue our drive north and enter I-90 W toward Chicago. The early afternoon traffic is flowing fairly well, and I figure we're about an hour away from Chicago. I ask Maggie to call Lucretia to let her know when we should arrive at the Land Foundation office. Thankfully, Maggie and Tori are enjoying their conversation with Lucretia and have stopped asking me probing questions, for now anyway. Before long we see the Chicago skyline looming in the distance.

"You know, even though I've been able to see for a year now, I still get excited seeing a panoramic view of the city like this," Tori admits.

"I think we all do, Tori," Maggie confirms. "Chicago's pretty amazing. The lake, the tall buildings … the shopping!"

Thirty minutes later we turn onto Erie Street and see the Art Deco facade of the Land Foundation's edifice. I pull into the underground garage, take the parking stub to be validated by the Foundation staff, and we ride the elevator to the twenty-sixth floor. When the doors open we exit to a spectacular foyer that is decorated with midcentury modern furniture and paintings that would be the envy of any museum's collection. I don't recognize all of the artists represented on the foyer's walls, but a few by Winslow Homer, Edward Hopper, and Edward Hicks are unmistakable. We approach the main desk and introduce ourselves to an attractive associate named Bella.

"Of course, Mr. Arnold, Ms. Land is expecting you, Ms. Arnold, and Ms. Rawlins. She's just finishing up a phone call and will be with you momentarily. You're welcome to have a seat," which Maggie and I accept, but Tori instead walks over to a large picture window and takes in the sweeping vistas of Lake Michigan and downtown Chicago. "Whoa!" she says as she steadies herself at the window. "I'm not used to being this high up. Pretty amazing!"

Bella offers Tori a chair by the window, but before she can sit down, a large door behind the receptionist's desk opens up, and Lucretia Land comes waltzing into the room with her arms spread wide open in warm friendship.

"You made it!" she says as the three of us rise to greet her. Lucretia gives me an energetic hug and then turns her attention to Maggie and Tori. "I am so glad that you're here. Our getting together is so long overdue, and I'm delighted that you were able to entice Clay to come too, but where's Mace?"

"I told him you'd be disappointed that he didn't come, but he sends his regrets and said there are things that he needed to tend to at home. Please don't take his absence personally, Lucretia, I just think that he's most comfortable staying closer to home these days."

"Of course I don't take it personally, Clay, but please tell him I miss his handsome face. And you, Maggie, you look as lovely as ever. I have some fun things planned for your visit, all expenses paid, of course, by the Land Foundation."

Lucretia then turns her full attention to Tori and takes both of her hands and looks sympathetically into Tori's eyes. "I've wanted to meet you in person for a long time now, Tori." A tear comes to Lucretia's eye as she says. "I can't tell you how very sorry I am about your brother, Weed. His death still haunts me, and I'll never, ever forgive my brother, Malcolm, for causing his murder."

"Thank you, Lucretia. Weed's death will always be an open wound for each of us. I appreciate your kind words very much though. On a happier note, Maggie and I are thrilled to be spending time with you, and I can't wait to see more of the art collection."

"Let's all go in my office, and we can have some coffee and make some plans, okay? Bella, would you please hold my phone calls for a while?"

"Of course, Ms. Land. No interruptions. I can tell these are very special guests."

We follow Lucretia into her spacious office whose walls are adorned by paintings as equally impressive as those in the foyer. We take seats on plush sofas and chairs around a low carved table supporting a gorgeous silver coffee service. Maggie gives Lucretia a hand in dispensing cups for each of us, and we settle in.

We spend the next several minutes discussing various places to visit and dine, and Lucretia insists that we all stay at her place. "I have plenty of room, and it'll be easier to coordinate our comings and goings."

"That shack!" I joke, and Maggie shoots me a threatening look.

"But first, if you're up for it, I'd love to share some of our artwork with you," Lucretia asserts. Before we can accept her invitation, there's a knock on the door, and Bella steps inside looking very anxious.

"Yes, Bella, what is it? You look like you've seen a ghost!"

"I'm so sorry to interrupt, Ms. Land, but there's, uh ..." She approaches Lucretia and whispers in her ear.

"What do you mean there's a large man with a huge dog in the foyer? Just call security. I'm sure they can handle it."

The door swings open and Robert Midew steps inside with his wolf, Grey, at his side.

I immediately stand and stride over to them with a broad smile on my face. "Robert, I didn't know you were coming too. It's wonderful to see you. How'd you know we'd all be here? Don't tell me; information has a way of flowing to you."

Robert smiles and nods affirmatively. "It's great to see you too, Clay, and please pardon my intrusion, Lucretia."

Meanwhile Grey casually dogtrots over to Lucretia who stands frozen in apprehension. Grey sniffs her crotch and then moves on to "introduce" himself to Maggie. Robert and I watch the introductions with amusement. Maggie looks to me for help, and I just smile and shrug. Grey then moves on to Tori and repeats the same introduction that he did with the Lucretia and Maggie, but this time after sniffing her, he lies down in front of her with his head resting on her feet.

"Ladies," I say, "It's my pleasure to introduce you to Robert Midew and Grey." Immediately, the ladies relax, and Lucretia says, "It's all right, Bella, we're all friends here." Bella nervously smiles, backs out of the room, and closes the office door.

Recognizing that she's now meeting the legendary Robert Midew for the first time, Tori gets up and walks over to Robert with tears streaming down her cheeks. She can barely muster a complete sentence as she envelops Robert in a huge embrace knowing that she's finally met the person who imbued her with the gift of sight.

"I, I can't thank you enough, Robert," and her tears continue to flow. Robert bends down and places his forehead on Tori's, and Grey walks over to join them as a kindred spirit. "It is my pleasure, dear lady, any friend of Clay's is a friend of mine."

"Well, that was quite an entrance, Mr. Midew," Lucretia says, "Won't you please join us for some coffee? I sincerely appreciated our recent phone conversation, and I'm delighted that you and your really large companion are able to join us."

"Thank you, Lucretia, and please call me Robert, and this is Grey. I know this is an unexpected intrusion, but I became aware that you'd all be together, and since I was in the neighborhood, I thought I'd drop by and discuss our ancient cave art with you."

"I'm delighted that you did," Lucretia replies. "What neighborhood were you in?"

"The Keweenaw Peninsula in the Upper Peninsula of Michigan," Robert says in all seriousness.

"But that's not ..." Lucretia begins to say, and I interject, "Lucretia, our friend, Robert, has, uh, very unique abilities. Perhaps over time you'll come to recognize that."

"Okay," Lucretia says in confusion as she looks to Maggie and Tori for more explanation, but they're both as befuddled as she is.

"Let's have a seat everyone," I suggest, "and perhaps Robert and I can shed some light on a few things."

Over the next thirty minutes or so Robert and I take turns talking about some but not all of the tragic events that occurred under Brockway Mountain last summer. Robert first explains that he comes from a very long line of Chippewa Indians who lived on the Keweenaw Peninsula near the present site of Copper Harbor prior to white Europeans arriving, and that he serves as the president of the Keweenaw Bay Indian Council. I describe how I went up there to visit with our son, Rennie, who was doing a summer internship for his doctorate at the National Park Service, and that Rennie and Ranger Kelli Katterman had been entombed under Brockway Mountain by the owner of the Brockway Mining Company, Rex Trammer, and his associate, Digger Finn.

"But how did you know that they had been trapped under the mountain and how did you find them?" Lucretia asks. Maggie sits next to me in rapt silence because she's hearing some things that I had chosen not to mention to her. From time to time she looks at me, and I know I'm in for more questioning when she has me alone.

"As I mentioned, Robert possesses some very special cognitive powers, most of which I don't have a real clue about, and it's best if I leave it up to Robert to share what he's comfortable with."

Robert changes the subject and describes how Rennie and Ranger Kelli had discovered the magnificent Paleo-Indian cave art under the mountain, and that he and his Chippewa people had agreed it was appropriate to share it with the rest of the world now.

"Robert had asked me if I could recommend a highly reputable arts organization that could help facilitate the dissemination of images of the cave art after I've photographed the scenes in situ. Lucretia, given our shared history and your impeccable reputation, I naturally thought of the Land Foundation. And, since then, you and Robert have had an opportunity to speak by phone. Correct?"

"Yes, that's correct, Clay, and as I said to Robert, the Land Foundation would be honored to work with him and that we'd be happy to respect his and his peoples' wishes at every step of the way." She then laughs and admits, "I just didn't know we'd be meeting today." Grey walks over to Lucretia, spins around in front of her, and leans against her legs. "Yes, including you, Grey!" she says as she scratches him behind his ears.

We continue to talk, and Robert suggests that we return to the Keweenaw with him and begin the process now. I detect a sense of urgency to his suggestion.

Maggie stutters and says, "But, I don't know if I have the right clothes, and this is all so sudden." Tori has her eyes fixated on Robert still trying to comprehend the special powers this man possesses that would permit him to give her eyesight and to refresh Mace's health. "I'm game!" she says without hesitation. "C'mon Maggs! Bodie's at camp, and Mace can handle everything at home."

"Wattya say, Lucretia? Can you get away for a few days of adventure?" I ask.

"I wouldn't miss it, Clay, although the last time we went on an adventure together, we darn near got entombed forever with Samuel F. B. Morse. And don't worry about the clothes, Maggie, there may be one or two stores along the Magnificent Mile that have suitable attire."

Maggie looks at me, then at Robert, and back at me again. "Sure, why not?!" she declares. "What's the worst that could happen?"

I give her a hug and look over at Robert who puts his finger to his lips indicating that it's better to say less rather than more. I nod my understanding.

"Then, it's settled, Robert! We accept your invitation," Lucretia says as she pets Grey, "provided this big baby can come too!"

"Not a problem, Lucretia, Grey and I are a package deal."

We talk a few minutes longer about logistics, and Lucretia invites Robert and Grey to stay at her place with Maggie, Tori, and me which he accepts. Then there's a knock on the door, and Bella reenters. "Sorry to interrupt again, Ms. Land, but Mr. Thomas and Detective Cioffi are here to see you and say it's very important."

"Well, this is a day full of surprises!" Lucretia exclaims. "Please show them in." Uncle Drew Thomas and Chicago Homicide Detective, Christopher Cioffi, enter a few moments later.

To offer a little backstory here, these two gentlemen saved my life. They not only saved mine, they saved Lucretia's and Mace's as well. After Weed was murdered by Malcolm's henchman a few years ago, Mace joined Lucretia and me as we went traipsing all over the country looking for Samuel Morse's hidden trove of rare Renaissance paintings. We found the treasure in an underground crypt attached to Morse's mausoleum, but Lucretia's evil brother, Malcolm, surprised us and locked us inside the crypt to die. Fortunately, wise Uncle Drew and Detective Cioffi had also deciphered the clues to the art trove, and traveled from Chicago to the Green-Wood Cemetery in Brooklyn, New York, sensing we were in grave trouble. They apprehended Malcolm and saved our asses just in the nick of time. Malcolm was sentenced to twenty years at the Joliet Correctional Center for attempted murder, and Lucretia was able to reclaim her rightful position as the chairman of the Land Foundation.

"As usual, Drew and Chris, you guys are sights for sore eyes!" I give each guy a hearty hug, and Lucretia and I introduce them to Maggie, Tori, Robert, and Grey. We all sit down to get acquainted and reacquainted.

A few minutes into the conversation Robert turns to Uncle Drew and says, "You aren't Lucretia's uncle by blood, are you?"

"No, I'm not," Drew replies. "I worked for Lucretia's father for nearly fifty years, and I've been around all of Lucretia's life."

Lucretia interjects, "I've called him 'Uncle Drew' since I was a little girl because he was always so kind and helpful to me. Drew's the closest family I've got!"

"I can tell," Robert says. "You're both very fortunate."

"And you, Detective Cioffi, you come here today with a heavy heart, yes?"

"You're very intuitive, Robert. I'm actually here on official business."

"Official business, detective? Has the Land Foundation done something nefarious?" Lucretia queries.

"No, of course not, Lucretia, but it does involve the Land family."

"In what way? I honestly can't think of anything that I've possibly done to warrant your attention."

Detective Cioffi pauses a moment. "It's not you, Lucretia. It's your brother, Malcolm. He's escaped from Joliet, and he's on the loose."

I shift my look from the detective to Lucretia, then to Maggie and Tori, and finally to Robert who's staring into the expanse of Lake Michigan with Grey standing at his side.

Lucretia sums up her reaction with one word, "Shit!"

Chapter 7

TWENTY MINUTES LATER we all arrive at Lucretia's home nestled in a secluded section of the Gold Coast. Her father had purchased this Victorian mansion some seventy years ago as a gift for Lucretia's mother, and it's been the only home she's ever known.

Detective Cioffi says, "I've got to get back to the office for a meeting with the commissioner, but I've ordered round-the-clock security for your home and the Foundation's building. I'll keep you posted the moment we know anything further about

Malcolm's whereabouts. We'll get him. I promise you." Just as he finishes two police cruisers pull up, one with three police officers to keep an eye on Lucretia's home, and another to bring the detective back to headquarters.

"C'mon inside everybody, and I'll get you settled. Maggie and Tori, when you're ready, meet me in the den, and we'll go online to a trendy outdoor clothing store I use, and we can order your new duds and accessories, my treat. Clay and Robert, if you need anything, let me know too."

"But, won't it take a day or so for the clothes to get here?" Tori asks.

"Not the way I drop dough in their store. We should have everything by dinner. I realize this is putting a major crimp in what we'd originally planned to do with looking at art and shopping, but I believe that Detective Cioffi's concerns about Malcolm are justified, and Robert's suggestion that we leave for the Keweenaw Peninsula soon gives us a good opportunity to get out of town until the police can catch my crazy brother. I'm thinking we stay at my place this evening, have dinner, hang out and visit for a while, then call it a night around ten o'clock. How's that sound? We can leave in the morning right after breakfast."

We all voice our agreement with Lucretia's plan, and Robert nods his head affirmatively. He touches the large wolf's head and says, "Grey, go scout, protect!"

"Crap!" I blurt out. "I just realized that I don't have any of my photography gear with me. I have it all set aside and ready to go. I just didn't think I'd need it for our trip to Chicago. I'll call Mace and see if he can safely ship it overnight to the Keweenaw Peninsula or think of something else."

Somewhere on I-80 East between Joliet, Illinois, and Chicago, Malcolm Land slumps down in the front passenger seat of an unmarked prison transport vehicle with a jacket and hat concealing most of his features. The car is driven by Felix Falmann, Chief Security Officer for the Joliet Correctional Center. In reality, Falmann is now the former Chief Security Officer having sacrificed his career for the promise of making a ton of money by helping Malcolm Land escape. They listen intently to the vehicle's police scanner hoping to stay at least one step ahead of the authorities who have issued an all-points bulletin for their apprehension. So far, their luck is holding. Their goal is getting to Chicago where Malcolm hopes to retrieve a cache of cash and weapons that he'd secreted away prior to his arrest for being an accessory to murder, etc. etc. nearly four years ago now.

"Where are we going, Land?" Felix asks his prisoner turned partner-in-crime.

"Just keep driving, Falmann, I'll let you know where to go once we hit Chicago."

Felix stares at his passenger. "You better not think about screwing me over, Land. Once I get that $1 million you promised me we're history, understand?" Felix pats his handgun to emphasize his point.

"I understand perfectly. Just keep driving and head for the Chicago River. I have a private warehouse nearby where we can hole up while I get you your money."

"Just don't go pulling any tricky moves, Land, or I'll shoot your ass faster than you can say 'escaped convict'. Capisce?!"

"Yeah, I 'capisce.' Just keep driving, and I wanna listen to the scanner instead of you flapping your gums."

They listen to the police chatter on the radio, and Malcolm smiles. "I guess we got their attention, didn't we, Falmann? Malcolm Land on the run, like it's a big, damn deal. These guys are such morons!"

"They're not all morons, asshole. I've worked with some of them a long time. There are some pretty sharp guys in law enforcement. People like this Chris Cioffi guy who you don't want chasing after you."

"Yeah, I've met Cioffi already. He's the reason I was your guest at Joliet. I wouldn't mind evening the score with him."

"Well, good luck with that, Einstein!"

"Yeah, and so much for your professional loyalty, huh Falmann? All for a few bucks! I don't need you lecturing me," Malcolm lobs acidly.

"Screw you, Land! I'd hardly call $1 million a few bucks. You're out, aren't ya!? Just sit there and shut up, you prep school prick!"

A few minutes later the chatter on the radio heats up, and Christopher Cioffi's voice is heard, *"This is Homicide Detective Cioffi. We've got an APB out for a Joliet Prison transport car carrying escaped prisoner, Malcolm Land, and Joliet Security Chief, Felix Falmann, who orchestrated Land's escape. Both are considered armed and dangerous. We have reason to believe they're headed for Chicago, and if you spot their vehicle you're instructed to notify me immediately and call for back-up. We've got officers guarding the Land Foundation office on Erie Street and Land's sister's home on the Gold Coast. Joliet's less than an hour away, so keep your eyes pealed and your radios tuned to this frequency. That's it for now. Cioffi, out!"*

"Handy little radio, you've got there, Falmann. We're gonna need to dump this car though. I've got a vehicle stashed at the warehouse, provided it still starts after sitting idly for four years."

Thirty minutes later Malcolm directs Felix through a series of turns and finally has him pull slowly down an unlit alley. "Pull over here and kill your headlights, Falmann." They sit still in the dark car for a few minutes to see if their arrival has attracted any unwanted attention.

"Let's go," Malcolm says. They exit the car and approach an old, windowless, brick building with a metal garage door and stout-looking lock.

"Now what, wise guy? I suppose you brought a key with you, Einstein."

Malcolm doesn't bother to reply. He walks to the side of the brick building and moves a heavy rock near the foundation revealing a small metal box holding an old key. He returns to the door, inserts the key, unlocks the lock, and slides the garage door up. "Pull your car inside, Falmann."

Felix drives the prison car inside, and Malcolm motions to a stall on the side where he wants him to park it. He closes and locks the garage door and turns on the interior lights. They stand still and again listen for any unwelcome sounds.

"Okay, I think we're good," Malcolm says. They both smile sly grins. "I told you those cops are a bunch of morons."

"Enough small talk, Land, I don't plan on spending any more time with a con like you than necessary. Where's my dough? I wanna get out of this city pronto."

"Ease up, Falmann, it's over here. I'd planned on using it as my little nest egg if and when I ever got out of Joliet. Guess I'm gonna have to view the $1 million as the cost of doing business, huh?"

"Guess so, Einstein," Falmann replies snidely. Malcolm leads him over to a dingy interior office and approaches a large, locked cabinet. This time he grabs a wrench, and with some effort, he muscles the lock free and the door swings open. Malcolm drags a wooden chest from the bottom of the cabinet and drops it on the floor.

"Go ahead and open it, Falmann. This is what you came for!" Felix Falmann kneels down on the concrete floor and opens the latch to a large, carved wood chest. In his mind it looks like a treasure chest. He opens the lid and stares in rapt excitement. There are wads of hundred dollar bills, two rows of neatly organized gold coins, and a Kimber 1911 handgun which Falmann quickly grabs and stuffs in his belt. He laughs greedily and turns to face Malcolm and is rewarded with a skull-crunching blow from Malcolm's wrench. Then he delivers another blow, then another and another until Felix Falmann, the former chief security officer for the Joliet Correctional Center, lies on the floor, his head a bloody, pulpy, lifeless mess.

"And that's what you get for calling me Einstein, ass-wipe!" Malcolm grabs the Kimber, Felix's other handgun, and the police radio; then awkwardly lofts Felix's body and crams it into the cabinet. He uses an old rag to clean up the mess he's made and tosses it inside the cabinet. "Neatness counts," he muses out loud.

Next, Malcolm walks over to the Lexus SUV he'd stored away, climbs inside, grabs the key from the sun visor, and tries to start it. Dead battery. He takes another wrench and screwdriver and goes over to Falmann's prison vehicle and lifts the hood. He frees the battery from the car and carries it over to the Lexus and attaches it to its terminals. He spies a five-gallon gas can and carefully pours it into the Lexus. The car's interior lights gleam brightly as he opens the driver's door this time indicating that he's got juice. He turns the key, and voila, the engine roars to life. "Gotta love these Jap cars!" he praises.

With effort Malcolm then drags the wooden chest over to the Lexus, puts a few hundred dollar bills in his pocket, and lifts the heavy chest into the trunk. He drives out of the building, then returns inside for a final scan of the building's interior. Everything looks okay. Malcolm turns off the building's interior lights, steps outside, closes the garage door, relocks it, and tosses the key into the bushes.

"Free at last!" he murmurs to himself as he drives off into the night. "Now, I need to settle a few scores!"

Chapter 8

W E ALL SIT AROUND Lucretia's elegant dining table in a pecan-paneled room displaying vases of flowers, sculptures, paintings, art glass, and a panoramic view of her impeccable gardens and Lake Michigan beyond. Despite the palpable, uneasy feeling we share about Malcolm's escape, we're actually having a very good time. In fact, I can't recall the last time I had so much fun in a kitchen as when we each bumped and excused our way though the preparation of various salads, breads, pasta, and side dishes. No doubt, the consumption of a few bottles of wine

and lively music helped. I look at Robert and wonder if he's ever been in a home as elegant as Lucretia's, but then I can't recall if I've ever been either, and I've been in some pretty impressive digs. Maggie and Tori are definitely in their cups and appear to be having the time of their lives. And Robert, forever stoic in manner and speech, is beaming at the camaraderie we're experiencing.

And now, the food is on the table and the candles are lit. Lucretia uses a remote control device to dim the lights, change the tempo of the music, and lower the volume. With a wine glass in hand and a smile on her face, she stands to offer a toast.

"So, here we are, old friends and new, cast together for a 'first supper' of sorts as we prepare for a new adventure in the Keweenaw Peninsula." Lucretia takes an uncharacteristically large slug of wine and looks at each of us, and continues. "To my trusted friend, Clay Arnold, with whom I have shared some of the most thrilling and terrifying episodes in my life, I can't adequately say how great it is to be together again, my friend, and hopefully we'll escape the trauma and turmoil of our first adventure." We solemnly nod at each other, knowing all too well the heartache we endured on our search for Samuel Morse's art treasure.

"To Maggie and Tori, with whom I'm only just now getting acquainted. It's a joy to be with you, and I look forward to our all being friends ever after!" Lucretia takes a dainty sip from her wine glass and politely stifles a burp. "And I promise you once the authorities finally get their hands on my nutcase brother, Malcolm, we'll find a time to meet again in Chicago, look at art, wine and dine ourselves silly, and shop till we drop." There's a rousing "hear, hear!" from Maggie and Tori.

"And to Robert Midew, man of mystery, with one really big canine, I can't thank you enough for trusting the Land Foundation to help present what promises to be the most significant ethnographic art find in North America. I pledge to you that our foundation will do everything we can to respect your peoples' heritage. By the way, Robert, I know that I'm rip-roaring drunk, but I sincerely mean every word I'm saying."

Robert respectfully raises his glass to Lucretia and nods understandingly. "After this upcoming trip to our home in the Keweenaw, Lucretia, you will be one of us, like Clay and his family. My people and I are grateful for your help, and I promise you a memorable adventure, dear lady." Robert briefly looks my way, and our eyes meet. I sense something that I have rarely felt or seen in him before … concern.

There's a knock on the front door and a moment later Uncle Drew Thomas enters carrying a cake box and another bottle of wine. Lucretia is still standing, albeit now leaning against her chair, and calls out, "And to my beloved Uncle Drew who has forever been my knight in shining armor."

Drew realizes that he's entered in the middle of a toast by Lucretia, and he raises his unopened wine bottle to her in acknowledgement. Lucretia finally concludes her inebriated praises and plops down between Tori and Maggie. She places her hand over her glass when Maggie offers her more wine. "I think I've already had *tar foo much,* but bon appétit, guys!"

We enjoy dinner, and spend the next two hours getting to know each other. Everyone is curious about Robert, mainly because I've told our family on more than one occasion that he is endowed with very unique mystical powers. Last year Rennie and I witnessed firsthand what some of those supernatural abilities are, but out of respect for Robert and to protect his privacy and the sanctity of their culture, we've pledged not to discuss specifics with anyone. Besides, I've already freaked Maggie out enough with some of the stuff I get involved in. Nothing to be gained by giving her the full monty!

"So, Robert, what can you tell us about the work that Rennie and Ranger Kelli are doing with you?" Maggie asks. "Clay and Rennie have told us some impressive things about the art, but I think we'd all enjoy hearing more from you."

"Yes, Robert, please do," Lucretia adds.

Without preamble, Robert stands and walks over to the large picture window with his back to us. He stares into the distance at Lake Michigan and begins, "Several millennia ago, my Chippewa people descended from the Anishinaabe, the original people. The extensive cave art under Brockway Mountain that Rennie, Kelli, and I are working on illustrates our migration story. It is said that our people originally came from a place near a great salt sea. We believe that region was the Canadian Maritime Provinces."

Robert turns to face us with a solemn expression. "The legends state that the seven prophets warned that the Anishinaabe must leave this place, seek the sacred Megis shell, and find a new home where food grows on the water. They proclaimed that if we did not do this, we would perish. It took nearly five hundred years, with long sojourns along the way, but our Chippewa people, along with our sister tribes, the Ojibway, the Ottawa, and the Potawatomi, eventually settled in the northern regions of Michigan, Wisconsin, Minnesota, and central Canada. The artwork we are studying and now wish to share with the world is a pictorial history of our journeys and our travails."

Robert looks in my direction, and nods his head affirmatively. "My people have always struggled with the white-skinned race. We are wary because the faces of friends and foes often look the same. Words and promises often turn hollow. Last summer when Clay and I searched for Rennie and Kelli under the great mountain, we came across wondrous things, not just the artwork, things that are deeply rooted in our culture, things that we protect from the egocentric greed of the white-skinned world. And, because the four of us banded together and survived terrifying tribulations, we've forged an uncommon bond. It is because of this bond, Lucretia, that I trust Clay's recommendation to work with you and the Land Foundation."

Lucretia looks deeply into Robert's steel-gray eyes. "I understand, Robert, and I respect your concerns about letting outsiders into your world. I promise to be a gracious guest in your homeland." Robert pauses contemplatively and offers her an agreeable expression in return.

I look at Maggie and Tori who are spellbound by Robert's words. "What tribulations, Robert?" I hear Maggie ask. "Can you tell us about the tribulations the four of you faced last summer because Clay has been very adamant about not saying anything?"

"Your husband is a wise man and a trusted friend. He would have done you no favor by being too forthcoming. Perhaps there may come a time when you will understand, but this is not something I choose to speak about tonight. I hope you can accept this."

Maggie nods her acceptance, but I have a feeling that before we fall asleep tonight my wife and the mother of our children will try to stealthily broach the subject with me again. I honestly can't blame her though.

Over the next hour or so we all continue to get acquainted. Tori spends a good deal of time speaking with Robert about now being able to see, and how he changed her and Mace's lives through his "gifts" to them. Maggie joins in their conversation but doesn't try to ply him with more questions about last summer's tribulations. Then around eleven o'clock we hear the doorbell ring again, and Lucretia and Drew go to answer it. A police officer stands at the door with another figure. "This gentleman says he's a friend of yours. I told him it was a little late to be making a social call, but he insisted."

"Mace, you came!" Lucretia calls out, and I turn to see our friend beaming his quintessential grin in the doorway. Lucretia gives him a warm embrace, and Drew helps him carry his gear inside. I walk over to greet him.

"Good lord, Mace, I didn't expect you to drive all the way up here tonight. You must be pretty tuckered."

"I'm a little weary," he admits, "but since you said you had all of your gear ready to go, I decided I might as well load it in Maggie's car and not mess with finding a shipper at this late hour. Besides, I brought you something else, just in case."

"Oh?!" I say, but I have a pretty good idea what he means.

Now, Mace has a chance to spend time with Robert, and their connection is instantaneous and positive. It's the first time that they've met in person and now Robert has had a chance to personally meet everyone in my family of friends, with the exception of Bodie and Satchmo.

"It's good to see you looking all hale and hearty," Robert says, and Mace acknowledges, "Thanks to you, my friend."

While Mace grabs a late dinner, we all help clear the leftover food and dishes from the dining room and clean up the kitchen. Maggie and Tori help Lucretia set the breakfast dishes out and prep the coffee maker. I look around at our assemblage of friends and feel very fortunate. Knowing that Malcolm Land is on the loose somewhere is a very unsettling thought, but having the cops and Grey and Robert on the scene assuages my concerns.

"I'm heading to bed!" Lucretia announces, and then the doorbell rings again. It's a different police officer this time, and he's standing in the doorway with Grey.

"Uh, any of you folks missing a really big wolf?" Grey leans against the officer's leg and appears to have a smile on his face. "Good boy," the cop says nervously. "He came out of the bushes, gently took my jacket sleeve in his teeth, and walked me to the door. Damndest thing!"

Grey strides inside and goes to Robert's side who scratches him behind the ear. "Good wolf," he says softly. With Lucretia's permission, Robert retrieves a raw lamb-shank bone and gives it to his lifelong friend. "Now, go back out with your new buddy and search and protect." Grey nudges the officer back out the front door. We hear the cop say, "I'm coming, I'm coming. Glad to see you enjoying your lamb bone instead of one in my leg."

Ten minutes later we say our goodnights and wander off to the bedrooms Lucretia has prepared for us. To her credit, Maggie surprises me by not asking me any further questions about last summer's turmoil under Brockway Mountain. All in all it's been a cozy and engaging evening, but I can't get that nagging sense of Robert's preternatural concern out of my mind. When it comes to Robert Midew, I've learned to trust his instincts … and mine.

Chapter 9

EARLY THE NEXT MORNING Malcolm Land wakes up in a grumpy mood having spent the night inside his cramped Lexus. He feels tight and cold and tries to stretch his legs inside the car's confines without much relief. He turns off the car's dome light, opens the door, and steps outside to pee. After he relieves himself, he returns inside and hunkers down, looking and listening for any sign of activity. He's parked on the secluded street where Lucretia lives, about a hundred yards from the entrance to

her driveway. From this vantage point he's able to see any cars that enter or leave her property.

"This is bullshit," he mutters to himself. "I was better off in prison. At least I'd be warm and could have a crappy cup of coffee, and what the hell was all that howling I heard last night." He pulls his jacket tightly around his torso and shifts lower in his seat to conceal his presence. Even though the car has darkly tinted windows, he saw the two police officers patrolling Lucretia's property last night and doesn't want to risk getting caught. "I'll give this bullshit surveillance another hour max and then move on if I need to, but I'd sure like to surprise my dear sister."

Inside the house Robert Midew awakes, dresses, and quietly slips outside into Lucretia's garden. He's greeted by a rosy-fingered dawn and his friend, Grey.

"There you are, big fella," he says as he bends down and touches his forehead to the great beast's. "Any trouble last night? You didn't eat the police officers did you?" Grey wags his tail and goes running off into the bushes. A few moments later he reappears bringing one of the cops with him.

"G'morning, officer," he says. "All quiet last night?"

"Yeah, all quiet with the exception of a little rustling in the bushes and some occasional howling.

You've got yourself quite an animal, sir. Have you had him long?"

"Pretty long," Robert replies. "We grew up together, didn't we fella?" Grey wags his tail and gives an agreeable yelp. "C'mon, Grey, let's go inside, and we'll get some breakfast." They leave the officer to his appointed rounds and walk back inside to the kitchen. They find me alone with a cup of steamy coffee in my hand, and I extend another cup to Robert. Robert opens the refrigerator and pulls out another lamb bone for Grey and fills a bowl with water.

"I think we're the only ones up. Not surprising given the amount of wine we downed last night." A moment later we turn to see Mace enter the kitchen. He grabs a cup of coffee, and the three men, plus Grey, walk into the dining room to enjoy the view and wait for the others to regain consciousness.

"I still can't believe that you drove up here last night, Mace, but I'm glad you did. Thanks for bringing my camera gear."

"You're welcome, Clay, I figured it would save you a lot of time if I just brought it all up here. No sense in trying to ship delicate photo equipment. Besides, I wanted to thank Robert in person for his gift to me and finally meet the living legend in the flesh."

"It is a pleasure to meet you as well, Mace. Clay has told me much about you and your friendship, and I can sense much more too."

"Oh?" Mace says. "And what do you sense?"

"That you're a man of honor who sprang from very humble beginnings, and that you'd do anything to protect your family."

"Yeah, kind of a family trait, right, Clay?" I nod my head affirmatively.

"I also sense you and Clay have shared and survived many life-threatening adventures and that there will be others in your future."

"Oh, and how do you know that?"

"Let's just say that information has a way of flowing to me," Robert replies.

I look at Mace as he tries to comprehend the gravitas of Robert's words. "Trust him, Mace, our friend Robert is able to see into the heart of things like no other person I've known."

"I also sense, Mace, that you and I are destined to be trusted friends."

"That's good to know. I'll try not to screw that up," Mace quips.

Several minutes later Lucretia comes staggering into the kitchen. Her hair is in disarray, and she has no makeup on. "Coffee!" she blurts aloud. "I need coffee!" She then walks over to Mace and buries her face in his chest.

"Gee, Mace, when did you get here?"

"Uh, last night, Lucretia. Remember? You and Drew opened the front door for me."

"Oh yeah, I think I may have had a little too much to drink last night. Did I sing any opera?"

"No opera, although I'm sure you have a very good voice. How are you feeling this morning?"

Lucretia rolls her eyes and offers a faint smile. "Like twelve miles of bad road." She buries her face in Mace's chest again and then says, "C'mon guys, why don't you cook up some breakfast, and I'll get Maggie and Tori up and at 'em."

A few minutes later Lucretia returns with Maggie and Tori in tow. "Got any coffee left?" Maggie pleads. Tori sits down and rests her head on the breakfast table. "At least when I was blind I couldn't see how bad I look in the morning after getting blotto."

"On my best day I wish I was as good looking as you are now," Lucretia confesses.

"Here," Mace responds handing Tori and Maggie each a cup of strong, black coffee as Robert and I take turns scrambling eggs, frying sausage, and preparing toast. "That was quite a soiree you threw for us last night, Lucretia," I offer.

"Well, with Malcolm on the loose, it seemed like a good idea at the time. We better get a move on though. No telling what my brother might want to do after spending four years in prison. The last time we spoke he swore he'd get even with me for taking everything away from him."

"Pretty damn delusional, I'd say, Lucretia, considering he was the one who took everything away from you and wanted even more."

"Was he always this selfish and mean?" Maggie asks.

"He was always a difficult child, but manageable, although I once overheard my father tell my mother that *there's something not quite right about that boy*. Over time he got worse, and as we got older, and he had a lot of money in his pocket, he felt that he no longer had to follow rules … house rules or societal rules. Then our mother died, and you could tell that Malcolm just didn't care what anyone thought anymore. He decided that the family wealth insulated him from listening to anyone."

"There's much more, isn't there?" Robert asks.

"Yes," Lucretia replies soberly. "Then, he decided that he wanted all of the family money and control of the Land Foundation and its vast art holdings. Around the time that I met Clay and Weed, Malcolm was already slowly but systematically poisoning our father, and he coerced an outside attorney to change Father's will. In the end Father was so sick from the poison he signed away the family fortune to Malcolm, leaving me with nothing except this house."

At this point we're all captivated by the tragic family story Lucretia is sharing. "Couldn't you stop him?" Tori pleads. "You and Uncle Drew?"

"Believe me, we tried, Tori, but Malcolm had hired an evil henchman named Ernst Kline. Kline killed our family attorney, Benton Pettengill, and then the bastard murdered your brother, Weed."

I can't bear to make eye contact with Tori and instead look at the floor with the devastating memory of my closest friend dying in my arms.

"I remember him all too well, Lucretia," Mace says. "That Kline guy got the drop on us at home in the brewery complex. He shot me in the shoulder and was about two seconds away from killing Clay, Maggie, and Tori when Rennie shot him first."

I look at Maggie and Tori sympathetically and then at Robert.

"You've all endured great heartache and suffering," Robert offers. "No wonder why you stay so closely connected."

We finish eating our breakfast and clean up the dishes. Lucretia telephones Detective Cioffi to let him know that we'll be leaving very shortly. She tells him that Uncle Drew has agreed to look after operations at the Foundation while she's in the Keweenaw and keep an eye on her home too. I call Rennie to let him know we're getting ready to depart Chicago, and that we'll see him later in the day.

Twenty minutes later Mace and I have transferred my camera gear to my truck, and we're set to go. Lucretia, Tori, and Maggie will follow us in Lucretia's car, and Robert and Grey will lead our three-car caravan in Robert's Jeep. We leave Maggie's car at Lucretia's home and will pick it up on the way home.

"Everyone ready?" I ask. "Destination: Copper Harbor, Michigan, about eight hours away due north." Robert slowly drives down Lucretia's driveway onto her street, followed by the rest of us.

In his car Malcolm suddenly sees us all pull out together and form a single-file line. He scrunches further down in his seat as we approach and pass his car. He sees that Lucretia's car is the third in line. "Hmm, I wonder where they're all going together. No doubt they know I busted out of Joliet. I bet they're trying to get out of town for someplace safe." Malcolm starts the Lexus's engine, turns his car in their direction, and decides to follow them maintaining a safe distance behind.

"Won't good ol' Lucretia be surprised to see me again?" he scoffs. "Slow and easy does it, Malcolm, my boy. All in good time. If nothing else, prison taught me patience … and the sweetness of revenge."

Chapter 10

EVEN AT THIS EARLY morning hour traffic heading north out of Chicago is congested. We all stay in the middle lane and follow the highway signs for Milwaukee and Green Bay. I look in the rearview mirror and see Maggie, Tori, and Lucretia maintaining a safe distance. I'm delighted that they're all together, bonding.

Mace and I have traveled together enough over the years that we're comfortable not speaking for long stretches at a time. After a while, though, Mace says, "I see what you mean about Robert and Grey,

Clay, there's a certain mysticism about them that's hard to explain."

"You have no idea, my friend. I've never been a big believer in the supernatural world, but then I met them … and Nokomis."

"Who's Nokomis?" Mace asks. "I've never heard you talk about her before."

"Uh, yeah, that's because I haven't, Mace, and I probably shouldn't have mentioned her now." I see that Mace looks a little hurt. "Please don't misunderstand, Mace, you know that I trust you implicitly, but some things are best left unspoken, and I'll bet you dollars to doughnuts that Robert knows that I just told you that."

"That's crazy talk, Clay, there's no way he could know that. So, who's Nokomis?"

I look at Mace. "Wanna bet?! Nokomis is Robert's grandmother, and even Robert would admit that when it comes to the supernatural world and sorcery, Nokomis has him beat hands down."

"You're serious about this, aren't you? Are there other things that you and Rennie haven't shared with me about your experience under Brockway Mountain last summer?"

"Yes," I answer truthfully.

"And?" Mace replies, "Are you gonna share any more details?"

"Nope!" I say without hesitation. "Look, Mace, like I said a minute ago, I trust you with my life, and you know more of my secrets than anyone on the planet. But … I've seen things and witnessed an evil being that I never would've dreamed possible. Over time I think Robert will share information with you, and I prefer to leave it up to him to decide when. I know this is probably frustrating for you, but I want you to trust me on this, okay?"

"Okay," Mace agrees reluctantly. We drive another few miles in silence, and then Mace reaches in his pocket. "I brought something to show you."

"Oh?!" I ask, and then I see him holding the harmonica that he showed me in our subbasement work room.

"Ah! The Weed Killer!" I exclaim and see Mace beaming with pride. "Have you tried it yet?" I ask.

"Oh, yeah! I fine tuned the microwaves with the harmonics and stabilized the targeting mechanism. It's one bitchin' sweet device. I thought you could carry the Demon camera, and I could carry the Weed Killer until you've had a chance to become better acquainted with it. How's that sound?"

"Sounds good to me, my friend, and thanks for getting everything worked out. I just hope we don't have to use them."

An hour or so later we take the entrance ramp for I-43 North through Milwaukee and head toward

Green Bay. Having traveled this way last summer to visit Rennie in the Keweenaw, I know that we'll have to endure congested traffic until we get past Green Bay. Then, the terrain will gradually change into woods and lakes with far fewer people. When we see signs for the city of Manitowoc, Robert takes the exit, and we follow him so we can gas up, pee, and stretch our legs. Unbeknown to us another vehicle takes the same exit and pulls into a gas station on the other side of the road. Malcolm gets out and quickly runs inside to use the restroom and grab some coffee and a box of doughnuts and sandwiches. He gasses up his car as he devours a couple of glazed twists and watches us.

"Oh, Clay Arnold," Malcolm mutters aloud, "and that old black man, Mace something or other. I don't think they'll get away from me this time. If it hadn't been for that meddling old fool, Drew Thomas, and that asshole cop, Cioffi, I would've had them and dear sister, Lucretia, entombed in Samuel Morse's mausoleum for eternity. Oh well … patience and revenge."

I join Maggie, Tori, and Lucretia at their gas pump to see how they're getting along. "We're happy as clams, aren't we, girls?" Maggie exclaims. "Sure enuf, Sugar!" Tori adds with an exaggerated Southern accent. Lucretia nods affirmatively, and the three of them climb back inside Lucretia's car and strap in for the next leg of our journey.

Mace and I walk over to Robert and Grey who is lifting his leg on a nearby tree. We look at a map to see where we want to stop for lunch. Robert knows the area well and suggests a diner that he's familiar with in the town of Crivitz, Wisconsin. "There's also a Piggly Wiggly grocery store there in case the ladies and you guys need to pick up some things you weren't able to get because of our abrupt departure from Chicago. A little north of Crivitz we'll enter the UP of Michigan, and towns with larger stores will be far and few between."

Mace looks at Robert with quizzical interest because I mentioned his and Nokomis's special powers. Robert sees him staring at him and smiles knowingly. "Ready to get on the road again?" he asks us. We say yes, and walk over to my truck. As we're about to get in, Robert shouts over to Mace, "Don't worry, Mace, Nokomis is unusual but perfectly harmless … unless you really piss her off." He laughs, and he and Grey get back inside his Jeep.

Mace gives me a stupefied glance. "But how'd he know?" Mace starts to ask. I look at him sympathetically. "Now do you believe me?" I reply, and then we strap our seat belts for the next leg of our journey. Mace looks at me for more of an answer, but I return his bewildered stare with an *I told you so* expression.

Our little caravan pulls out of the gas station, heading north toward Green Bay and then Crivitz for lunch. A hundred yards behind us Malcolm Land trails Lucretia's car as he munches on another glazed doughnut. He licks his fingers and wipes them dry on his pant leg.

Meanwhile three hundred miles north in the Keweenaw Peninsula, Rennie and Ranger Kelli take a break from their curating the Paleo-Indian art under Brockway Mountain and drive over to Evergreen Point Lodge to have lunch with Thomas Arrowsmith. Thomas is Kelli's retired mentor at the National Park Service and someone who has lived for many years in the area around Copper Harbor and Brockway Mountain. They pull Kelli's Forester into the lodge's parking lot and get out.

"Thomas is already here," Kelli says.

"How do you know?" Rennie asks. She points at a vintage Studebaker pickup truck parked under an enormous pine tree. "Look at the truck's door."

"Of course!" Rennie exclaims. Neatly painted on the door is the image of an Indian arrow with the name Smith underneath it … Arrowsmith. "I remember now. Thomas used the same image on his mailbox. I recall seeing it when we visited him at his home last summer."

"Good memory, Rennie, let's go see what he's been up to." They walk inside the lodge's dining room and spot Thomas sitting by himself next to a large picture window overlooking the town of Copper Harbor. He sees them approach and rises to say hello. "Kelli! How good to see you. As usual, it's been way too long. I imagine you're keeping yourself pretty busy at the park service."

Kelli gives her old mentor a warm hug. "It's always great to see you, my friend, and I trust that you remember my partner in crime, Rennie Cotton," she jests.

"Of course I do. Rennie, very nice to see you again. Have you come back for another summer internship with Kelli?"

"Well sorta, actually I never left, Thomas, I imagine you got wind of Kelli and me working with Robert Midew on a special Paleo-Indian project."

"Yeah, I had some personal business in Baraga a while back and stopped in to see Robert at the Chippewa Council office. We had a very good conversation about the cave art you guys stumbled upon last summer, but I could tell that Robert was only comfortable sharing certain details with me. I'm sure he has his reasons."

"Well, you know Robert, he is a man of mystery, and he knows how to protect secrets, especially as they relate to the Chippewa people and their culture. So, how've you been keeping yourself busy, Thomas?"

"Oh, looking after my property keeps me busy, and I try to stay fit by walking the woods around here and on Brockway Mountain. Now that the winter snows are finally behind us, I've been getting out more and trying to keep these aging legs from crapping out on me."

"Well you look fit to me," Rennie replies. "And by the way thanks for suggesting that we have lunch here. Ordinarily, Kelli and I bring our lunches with us and eat inside the mountain near the cave art. My parents, my Aunt Tori, and a family friend from Chicago are on their way up here with Robert Midew now, and we've booked several rooms for them here at Evergreen Point Lodge. You may recall that my dad's Clay Arnold, and Robert has asked him to photograph the ancient Chippewa cave paintings."

"Indeed, I do remember that your dad is the famous photographer. You guys must've had a very memorable experience last summer with Robert for him to want to work closely with you."

Kelli and Rennie look at each other briefly, and despite her positive relationship with Thomas, Kelli chooses not to give away any information that she feels Robert, himself, would be reluctant to share. "Yeah, it was quite an unforgettable experience, and what we're learning from the stories illustrated in the cave art is opening up a whole new understanding of the native people who lived here hundreds, even thousands of years ago."

"You may recall, Kelli, that my mother is full-blooded Chippewa. She's over a hundred years old now with no immediate signs of slowing up. She lives in a nursing home near Baraga, but I swear she's got more on the ball than most of the aides. When I was young my mother told me stories of her people and the ancient ones, including some pretty fantastical tales that she swore were true. My father often chided her for filling my head with nonsense, but she always stuck by the stories. As an adult working at the park service, I once ridiculed one of the stories about an evil, man-eating spirit called a Windigo to Robert."

Rennie and Kelli shoot each other a cautionary glance, knowing full well that the Windigo is not a subject for discussion. "Anyway, Robert made it clear he didn't appreciate my belittling remarks, especially since I have some Chippewa blood running through my veins. I don't think he ever fully trusted me after that."

"I'm sorry to hear that, Thomas," was all Kelli could think to say.

They enjoy a leisurely lunch talking and catching up on local news and gossip. Then, Thomas says, "Well, I suppose you two need to get back to the Brockway caves. If you ever want me to tag along and help with your work, I'll be happy to do it. Some days I miss my old work, and it could be fun to see what you're working on before it all goes public."

"It's always good seeing you, Thomas," Rennie says. "Kelli and I need to get going though. We need to stop by the lodge's front desk to make sure everything is ready for my mom and dad and the others when they arrive this evening."

"Well, keep my offer in mind, Kelli. Heck, You never know, I might just drop in on you unannounced since I sometimes walk that way."

"Okay, Thomas, well it's been great seeing you. Take care of yourself."

Rennie and Kelli walk off toward the lobby of the lodge. "I think he's really bored," Kelli remarks, "but I hope that he doesn't just show up unannounced. I've always liked Thomas because he was helpful to me when I was a rookie ranger, but I can't say that I know him very well. He retired from the park service about six months after I was hired. I think he took early retirement which always surprised me because he seemed to enjoy the field work so much. His comment about Robert not entirely trusting him doesn't sit well with me though. I doubt that Robert would feel that way without good reason."

"I agree, Kelli. His comment got my attention too, but for now let's put Thomas behind us and make sure all the accommodations are ready for everyone at the lodge. Then, we need to get back to work."

"Ah, spoken like a true, dedicated drudge, Mr. Cotton!" she teases. "Back to the mines!"

Chapter 11

WITH ROBERT AND GREY leading our mini caravan, we cruise through Green Bay, Wisconsin, and continue north on US Route 141. We pass through small towns with charming monikers like Little Suamico, Lena, Coleman, Pound, and Beaver.

"Who comes up with names like these?" Mace asks sarcastically. "I mean, I get Beaver because we're getting pretty far north, but couldn't they come up with something more colorful like Maceville or Macetown?"

I look over at my friend and see him grinning. "Clearly, you need something to eat, Mace, because I think your low blood sugar is addling your brain function. Do you think you can hold out for another hour, or do I need to contact Washington and ask how we can change the names of towns?"

"That would be interesting, Clay, but I think I'll hold out for a cheeseburger and fries." Then Mace's tone turns serious. "So, Clay, how do you feel about going back up to Brockway Mountain?

"Well, it'll great to be with Rennie, of course, and I'm looking forward to seeing Kelli again, but I have to admit that I'll feel some trepidation going into the mine and its side caverns. If we were doing it without Robert and Grey, I'd probably be micturating myself."

"But, Rennie and Kelli have been spending time curating the cave art. They seem to deal with being underground okay."

"I guess you're right, Mace, but Rennie told me that he and Kelli stay in one centralized area of the caves and haven't ventured into other regions because doing so would dredge up memories they prefer not to think about. Rennie also shared with me that he and Kelli swear they hear disturbing sounds from time to time. Like I said, if it weren't for Robert's and Grey's presences, I don't know that any of us would venture back inside Brockway Mountain."

"It was that bad, huh?" Mace asks seriously.

"The worst, most terrifying experiences I've ever had," I reply frankly, and then I shiver just thinking about the Windigo. "But, the cave art is unbelievable, and I'm really glad you're along to see it firsthand."

"It's great that Maggie and Tori are along too. I'm sure Rennie will be very excited to show them around, and to finally introduce them to Kelli. He's developing into a very fine young man."

"Yeah, he is, and I'm really pleased that we're all gonna be together." A few moments pass, and I say, "You know, Mace, I was thinking a little while ago how having Robert and Grey involved with Lucretia and our family of friends is a fascinating blend of people from my past experiences. I find it to be a very curious intersection of lives; although I imagine that Robert might say that there's nothing curious about it, that it's the nature of our spirits that brings us together. One thing's for sure though, Mace, last summer taught me that there are other forces in play in our little planet than most of us haven't any clue about. I now know that for a fact, my friend."

Mace glances at me and sees the earnest look on my face. "I take you at your word, Clay. Not having been there, though, it's hard for me to grasp the full weight of what you're saying."

About an hour later we arrive at the bustling metropolis of Crivitz, Wisconsin, boasting a population of some 984 hardy souls, and Robert guides us into a parking space at the Bon Ton Diner. We don't notice another vehicle pull into the parking lot of a fast-food restaurant across the road. Malcolm Land manages to conceal his presence, then leaps out to use the bathroom and order a take-out lunch.

We all get out of our vehicles and stretch our legs. Grey spots a fake fire hydrant and takes a real leak on it, then jumps through the open passenger window of Robert's Jeep to await our return. Lucretia looks around and says, "Well, ladies, it's not the Magnificent Mile, but if they have a clean bathroom and a salad bar, I'm okay with that!"

"Gee!" Maggie adds as she looks at our attire of trendy denim jeans and fashionable tops. "I think we may be a little overdressed for the restaurant. Wattya think, Tori?!"

"Well, it's not Stella's Diner, but if Robert endorses it, I'm game."

We enter the diner, and I inhale the fat-filled aroma emanating from the kitchen. There's something about the homespun ambience and welcoming smell of diners that's pretty universal, and this one is no exception. A portly, middle-aged woman named Claire welcomes us as we enter and leads us to a large table near a picture window. "Hello, folks, we serve breakfast all day if you're interested, or you can order off the menu, or visit our salad bar." She pours coffee for Mace and me and gets drink orders from the others. At this hour most of the lunch crowd is gone, and we take turns using the bathroom facilities.

A few minutes later Claire returns and asks what we're having. The ladies decide to try the salad bar, and Robert requests the walleye dinner. True to his word, Mace gets a cheeseburger and fries.

"How's your Reuben sandwich?" I ask Claire.

"It's okay," she replies evenly.

"Not exactly a ringing endorsement," I say. "How about your ham salad sandwich?" I ask hoping for a more encouraging reply. I see Robert give me a private little head shake indicating no.

"Not as good as the Reuben," Claire responds frankly.

"Well then, how about your fish tacos?" I ask. "Your menu says they're world-famous."

"We ran out of the tacos. You shoulda been here an hour ago."

"Okay," I say. "What do you suggest?" I ask Claire since I'm not in the mood for the picked-over salad bar fixins'.

"The turkey club sandwich is popular," she offers. "It comes hot or cold, open or closed face on white, whole wheat, sourdough, multigrain, raisin, or pumpernickel bread."

"Gee willikers!" I guffaw all giddy-like. "So many options! I think I'll have the Reuben on pumpernickel and onion rings!" Maggie rolls her eyes at me, and Claire waddles off to the kitchen shaking her head.

Once our food arrives and the ladies have loaded up their plates at the salad bar, we settle in for a leisurely lunch. Everyone around the table remains curious about Robert and his life in the Keweenaw Peninsula.

"My interests?!" he replies to Lucretia's question about how he spends his time. "Well, as president of the Keweenaw Bay Chippewa Council, I spend a portion of every day making sure that the needs of my people are met, mostly issues dealing with government funding for education, healthcare, and infrastructure. We have our own police force on the reservation, and I work closely with our officers to settle various disputes. During the winter I help with a lot of snow removal. We get about three hundred inches of snow every year, so it doesn't do us any good to have schools and medical clinics if people can't get to them."

"Three hundred inches of snow?!" Maggie asks incredulously. "Have you ever considered moving the tribe to Miami?" she teases Robert.

"Only once," he teases her back, "but our Jewish friends in Miami didn't believe me when I told them we're one of the ten lost tribes of Israel."

Mace damn near chokes on a french fry. "That's really funny," he hoarsely replies. "And here I thought you were a serious dude all the time."

"When you've been around as long as we have, Mace, you eventually develop a sense of humor or go nuts, right?" Mace nods affirmatively.

"So, how old are you, Robert? You have kind of a timeless appearance." Tori asks.

"Thanks! I turned five hundred and two last autumn, but I don't think I look a day over three hundred, maybe three fifty, max."

Everyone laughs, including me, but I believe that he's actually telling the truth. He glances my way briefly, flashes me a snarky *I-know-what-you're-thinking* grin, and takes another bite of walleye.

Meanwhile outside in the parking lot five teenage boys pull up near our vehicles playing loud music and taunting each other out of boredom. A meaty-looking lad named Billy Wormpter is the alpha male of their little, pimply-faced, testosterone-filled Crivitz Clodhopper Club. Granted, living in a small town has its limitations for compelling entertainment, but these juvenile delinquents always manage to create their own excitement.

They get out of their old Chevy Blazer and approach our three vehicles peering in the windows, looking for stuff. They approach Lucretia's vehicle first. "Hey, you goobers, check out the Mercedes SUV! Now that's one sweet ride!" Wormpter exhalts.

"Sure beats that rusty piece of crap Blazer you're driving, Wormpter!" Eddie Kissinger chides. They shade their eyes from the sun as they peer inside. They notice a couple of suitcases and then spy Tori's iPad and Lucretia's laptop. "Cool! I bet they've got other neat stuff too."

Another vehicle pulls into the parking lot, and the band of small-town delinquents tries to act non-chalant until the new guests are inside the diner.

Wormpter announces, "Let's check out the other cars and see what else is, uh, available."

They walk over to my Tacoma that Mace and I are traveling in and begin inspecting the interior. They see studio lights, tripods, and cases of my camera gear bearing the name Canon. It's all of my equipment for shooting the cave art. Then, they notice my Canon 5D Mark IV camera that Mace left partially concealed on the passenger seat. Billy Wormpter directs his pals to keep an eye out as he tries to open the door. He tugs at it with no luck. Locked.

From his vehicle across the road Malcolm munches on a chicken sandwich with unremarkable flavor and wipes away a dollop of mayonnaise that had dripped onto his thigh. He's amused at the brazenness of these founding members of the Clodhopper Club as they hover around the three vehicles, peering inside, and trying to open doors. "Well fellas!" he muses out loud. "I'd certainly give you an A for being ass-wipes … and in broad daylight no less."

Inside I suddenly notice Robert sit up straight and look out the picture window. I follow his gaze and so does Mace who gets up and walks to the front door. Robert's eyes squint intensely as he intuits the motives of these dropouts from charm school. Fortunately, Maggie, Tori, and Lucretia are heavily engaged in talking about stuff and don't notice our shift in mood.

Mace looks back at Robert and me looking for a signal about what to do next. Robert surreptiously raises his index finger to Mace indicating that he should hold off confronting the boys. I see Robert slightly squint his eyes again and hear him whisper, "Grey, protect."

Billy and Eddie leave my truck and move on to Robert's Jeep to see what treasures its interior holds. They bend down low and crab-walk over to the passenger side, and Eddie slowly rises to peer inside the open window. As his eyes reach the bottom of the window, he suddenly sees another set of eyes three inches away that causes his bladder to give way. "Mother!" he beseeches feebly as Grey lunges forward at the intruder grasping his fleshy, sweating, quivering throat in his powerful maw. Eddie tries in vain to swat the great canine's mouth away, but Grey leaps out of the window still holding on to the hapless lad. If Grey had intended to kill the boy, his death would've been instantaneous, but Grey's intention is only to scare the crap out of the boys and do as Robert had instructed him … to protect. Billy Wormpter sees his friend helplessly lying on the ground with the largest canine he's ever seen holding his buddy's neck and growling with a horrifyingly low timbre. Eddie pitifully looks to Billy for help as all of his friends run for the Blazer. From the front door Mace watches the spectacle unfold, and we both look at Robert to see what the boy's fate will be. Robert takes another bite out of his walleye dinner and quietly says, "Grey, release." Instantly, the huge wolf follows his human friend's command, jumps back inside the Jeep, leaving Eddie with wet dungarees and wolf slobber on his scuffed but mostly uninjured neck. Mace walks outside to check on the boy as the Blazer sprays a rooster-tail of gravel as its occupants flee the parking lot. Across the road Malcolm sits gape-mouthed wondering what the Sam Hill just happened. "That's one big friggin' doggy!"

"Are you okay, boy?" Mace asks unsympathetically. "Can you get up?" Grey watches closely from within the Jeep to see if he'll need to leap into action again. Mace pats the wolf's broad head and says, "Good wolf, Grey! And you, young fella," he says to Eddie, "I suggest you get out of here while you're still in one piece."

Eddie looks at the huge wolf and doesn't need to be told twice. He gets his feet under him, feels his neck for any serious damage, and staggers away with a look of bewilderment etched on his pimply face. Mace checks out the three vehicles for any damage and seeing none, he praises Grey again and walks inside to rejoin his companions. Mace sits down at the table and looks at me and Robert for any commentary about what just transpired. He receives nothing verbal from us, only amused smiles on our faces. Claire returns to our table and asks if we want dessert which we all decline.

Oblivious to the drama that transpired in the parking lot, Maggie says, "Well, I think the three of us are finished with lunch. Are you guys ready to hit the road again?"

"Yep!" I say. "Nothing exciting happening in Crivitz today! I'm ready if you guys are." We pay our bills, make final restroom pitstops, and exit the Bon Ton Diner for the remaining two hundred mile drive to the tip of the Keweenaw Peninsula.

From across the road Malcolm watches us get into our vehicles. He starts his engine and plots his clandestine pursuit with sweet revenge on his mind. "Man! That was one big ass doggy. I think I'm gonna need a bigger gun!"

Chapter 12

WE HEAD NORTH out of Crivitz and soon enter the sprawling Chequamegon-Nicolet National Forest. Vast stretches of pines, maples, and birch trees loom on either side of the highway as far as the eye can see. Mace and I settle in for the four-hour drive and listen to the steady drone of our tires on the pavement. Several minutes into our trip Mace turns to me and says, "I'm beginning to get a feel for what you've been saying about Robert's unusual mystic abilities."

"What do you mean?" I ask looking for further explanation.

"Back there in the diner's parking lot in Crivitz. Those boys and how Robert communicated with Grey. Any idea how he and Grey telepath with each other?"

"Not really," I say honestly. "That's a question you should ask Robert at some point. I'd be curious to hear what he says. I'll tell you this. Anything you've witnessed so far and anything that you imagine to be true is just a small portion of what he's capable of. I've seen some things that I never would've thought possible, and I'm dead certain that I can't fathom the extent of his powers. I'll tell you something else. My friend, Banks, up on the Brule River, was Robert's commander in the Marines. Small world, huh? They did a couple of tours together in Iraq and Afghanistan. Banks said he never knew a more effective fighter than Robert Midew. Banks felt certain that Robert possessed superhuman abilities, and trust me, Banks doesn't tell tall tales."

Mace knows that I'm not exaggerating because he knows full well that he wouldn't feel as strong and healthy as he does for his age if it weren't for Robert's gift to him of enhanced physical fortitude. "But how, Clay? How does he do it?"

"All I know, Mace, is that when he found their tribe's sacred Megis shell as a young boy many,

many years ago that he and their medicine men, the Midewin, were able, over time and with great study, to unlock the magical healing and spiritual powers that made him and Grey who they are today. There is a knowledge that is beyond what Western man has been able to comprehend, mainly because our hubris and greed blocks our ability to learn the ancient secrets."

"The Megis shell. Have you seen it, Clay?"

"Yes, I have and so have Rennie and Ranger Kelli."

"And?!" Mace presses.

"And anything else you wish to know you should either ask Robert or wait to see what presents itself during our visit to the Keweenaw Peninsula and Brockway Mountain. I don't mean to frustrate you with obtuse answers, but that's really the best answer I can give you now."

A few minutes later I feel my phone vibrate and see that it's Rennie calling.

"Where are you, Dad? Any idea what time you guys will get here?"

"Hi Rennie, yeah, we're near a little town named Crystal Falls, probably about three hours away from Copper Harbor. We should see you about five o'clock. Where do you want to meet?"

"Let's meet in the lobby of the Evergreen Point Lodge where we made reservations for all of you.

It's just a little way up the mountain from Copper Harbor. I booked three rooms, one for you and mom, one for Lucretia and Tori, and another one for Mace. Robert had told me earlier that he didn't need a room since he expected to be in and out on tribal business. You may recall that we drove past the lodge last summer. It's a tidy, upscale place that you should all be comfortable in, and the restaurant's decent and has a bar. Actually, Kelli and I had lunch there with her former park service mentor, Thomas Arrowsmith, earlier today."

"I vaguely remember it, but that sounds fine, Son. Everything going okay for you inside the mountain?"

"Yeah, everything's fine. We're getting some good work done studying the cave art, but I'd be less than honest if I didn't admit that both Kelli and I get a little spooked when we hear certain creepy sounds every once in a while."

That comment sets the hair on my arms standing on end. "Oh, what kind of sounds?" I ask evenly.

"Not sure exactly. It sounds like a voice but it's garbled and doesn't sound very human. Kelli reminds me that there are lots of legends about miners who worked the Brockway Mountain copper deposits that went into the mine but never came out. Creepy, huh?"

"Uh, yeah, very creepy. Do us both a favor and don't say anything to your mother about this, okay? She already thinks I'm a little wacko. No sense scaring the bejesus out of her on the first day." We talk for a few minutes longer, and I tell him about the photo equipment Mace and I are bringing. He tells me he has some extra power packs and lights in case we need them, and then I turn the phone over to Mace so they can catch up. We put the phone on speaker so we can all communicate.

"Hi there, Mace, how're you enjoying the trip north? It's been a while since you and dad have been on the road together."

"Well, you know your dad. Never a dull moment. Nobody's gotten killed or seriously injured which is an achievement when Clay Arnold is around." Mace looks at me, grins, and rolls his eyes.

"And what about Robert and Grey? Have you been able to get to know them a little?"

"Uh, yeah, but just a little, and the little bit that I've witnessed so far is hard to describe."

"Yeah," Rennie replies. "I've noticed that. The good news is that he and Grey are playing on our team. Just wait till you get to know them even better. How about mom, Tori, and Lucretia? How're they doing?"

"I think they're bonding very well. I'm not sure if we told you that Lucretia's brother, Malcolm, busted out of the Joliet Correctional Center and is somewhere on the run. Lucretia's Uncle Drew and Detective Cioffi are keeping an eye on Lucretia's properties in Chicago, but your dad and I have a nagging feeling that he'll want to get even with Lucretia and us for getting him shipped off to prison."

The thought of Malcolm Land being on the loose sends a shiver down Rennie's spine. He remembers that Malcolm's assassin, Ernst Kline, was the man who murdered Weed. Rennie also knows all too well that he was the person who killed Kline when he nearly executed everyone in our family at home.

"That's not good news about Malcolm. Please keep your eyes and ears open. Are you and dad armed?"

"Yeah, we're both armed and having Robert and Grey with us is a definite comfort. I sorta wish the women weren't with us now though. I hate the thought of them being subjected to any violence."

"Amen to that!" I chime in. "Rennie, our cell phone signal is starting to break up because of our remote location. We're going to hang up now, and we'll see you in a few hours at the Evergreen Point Lodge, okay?" A moment later the cellular signal is lost, and Mace and I are back to listening to the hypnotic sound of our tires on the pavement.

In the car behind us, Maggie and Tori are enjoying getting to know Lucretia better and no doubt making me the subject of their discussion more than I'd prefer. How do I know that? Well, I absolutely love Maggie to the moon and back, and that's why I've chosen to not share every detail of my harrowing adventures. She knows this and still probes and prods me with leading questions, along with threats to suspend all sex, unless I tell her more. I tell myself that it's a balancing act with Maggs. I try to be a little forthcoming on already established information and practice my convincing theatrical skills in dodging stuff that isn't pretty in the light of day. Fortunately, they're talking about other things too.

"So, Lucretia, do you really think your brother will try to find you? I mean, if I managed to escape from prison, I think I'd want to get as far away as possible. Surely, he's got to know that the police will be on the lookout for him in the Chicago area."

"Yeah, Tori, you would think so, but my brother, Malcolm, likes to make his own rules, and honestly, it's worked pretty darn well for him over the years. Think about it. Money was never an issue for him. We both had access to a lot it, as well as social prestige. Fortunately, I listened to my parents and to Uncle Drew when it came to being a little thrifty and charitable at the same time. Malcolm never did quite think like the rest of us in our family, and he always resented the way my parents favored me. Malcolm wanted it all … leadership of the Land

Foundation and its art holdings, stocks, properties, cash, and he damn near pulled it off. He slowly poisoned my father. He had Ernst Kline execute our family attorney and your brother, Weed, and if it weren't for the quick thinking of Uncle Drew and Detective Cioffi, he'd have murdered Clay, Mace, and me. So you wonder why he'd want to hang around Chicago and risk getting caught or killed, it's because he's hell-bent on showing me he's the king of the hill, and he'll do anything to hunt me down and finish the job."

"I had no idea how frightening a person he is," Maggie says sympathetically as she takes Lucretia's hand. "But, for what's worth, Tori and I have your back, don't we, Tori?"

"Sure do! And for a second there I was actually hoping he'd show up. We could each take turns kneeing him and then turn him over to Grey to enjoy whatever's left."

Lucretia loves the bravado and gives hugs to her pals. A moment later Tori's cell phone rings, and she see that it's her therapist, Dr. Adrian Dale, calling. She thinks about letting it go to voice mail but figures he'll just keep calling so she decides to answer it.

"Hello, Adrian, this is a surprise."

"Uh, yes, well, I couldn't remember when you were leaving town and just thought I'd call and see if you're okay."

Tori glances at Maggie and Lucretia with an expression that says, *"I have no idea why he's calling."*

"Yes, Adrian, I'm quite okay. I'm in a car with two friends, and we're on our way north to the Keweenaw Peninsula."

"The Keweenaw Peninsula? Where in God's name is that?"

"It's the uppermost part of the Upper Peninsula of Michigan."

"I thought you were going to Chicago," he says petulantly.

"We were in Chicago and now we're going to the Keweenaw. Look, Adrian, I can tell you all about it when I return home. I have an appointment on your calendar, okay. Now isn't a good time to talk, but it was thoughtful of you to call."

"Well, of course, I'm sure you know you're my favorite client."

"No, I wasn't aware of that. I'm sure you have many special clients. But, we can talk when I get back to town, okay?"

Dr. Dale doesn't want to hang up just yet, though, "So, where will you be staying on this Keweenaw Peninsula?"

"Near a town named Copper Harbor. Rennie has booked lodging for all of us at the Evergreen Point Lodge. But look, seriously Adrian, I need to go now, thanks for calling." She hangs up and stares into the phone. "That was bonkers!"

"Who was that?" Lucretia asks incredulously.

"My therapist," Tori says. "I mean, he's been helpful to my dealing with the shock of being able to see after being blind all my life, but lately he's been crossing some professional lines that I'm getting concerned about."

"Me too!" Maggie adds, "but don't worry, Tori, if he shows up Lucretia and I'll knee him a few times and give what's left of him to Grey."

Chapter 13

ABOUT NINETY MINUTES later our little caravan cruises past the town of L'Anse, and we head toward Robert's hometown of Baraga. Robert sends texts to each car alerting us that the tribal center for the Keweenaw Bay Indian Community is just up ahead. "I need to stop in my office briefly to handle a few things and sign some papers. It'll only take me about twenty minutes."

We take the exit and Robert leads us to the parking lot of the tribal center. It's a contemporary looking facility constructed of wood, copper, and stone. The

landscaping is adorned with finely crafted sculptures of wild animals and scenes of native life. It's a welcoming place. In a little niche I see a facsimile of an artifact I've come to recognize and respect, the Megis shell, the ancient mystical conduit of well-being and thought. Robert told Rennie, Kelli, and me a while back that he, Grey, and his grandmother, Nokomis, had hidden the Megis shell in a remote shrine under Brockway Mountain. Robert also told us that he's sworn a blood oath to ensure that the Megis shell is never lost or taken from his people again.

"Why don't you guys use the restroom and look around the center? We've added some new things since you were here last, Clay."

We do as he suggests, and after relieving ourselves, Maggie, Tori, Lucretia, Mace, and I gather in the center's cultural wing. The walls are artfully covered with native clothing, ceremonial objects, and hunting and fishing gear. Nicely lit wooden display cases contain decorative beadwork, copper implements, animal skeletons, and bowls containing unknown herbs and leaves. An ancient birchbark canoe hangs from the ceiling, and a huge stuffed bear glowers menacingly at us from a corner of the room. But perhaps the most compelling feature in the room is a ten-foot wall of stone cave art that Robert and members of the tribe carefully extracted from Brockway Mountain and relocated here.

"This is amazing!" Lucretia says solemnly. "I'm certainly no expert on Great Lakes Paleo-Indian art, but this is as important a relic as anything I've ever seen." Mace and I hold back a little to let Maggie, Tori, and Lucretia take their time examining the artwork. Each of them is in awe with what they're seeing.

"Well, Clay, if the rest of the cave art that you've come to photograph is anything like this, we're about to rewrite the history books."

"Trust me, Lucretia, you haven't seen anything yet, and I know that you and the Land Foundation will respect what you see with the dignity it deserves."

She nods affirmatively, and after another minute the three of them move on to another gallery room. Mace and I then approach the wall to ponder its details. "Look here, Mace, these cave paintings depict the Migration Story that Robert shared with us during dinner at Lucretia's."

"I've never seen anything like this in person, Clay. I'm speechless."

I continue, "This first portion shows the Anishinaabe living by the great salt sea, presumably maritime Canada, and here after a centuries-long journey they've finally settled where they find food growing on the water … rice in the Great Lakes region."

We take our time examining the cave painting. We see their wigwams and fields that have been cultivated bearing corn, beans, and squash. We see fishing boats and nets and crude gaffs appointed with large copper hooks. I point out a symbol of the Megis shell which is being exulted by a throng of villagers. Mace moves toward the end of the cave painting and says, "Hey, Clay, look at this. It's a fight between the Chippewa and some huge, ugly, hairy thing. What is it because it sure doesn't look like a bear or moose?"

My bloods turns cold as I see what Mace is pointing at. A dozen or more natives lie mortally wounded at the creature's feet. I don't answer right away, and Mace turns to look at me. "What is it?" he asks me again.

I return his gaze. "It's the Windigo."

"The Windi-what?" Mace asks, and he notices beads of sweat on my forehead. "You and Robert fought this creature last summer, didn't you? This thing is real, isn't it?"

"Yes, it was real. Robert, Rennie, Kelli, and I ran from it, then battled it in the caves. It came very close to killing all of us."

"Did you use the Demon Camera on it?"

"Yes, more than once, and Robert summoned all of the strength and sorcery that he could to destroy it. It wasn't enough. Even Grey was nearly killed.

Not only was the Windigo big and mean and smelly, it was surprisingly clever and smart. This was the evil, man-eating spirit of ancient Chippewa legend, and it was preparing to feast on us."

"So if the Demon camera and Robert's powers weren't enough to defeat this thing, how did you do it … or is it still roaming around down there?"

"We got lucky. We got very lucky. At the last second Nokomis appeared and gave the Windigo a superhuman grandma ass-whupping. Basically, she somehow blew the creature to smithereens with Megis magic, and that's all I know because neither Robert nor Nokomis was willing to share details, and honestly, at that point I really didn't give a shit. We were alive and finally crawled out of the bowels of the mountain."

"Whoa!" Mace exhales. "And I thought Malcolm Land and Ernst Kline were bad dudes!"

"I never told you about it, Mace, because I knew that Robert didn't want the outside world to somehow catch wind of a supernatural being like the Windigo. Their homeland would never be the same again. Besides, it was the most terrifying experience of my life, and I just as soon forget about it."

Mace nods his understanding, although we both know he can't fully grasp what I'm talking about. We turn around to leave and follow the ladies into the next gallery when we get surprised by someone who has an uncanny penchant for showing up unannounced. Nokomis stands before us. Her sightless, milky white eyes stare deeply into mine and then Mace's.

"I see you have returned to us," the ancient grandmother states. "You have come to see your dark-skinned son and the young ranger, yes? And, you have brought new people with you. I sense that they are your family, yes?"

"Yes, Nokomis, and we come in peace and friendship. I want you to meet my close friend, Mace Davis."

"Ah yes, Mace Davis, the man you call family. The man who came from the islands many years ago as a boy, yes?"

"That's correct, Nokomis, and I am very pleased to meet you." Mace looks at me askance and says, "I reckon there are a lot of things from last summer that you and Rennie haven't shared with me."

"All in good time, Mace Davis," Nokomis advises. She then turns to me and grows even more solemn, if that's possible. "Robert needs your help, Clay Arnold. There are evil forces in play, and all of our people need you."

"But?!" I begin.

"You shall know everything soon enough, but for now know that we are pleased you have returned." I begin to speak, but all of a sudden

Nokomis, grandmother to Robert Midew, dissolves into a shimmer of golden light and disappears before our eyes.

"Please tell me that didn't really happen, Clay, and how the hell did she know I came from the islands?!"

"It happened Mace. Nokomis is a little, uh, gifted that way," I deadpan. "And, I hope you agree that there's nothing to be gained by sharing this episode with the ladies. Besides, when Nokomis says, *'All in good time,'* I have a feeling they'll find out about our uniquely talented friends before too long. For now, though, let's keep this between us and the dead Indians on the cave wall, okay?"

We move into the next gallery to find the ladies, and see that Robert is showing them a few special artifacts. He winks at us as we approach, and there's no doubt in my mind that he's well aware that we just had a surprise visit from his grandmother. He finishes talking with the ladies and then informs us, "I have to stay behind for a few hours now. Some things have come up that require my immediate attention, but Grey and I'll meet you at Evergreen Point Lodge in the morning."

He gives me directions for the lodge and says I shouldn't have a problem finding it with my phone's GPS. The ladies say goodbye, then walk outside and get into Lucretia's car. I turn to Robert and ask,

"Anything Mace and I can do to help you now? Is there a problem we need to know about?"

"Yes and no," he replies cryptically. "But, I need to go now. I'll see you in the morning."

Across the road and a few hundred yards away from the tribal center, Malcolm had managed to find a gas station, convenience store, and gun shop in a roadside strip mall. While we were occupied inside, he gassed up his car, grabbed a large bag of food, bottles of water, a fifth of Jack Daniels, and a high-powered rifle with a bunch of ammo.

"Yup, that was one big ass doggy back in Crivitz, but my new rifle should help even the playing field. I'm coming for you, baby sister … and your pals." Malcolm scrunches down in his driver's seat and munches hungrily on a Pasty pie. He has a clear view of our cars at the tribal center. When he sees the ladies get into Lucretia's car, he starts his engine and gets ready to follow. "Patience and then sweet revenge," he whispers to himself. "All in good time."

Chapter 14

MACE AND I SAY GOODBYE to Robert and walk outside to our car. I motion for Lucretia to follow us back onto the highway, and we settle in for an hour-long drive past the towns of Houghton, Hancock, and Calumet, then along the spine of the Keweenaw Peninsula to its very tip.

I feel Mace's eyes looking at me, waiting for me to say something. I turn to him with an impish smile on my face and say, "What?"

"What do you mean 'what'?! We just witnessed an ancient-looking Indian woman with milky white

eyes disappear into nothingness. Somehow she knew I came from the islands as a boy, and you finally tell me about fighting some abominable, man-eating creature last summer. Oh yeah! And then the million-year-old hag says that Robert needs your help, whatever the bleep that means."

"Oh that!" I toy with him. Despite my being coy with Mace, I find Nokomis's appearing and disappearing acts to be unsettling too. However since she saved all of our asses last summer, I cut her some slack in giving explanations.

"Yeah," I concur with Mace, "It's rather spooky, and no, I don't have a good explanation for Robert and Nokomis's mystical powers. All I know is that I've never experienced any ill will from them, and Robert has been a true friend to everyone in our family, including you, sir!"

"So, what was that big hairy beast that you guys fought last summer. You called it a Windi-something."

"The Windigo," I repeat and even saying the name out loud still creeps the crap out of me. "As I mentioned, it's an evil man-eating spirit according to ancient Chippewa legend, but this creature went far beyond being a legend."

"Do you think it has any, uh, relatives under Brockway Mountain?"

"Jeez, I sure hope not, but Robert hasn't mentioned that possibility to me so I tend to doubt it." I privately cross my fingers.

Before too long we come to the outskirts of Houghton, Michigan, the largest town on the Keweenaw Peninsula and home to Michigan Technological University. After driving through miles of forested highway, it's reassuring to know that even this far north civilization is alive and well. The university's reputation and architecture are impressive as are a number of homes near campus. We cross over the aerial lift bridge that spans the portage waterway and deposits us in the adjacent town of Hancock. We drive up a steep grade and soon see the looming presence of the shaft house for the Quincy Mine. It's a soft slate gray in color and blends in with the fog that enshrouds the elevation. Seeing the Quincy Mine confirms that we are, indeed, in what the locals call Copper Country.

"A lot of history in this area, Mace, more than I was aware of before I came up here to visit Rennie last summer."

"As if disappearing Indians isn't enough?!" Mace lobs back at me.

"Yeah, well, you'll have to take that subject up with Robert, but I doubt he'll give you a straight answer. No, the history I'm talking about is the history of copper mining in the Keweenaw. Millennia ago the Chippewa's ancestors collected copper rocks they found on the ground and in shallow earthen pits. They learned to heat the rocks to extract the copper ore which they fashioned into utilitarian objects like cooking utensils and hunting and fishing points. Over time they used the copper for ceremonial objects and ornamentation too. Then, white Europeans showed up in the early nineteenth century and that started the first real mineral boon in America. Scores of mines, large and small, cropped up all along the peninsula with dreams of riches for investors back east. It was an incredibly hard life. People of many nationalities immigrated here including some three hundred thousand hardy souls from Finland who sought a better life from the harsh Scandinavian winters and their Russian overlords. They escaped the brutal Russians but still suffered under the weight of three hundred inches of snow that annually falls here. Wait till you see the huge railway snow plow on display at the Keweenaw Historic Park in Calumet."

"So, what happened to all of the copper mines?" Mace asks.

"Many went bankrupt due to competition and falling copper prices. A few like the Quincy Mine and the Brockway Mining Company lingered on until just after World War II. Today, they're mainly tourist attractions. Then, of course, there's Gitche Gumee."

"Huh?" Mace laughs. "Does that Gumee come in spearmint?"

"Uh, no, Gitche Gumee is the Chippewa name for Lake Superior which has a long, colorful, and tragic history in its own right. It's huge and over a thousand feet deep and colder than a witch's bosom even in summer!"

About twenty minutes later we arrive at the outskirts of Calumet, Michigan, and Mace points out the huge snow plow I mentioned earlier. "Wow, it looks like a railroad car with a monster snow plow on the front!"

"Yep! And, over there is the National Park Service building where Rennie and Ranger Kelli work and a couple of blocks in that direction is Rennie's apartment."

I look in my rearview mirror and see Lucretia's car still following our lead. A moment later a text comes from Maggie stating, "We've gotta pee." I make a quick left turn and go a block or two, and we arrive at Rennie's apartment.

"C'mon guys," I say as we approach his front door. "He and Kelli are waiting for us at the lodge, but I remember where he keeps his spare door key. I find it under the quartz rock on his front stoop, and we enter to find a surprisingly orderly apartment with a few pictures of our family adorning a shelf.

A few hundred yards away Malcolm parks his car in a secluded spot, jumps out, and relieves himself behind a tree. While Lucretia and Tori avail themselves to the bathroom, Maggie rummages around in Rennie's refrigerator and kitchen cabinets to make sure her "baby" is eating properly. She sees that he's fairly well stocked which gives her a mixed feeling of pride and dismay that her baby is all grown up and perfectly capable of taking care of himself.

"Look at these, Clay!" she says as she points to several rough, egg-sized stones sitting on a recessed shelf. "Are these what I think they are?" she asks incredulously.

I nod affirmatively recognizing the collection of uncut, high-quality diamonds that Robert gave Rennie as thanks for helping to preserve the Paleo-Indian cave art and fight against the evil Windigo.

"Yeah, they are. Like the one that Robert gave to you."

"But they must be worth a fortune!" she blurts out.

I nod again and reply, "Well, let's just say that our 'baby' doesn't have to worry about his next meal … or college tuition, or a mortgage. Robert gave a similar number of stones to Kelli too, and we all promised to keep his gifts as our little secrets, so that's why I never told you about them."

"And, Sir Husband, what else haven't you told me?"

"A lot!" I reply evenly. "More than you can ever imagine. Now, it's your turn to use the bathroom, then Mace and me, and then we should hit the road, okay?" Maggie gives me a resigned look knowing that I'm not going to tell her more and slowly walks away.

I finally get my turn to take a leak, and as I'm finishing up, I look in the mirror above the toilet and see Nokomis staring at me. "Jesus, Nokomis! Is nothing sacred?! Can't a fella take a whiz in peace?" She ignores my protestation. "Robert needs your help," she repeats again. "There is much danger brewing."

"Robert mentioned something like that to Mace and me back at the tribal center, but he told us he'd share more tomorrow morning. Is there anything else I need to do right now?"

"Yes, indeed there is!" the sage old Nokomis replies. "Don't forget to wash your hands." And then she disappears.

After I finish, I wash my hands, collect my traveling companions, and replace the spare key under the rock on the porch where I'd found it. We climb inside our vehicles and wend our way back onto US

Route 41 north toward Copper Harbor. Unbeknown to us, Malcolm continues his clandestine pursuit from a safe distance while munching on the last of his Pasty.

"You look like you've seen a ghost," Mace says to me.

"Nokomis," I reply. "In the bathroom."

"How nice!" he laughs. "And?"

"She said Robert needs our help again, and that there's danger brewing. I've got an unsettling feeling that this trip isn't going to go as smoothly as planned, Mace. Just keep your eyes open and your Weed Killer handy, okay? I learned last year to expect the unexpected around Brockway Mountain."

"Swell," comes his one-word reply, and he slips his hand inside his pocket to feel the reassuring shape of his newly crafted weapon. "And, when was the last time you ventured anywhere, Clay, that things went smoothly?"

"Point taken," I admit, "but it's not like I go looking for trouble, well, not anymore lately."

"Uh huh. You're like a magnet for serious drama, Clay. Good thing you've got a spry eighty-something-year-old stud like me to keep an eye on you!"

"Uh huh," I parrot his words. "You and Nokomis."

Over the next several minutes Mace looks at a visitors guide that I'd kept in Pappy's door pocket.

"Looks like we've got a bunch of small mining towns coming up: Kearsarge, Allouez, Ahmeek, and Mohawk."

"Yeah, well, good luck seeing anything that remotely looks like a town because, believe me, I've looked. We might see a few rundown shacks and small buildings, but nothing that would indicate that thousands of people once populated this region. Further down the peninsula we'll see the remnants of more mining towns. They all have very little left to show but faint memories and abandoned dreams."

We continue driving along Route 41 until we come to the decrepit town of Phoenix, and I decide to turn left toward Eagle Harbor on the north side of the peninsula. I recall that it's a charming little tourist town near Copper Harbor, and I want the ladies to see the grandeur of Lake Superior before we head inland again to meet Rennie and Kelli at Evergreen Point Lodge. When we get to Eagle Harbor, Maggie texts me saying that she, Tori, and Lucretia want to stop and look through a couple of the tourist shops. Mace and I naturally oblige, and we find a weathered picnic table to occupy while Maggie and company go exploring for stuff that none of them really needs.

Unbeknown to us, Malcolm Land manages to find a secluded spot behind a dumpster to park his car. He intermittently watches Mace and me, then the ladies as they go sweeping in and out of shops with a growing collection of bags stuffed with goodies and tissue paper. Out of boredom Malcolm reaches into the back seat and retrieves several bullets which he loads into clips for his new rifle. For the first time since he escaped from Joliet prison, he wonders if he shouldn't just abandon his vengeful pursuit of his sister and her companions.

"Hell, I can go anywhere I want with the dough that I've got," and then he realizes that there's no where else that he'd rather be and nothing more that he'd rather do than whack his sister for being so goddamn perfect all of their lives. "Screw it!" he declares to himself. "In for a penny ..." He slaps one of his newly loaded clips into his assault rifle, leans it on the passenger seat, and continues his surveillance.

A hundred yards away Maggie and her pals enter the final shop after depositing their bags of purchased items in Lucretia's car. In addition to seeing a lot of touristy items that could populate any resort shop in America, they see some interesting copper items and things with nautical motifs that are unique to us Hoosiers. While Maggie and Lucretia explore one part of the store, Tori wanders into another room to see what wonders it possesses. She picks up a crystal figurine of an Indian boy and marvels as the sunlight casts a kaleidoscope of colors through its cut facets. She stares at it for several long moments thinking about when she was blind, and how no one would've been able to adequately describe the colors of the rainbow that she's seeing now. She decides to buy the little figurine and turns to leave the room and rejoin Maggie and Lucretia when she pulls up short. An ancient-looking, gray-haired woman stands in the aisle partially blocking her exit.

"Oh, excuse me, ma'am, I thought I was the only one in here. Here, I'll get out of your way."

The wizened woman doesn't speak at first but instead peers deeply into Tori's eyes with her own milky white orbs. Tori shifts sideways to make passing the old woman easier when the woman gently places her wrinkled hand on Tori's forearm.

"You were blind once, yes?" Nokomis asks already knowing the answer to her question.

Tori looks more closely at the old Indian woman and answers Nokomis's question with her own evasive question. "Are you totally blind, ma'am? It's pretty crowded in here. Do you need any help?"

A small smile appears on Nokomis's face. "Not totally blind. Sightless, yes, but I can see into the nature of things."

The inherent contradiction of that comment catches Tori by surprise, and she looks even more closely into the woman's milky white eyes. "How did you know that I'd been blind?

The ancient-looking woman shrugs and says, "Information has a way of flowing to me. I am happy for you that you can now see."

Tori is now feeling totally confused. "Who are you, and how do you know things about me?"

Nokomis shrugs again. "I just know."

Now, Tori is feeling more than a little flummoxed and decides that it's time to beat a hasty retreat. "Well, I hope you have a very good day. It was nice talking with you, but I need to catch up with my friends now." Tori turns to leave again, but Nokomis keeps her hand on Tori's forearm.

"It is good that you were once blind. Where you're going, your friends will need your sightless skills."

"What?! What do you mean, and how do you know where we're going?" Tori beseeches Nokomis.

"Once you've dwelled in the dark, Little Songbird, your vision sees more than the sighted ones. They will need your help. We will all need your help."

"But?!" Tori tries to say, but her stuttering voice leaves her in total shock as she sees the old Indian woman slowly dissolve into soft particles of golden light and finally disappear.

Tori looks around for the old woman and anyone else who might've seen what just happened, but she's alone in the room with only a carved glass

Indian boy as her companion. Tori absently walks down the aisle and finds Lucretia and Maggie by the shops entrance.

"Ready to go?" Maggie asks her. "Ah, I see you've found a little treasure," as she points at the crystal figurine.

Still stunned, Tori only manages to reply, "Yeah, a little treasure and a whole lot of questions."

Maggie looks at Tori with an inquisitive look. "Are you okay?"

"I'm not sure," Tori says. "C'mon, I'll tell you and Lucretia about it in the car."

Mace and I see the ladies exit the last shop, and we get up from our perches at the picnic table. "All set?!" I call over to them, and Lucretia replies that they are. We climb back in our respective vehicles, and I text Rennie to say that we're only about fifteen minutes away from the lodge. As if on cue, Malcolm starts his engine and stealthily falls in behind us.

The drive along the coast is stunning in both its grandeur and its subtlety. Pines, maples, spruces, birches, poplars, and oaks offer a verdant tunnel over the road, and the rock-bound beaches provide a colorful perimeter to the vast steel-gray waters of Gitche Gumee.

"So," Maggie begins, "You're telling us that you spoke with an old blind Indian woman in the other room, and then she just upped and disappeared."

"That's right and that she knew I was once blind and that everyone would need my help where we're going."

Lucretia and Maggie look at each other and then back at Tori skeptically.

"Has something like this ever happened to you before?" Lucretia asks.

"Never," Tori says. "I sure don't get it."

"Well, that's just plum weird," Maggie replies bluntly. "On the other hand, back at Rennie's apartment Clay did tell me that he'd experienced all sorts of unusual things when he was here last year. Well, guys, I think we need to have a frank conversation with Clay and Robert, and the sooner the better."

Before long we come to Copper Harbor, the last town near the tip of the Keweenaw Peninsula. We drive slowly through town, and I see Zak's diner where Robert, Kelli, Rennie, and I had a sumptuous breakfast the morning after we emerged from Brockway Mountain last summer. We turn onto Route 41 and begin ascending the road leading to the Evergreen Point Lodge. Three minutes later I see Rennie's smiling face by the side of the road, with one arm waving us into the parking lot and the other draped affectionately over Kelli Katterman's shoulders.

"He looks like a happy lad, eh, Mace?"

"That he does, my friend. Oh, to be young again …"

Chapter 15

"YOU MADE IT!" Rennie shouts as we exit our vehicles. "Welcome to the Keweenaw Peninsula!" Over the next couple of minutes we all stand in the parking lot stretching our legs and introducing Kelli and Lucretia to those of us they haven't yet met. Maggie envelops Rennie in big motherly hugs and looks appraisingly at Ranger Kelli. "Ah, so you're the young woman who drags my baby son into dark, creepy caves!" she says. Kelli looks at Rennie to see if Maggie is kidding and is relieved when he sees an amused look on his face.

"I assure you, Mrs. Arnold, that our relationship is strictly professional, isn't it, Rennie?"

"Uh no!" comes his quick reply as they both lean against each other.

"First of all, Kelli, please call me Maggie, and second of all I have all sorts of questions to ask you once we get settled!" Kelli gulps nervously and turns her attention to Mace.

"And you, sir, you must be the legendary Mace Davis that Rennie has told me so much about."

"Well, I don't know about being legendary, but this young fella and I have logged a lot of time together. Why, I could tell you stories that would make his antiperspirant fail."

"Mace!" Rennie protests. "Remember that road goes both ways! C'mon everyone, let's get you guys checked into your rooms and we can get better acquainted over dinner. How's that sound?"

"Like a great plan," I chime in. "We have a lot of catching up to do, and I'm sure we'd all like to hear more about your work on the cave art. Robert said he'd meet us all here in the morning, and then we'll go up to the Brockway mine. Why don't we newcomers take about an hour to get settled and rest up and meet at the restaurant, say around seven-thirtyish?"

"That sounds perfect, Dad, because Kelli and I still have to finish a few things before Robert comes in the morning." Mace, Tori, and Lucretia agree on the dinner plan, and we all go inside the lodge to get checked in.

Meanwhile just outside the entrance to the lodge in a roadside park, Malcolm Land eases his car into a spot with visual access to the lodge. He reaches into his bag of groceries and pulls out another pasty and the bottle of Jack Daniels. "Good thing I picked up a blanket and a coat in that store back by the Indian joint," he mumbles to himself. "If I need to spend the night here to be able to get a clean shot at Lucretia and that Clay Arnold prick, I'll do it. Then, maybe I'll head someplace new and just start over."

After we all get checked in, Maggie and I head to our room to rest up after a day of traveling. The room is spacious and clean but a little rustic with a large picture window offering a beautiful view of Lake Superior. Maggie and I put our stuff away, and she joins me by the picture window. "So, how are you and Tori and Lucretia getting along?" I ask. "Was it fun driving together?"

"Oh yeah, it was really a positive experience I think for each of us. Lucretia is a very intelligent woman, and I can tell you, Clay, she is very devoted to you and Mace for everything you did during the search for Samuel Morse's art trove. I think she and Tori were able to talk about losing Weed in a very sincere and sensitive way. She's a good woman, and I think you made a great call on introducing her to Robert."

We take off our shoes and lie spooning on the bed staring out the picture window at the panorama of pines and steel-gray lake water. After a few moments, Maggie says, "Tori told me about a very unusual experience she had at the last gift shop we visited in Eagle Harbor."

"Oh?" I reply.

"She told me she was confronted by an ancient-looking Indian woman who knew things about Tori that shouldn't have been possible." Maggie pauses.

Immediately, I know that Tori must've had a surprise visit from Nokomis, not unlike Mace's introduction to her at the tribal center, or my little visit from her while I was taking a leak in Rennie's bathroom.

"Clay, earlier you told me that there are things that go on up here that are, uh, beyond belief. Is Tori's experience an example of that?"

"Yes," I reply evenly. "Tori was visited by Nokomis who is Robert's grandmother. Mace had a similar surprise episode in Baraga. Nokomis has what I consider to be extraordinary magical powers derived from their sacred Megis shell. Two of those powers include a preternatural ability to see into the heart of things, and her ability to appear and disappear at will."

"Are you serious, Clay?"

"Yes, I am, and Robert, who is actually a Chippewa Midewin healer, has similar powers, but according to him he hasn't mastered the appearing and disappearing part yet. He says that Nokomis has a few hundred years of experience on him. And, to a lesser extent even Grey has instinctual abilities far beyond that of any canine, domestic or wild."

Maggie sits up and looks me squarely in the eye. "You're serious, aren't you?"

"Deadly serious, Maggie, and I suppose it's time to tell you what really happened under Brockway Mountain last summer." I spend the next several minutes giving Maggie a full disclosure of events with Robert and me searching for Rennie and Kelli after they were entrapped under the mountain by Rex Trammer and Digger Finn. I tell her about the incredible wealth in gold, silver, and precious gemstones that we encountered, and of course, the magnificent collection of Paleo-Indian cave art. I then tell her about the near-death fight against the evil Windigo, and how Nokomis arrived just in the nick of time to defeat the beast and save us all from certain death."

Maggie is stone still as she tries to comprehend everything that I'm telling her. "How come you never shared any of these details with me before? This is a lot for you to internalize on your own."

"It's a little burdensome, and even as I talk about it now it's hard to believe it really happened, but it did. The good thing is that Rennie and Kelli shared in that life-altering experience, so I'm not alone in trying to cope with the mystery of it all. And now you and Mace know the truth too. We've all formed a bond with each other and with Robert and Grey as well. But the main reason I didn't tell you, aside from not wanting to scare the bejesus out of you, was because Robert knew that leaking information about the Megis shell's special healing properties, plus the vast wealth and supernatural beings like the Windigo under the mountain would change his peoples' lives forever and not in a good way. So, Rennie, Kelli, and I agreed to stay mum about everything to protect their special way of life."

"Whew!" she exhales. "That's just beyond my wildest imagination. What should I say to Tori and Lucretia because Tori shared her experience with Nokomis with Lucretia and me in the car?"

"Robert will rejoin us in the morning. In matters such as these, I defer to him. This is his realm, and I'm sure he'll speak with all of us about the nature of things all in good time."

"You trust him that much, don't you, Clay?"

"I do," I reply fervently, "and you should too, Maggie."

"On a lighter note," she asks, "what do you think is going on with Rennie and Kelli? Their relationship seems to be more than professional to me."

I pull Maggie even closer to me and say, "I'm not sure, darling, perhaps like me, he knows a good catch when he sees one, or perhaps he just wants to ravage her like I want to do to you!" I move my hands gently over her tummy and cup an ample breast. "We've got a little time yet before we meet everyone for dinner. Care to get ravaged?! I could do my imitation of the evil Windigo for you."

"My, my, Mr. Arnold, you sure know how to get a girl's attention!" And at that, Maggie pulls my pants off, removes my Fruit-of-the-Looms, climbs on top of me, and begins to ravage the gee-willikers out of me. Thank goodness Nokomis is nowhere in sight!

Back at Baraga, Robert walks through the cultural wing of the tribal center. He's deep in thought and finds that he does his clearest thinking surrounded by his ancestors' belongings. The ceremonial objects, the clothing, the hunting, fishing, and farming implements all give off a special aura that spans generations of the Chippewa people. It's as if they're an extension of the sacred Megis shell. Robert stands in the middle of the cultural gallery and closes his eyes. Grey stands by his side with his eyes closed as well. Minutes pass and Robert remains transfixed, channeling an unseen energy that draws sensations, emotions, information to him. Grey moans quietly as the great wolf experiences something transcendental as well. Finally, the spell is broken, and Robert kneels down by the wolf he raised from a pup.

"You feel it too, don't you, Grey? You feel its presence. You recognize its innate vileness, its wanton lust for flesh, blood, and domination. Our greatest fear has been realized, Grey. The Windigo! The beast we thought was dead … it's back, and it's searching for the location of the Megis shell!"

Chapter 16

MAGGIE AND I BOTH have youthful springs in our steps as we walk through the lobby of the Evergreen Point Lodge and enter the dining room. Rennie and Kelli are already seated at a large table with Mace, and they wave us over to join them. Kelli blushes a little when she sees that Maggie notices Rennie holding her hand under the table. She gives Kelli's shoulder a soft pat as she walks by and sits beside her. Kelli instinctively retrieves her hand from Rennie's and places it in her lap. I sit next to Mace, and we await Lucretia's fashionably late arrival.

"How're your rooms?" Rennie asks. "Everything okay?"

"Yeah, it's a very nice place," Mace replies. "A guy could get used to living in a place like this."

"Except for the winters, Mace. We can get three hundred inches of snow up here. I mean, like every year."

"That's a definite bummer," Mace says. "I think I'll stay in Indiana."

"Good call," I chime in. "Besides, I don't want you moving anywhere. And yeah, Rennie, this is a very nice place."

I look around the dining room and the first things I notice are the huge, room-length windows. With the sun low in the evening sky, the shadows are long and dramatic as they stretch across the landscape. The commanding view of the deep-green forests and Lake Superior is truly awe-inspiring, and I typically don't use expressions like that. This view is stunning though. The interior of the room has rich pine paneling and softly lit north-woods chandeliers hanging above each table. The lights cast a warm amber glow. The white table linens and candlelight reflect a certain rustic nobility which I trust Lucretia will find appealing. And, as if on cue Lucretia enters the dining room wearing a broad smile and comfortably chic attire. Mace, Rennie, and I stand respectfully as she approaches our table, and Mace pulls a chair out for Lucretia to sit. We situate her between the two of us. A moment later Tori joins us as well.

"Well, isn't this a lovely room?!" Lucretia fawns as she takes in the view and our table settings. "A girl could get used to this. It's not the Magnificent Mile, mind you, but it's magnificent nonetheless."

"Mace was just saying the same thing," I offered. "Until Rennie told him that the peninsula gets about twenty-five feet of snow every winter."

"Oh my, that would be a deal breaker. Chicago winters are bad enough as it is!"

Our server is a friendly looking, portly lass named Molly. She comes to our table and takes drink orders, and we all settle in for what promises to be a cozy and tasty dinner together. "So, Rennie and Kelli, why don't you tell us what you've been working on with the cave art?" I request.

Rennie turns to Kelli and says, "Why don't you lead off with the perspective of the National Park Service, okay?"

Over the next couple of minutes Kelli shares the work that she and Rennie have been doing taking preliminary photographs of the cave paintings and other ancient artifacts and cataloging their locations and significance.

"Our National Park Service office in the Keweenaw is the lead agency on this project. The national office in Washington wanted to bring in a 'team of experts' to oversee the new find, but Robert Midew insisted that Rennie, he, and I would conduct and supervise the scope of work. We look forward to collaborating closely with Lucretia and Land Foundation once Clay concludes his photography. At this point we've made a good initial study of the art, and much of it would still be a mystery if it weren't for Robert's insights into what we've found. For example, he explained the Chippewa migration story in greater detail and pointed to the different eras of that five-hundred-year journey as reflected on the cave walls. He also described some but not all of the history and powers of the Megis shell. He knows so much detail about all of this that it's almost as if he'd been there himself." That brings a chuckle from Lucretia, Maggie, Tori, and Mace, but Rennie, Kelli, and I look at each other knowingly.

"So, what do you have in store for us tomorrow?" I ask.

"So, when Robert arrives tomorrow we'll head up to the old Brockway copper mine and enter into the caverns to see the discoveries," Kelli says. "Then, we can get Clay and Lucretia's recommendations on the best way to visually archive the art for global dissemination."

Molly returns with our drinks, and we temporarily shift the conversation to catching up and helping Lucretia and Kelli get better acquainted with our family of friends. A few minutes later Molly returns and asks if we're ready to order dinner.

"I'm sorry," Maggie says, "can you give us just a few more minutes please. We've been yakking away and have barely looked at the menu. Do you have any dinner specials this evening?"

Molly recites the specials, and Mace leans over to me and says, "I'm going for the elk. Never had it before. What're you having?" Maggie hears his question and looks at me pointedly. "Uh, I think I'll have the trout and vegetables," I reply, and Maggie gives me her approving look.

We all tell Molly our selections, and Lucretia quietly informs our server that she'll be paying for our dinners. She gives me a private wink.

Meanwhile, inside his car just across from the lodge's entrance, Malcolm zips up his coat against the evening chill and steps out into the twilight. He brings his loaded rifle with him and attaches his Leupold scope. He waits several more minutes for the night sky to grow even darker, then begins a clandestine walk to the rear of the lodge. A few minutes later he finds a secure hiding place opposite the dining room's large picture windows and scans the brightly lit interior. He estimates he's about fifty yards away from the windows. "Hell, from this distance and with this scope, I can hit the tipple off a nit!" he chortles to himself. "Now just a little patience, Malcolm my boy, and we'll see what develops." Malcolm tries to relax, but using the scope is taking a little more practice than he anticipates. Finally he gets used to the optics and slows his breathing. He spots us all sitting around the dining table, and a satisfied smile comes on to his face as he sees Lucretia sitting between me and Mace. He tries to anticipate wind direction and makes a small adjustment to his scope.

Inside, we're all enjoying the fellowship of our friends and family. Mace and Tori take turns telling stories about Rennie growing up. They're aim is to mildly embarrass him in front of Kelli and Lucretia which they do admirably well. Maggie chimes in with a couple of her own recollections while I just sit back watching my son squirm under all of the, uh, attention. Thankfully, none us tells the truly frightening tales like when Rennie was a young boy living alone in a shack on the streets of Indianapolis, or when he saved Tori from the Hacker twins' attack along the White River, or when he shot and killed Ernst Kline as he was preparing to murder all of us at home, or the terrifying events that befell us under Brockway Mountain last summer. No, the embarrassment stays mainly tame. Rennie looks to me for some salvation, and I shrug my shoulders as if to say, *"Deal with it!"*

Molly returns carrying a large tray holding our dinners. Lucretia asks her to please serve everyone else first. She hands aromatic dishes to Tori, Maggie, and Kelli and then moves over next to Mace, Lucretia, and me. Mace beams with delight when he sees the large portion of elk meat and potatoes Molly sets in front of him. Next, she places my savory rainbow trout in front of me which includes its head. Finally, Molly bends down to serve Lucretia her dinner when the sound of a large caliber bullet, intended for Lucretia, shatters the glass window behind us. The next thing I see is Molly, mortally wounded, falling face first onto the dinner table. Mace and I instinctively grab Lucretia, and everyone at the table dives to the floor.

"Stay down!" I scream as I look at everyone under the table. "Anyone hit?" I ask, but we all appear to be very shaken but unhurt. "Stay down," I repeat, but I don't think anyone needs me to state the obvious. We see other guests on the floor as well and hear an employee call 911. Outside Malcolm beats a hasty retreat from his hiding place and scurries back to his car under the cover of darkness. He starts his engine and sprays loose gravel as he speeds away.

Despite Maggie's protestations, I slowly get up and peer over the table top to see if it's safe to come out. The first thing I see are two sets of wide-open eyes staring at me, one belonging to the quite-dead

Molly and the other belonging to my beautifully prepared but equally dead rainbow trout.

"Shit!" I mutter aloud and look over at my friends who are shell-shocked. Mace and I stand up together, and the restaurant manager quickly joins us. It's obvious that there's no way to revive Molly, and we place another tablecloth over the body of our hapless server.

"The police are on their way," the manager says, and I imagine they'll want to speak with you and the other guests. Another server arrives and begins moving our dinner plates and drinks to another table where we all sit and await the cops. No one is very hungry at this point, although I see Mace take a couple of bites of elk. I look at Maggie who has a bewildered expression etched on her face. Lucretia leans over toward me and Mace and says, "I can't help but think that Malcolm did this."

"You honestly think he trailed us all the way from Illinois?" Mace asks.

"I wouldn't be a bit surprised," she replies. "Malcolm never was a person who believed in unfinished business." I listen to their exchange and come to the conclusion that Lucretia is probably right about her dear brother.

"But, that would mean that he's been following us every step of the way up here," Mace continues.

"Why would he do that when he just busted out of prison and could go anywhere he wants?"

"Oh, he knows that, but he always thought he could do whatever he wanted. I'm sure he's got another destination in mind."

Just then, two county sheriff deputies enter the dining room, and the manager leads them over to Molly who's still making eye contact with my trout. They confirm that she's as dead as a mackerel and radio for a transport vehicle to take her to the morgue in Calumet. A few moments later they approach us to get our statements. They quickly ascertain that none of us had a clue about the shooting, but Lucretia walks up to the lead officer and shares her thoughts about her brother and his motive of revenge. She suggests that they contact the Illinois Department of Corrections to get his photo and personal information which they agree to do.

Maggie comes up to me after the officers finish interviewing us and asks me, "Is this the kind of stuff you get involved in when you're not at home, Clay?"

Mace smiles at me sympathetically. "Uh, yeah, maybe, sometimes," I stammer. "But, not all of the time, honey," I say unconvincingly.

We all sit at our new table and order another round of stiff alcoholic beverages and pick at our reheated entrees. A new server comes up to me and asks, "Do you want a fresh trout, sir?" I politely decline and order the elk instead. "Good choice!" Mace offers. "It's really quite tasty, and it doesn't look back at you." Even Maggie manages to chuckle at his comment which helps break the seriousness of the tragedy that has occurred.

I look at Lucretia, Tori, and Maggie and say, "Look guys, given what's just happened, I think you need to decide if you still want to stay up here or head back home in the morning. I feel a need to remain and do the photography I promised Robert, Rennie, and Kelli that I'd do. Mace, you can stay or go. It's obviously your call, my friend."

At this point Lucretia informs everyone that she thinks her brother is the probable shooter and is very concerned for our safety.

"Don't you think he'd hightail it out of the area with the police investigating?" Tori asks.

"Maybe, maybe not," Lucretia replies. "When it comes to Malcolm, you can be sure that he does whatever he wants, regardless of the authorities."

"Well, I think I'm okay with staying, Maggie, if you are," Tori states. "We just got here, and I want to see what all of you have been raving about for months."

Maggie looks around the table and says, "Well, if you're okay, I'm okay. Besides, someone needs to protect these big strapping men," she lobs.

The remainder of our meal is understandably more subdued than it was before a bullet snuffed out the life of a woman who fortunately never knew what hit her. The other dinner guests eventually leave the dining room, and we all decide to call it a night. Mace and I make eye contact, and we both pat our jacket pockets. Clearly, there's a reason why we're glad to feel the reassuring shapes of my Demon camera and his Weed Killer. Rennie and Kelli watch us and nod their approval. They then leave to return to their apartments in Calumet and agree to meet us and Robert at the Brockway mine in the morning.

The officers and Mace and I head outside to search the area behind the lodge for any clues about the shooter. In the dark we locate a single brass shell casing, and a deputy places it in an evidence bag for fingerprint analysis.

"That's about all we can do right now," the lead officer says. "Deputy Johnson will remain on site overnight in case the shooter returns, and we'll let you know if anything else develops. The Michigan State Police are involved as well, but aside from Ms. Land's feeling that the shooter could be her brother, they have little else to go on."

Mace and I walk back toward our rooms, each of us shaking our heads in disbelief that we're involved in yet another tragedy together.

"I agree with Lucretia," Mace says. "I wouldn't be a bit surprised if asshole Malcolm isn't finished messing with our karma up here. I'll be curious to hear what Robert thinks when he arrives in the morning and learns about the murder."

I look Mace in the eyes and reply, "What makes you think he doesn't know about it already?"

"Uh, good point, Clay, he is a little spooky that way." We say goodnight.

In our room Maggie and I are both emotionally exhausted and quiet. We wash up and brush our teeth, then climb into bed. "I'm so sorry," I say as I move closer to her. "I'm sorry for our poor waitress. I'm sorry that you and everyone had to witness that, and I'm sorry that I can't do anything about the turmoil that happens in our lives."

"I know you are, honey. I don't know whether to be scared to death or royally pissed off. I'm glad we're all together though, and we'll still have a good time, plus you'll be in your professional element tomorrow." We hold each other tenderly, feel and hear the other's calming breaths until we fall finally asleep. And, I dream …

In my dream my family of friends is gathered around our dining table at home. Maggie, Bodie, Rennie, Tori, and Mace are all dressed in costumes that appear to be Native American, and they're wearing masks resembling woodland animals.

Maggie looks like a doe, Bodie a squirrel, Tori a rabbit, Rennie a fox, and Mace is a wise old owl. The scene changes, and we are in a vast, old-growth forest by a large body of water. We are walking along a mountain trail and come to a large opening in the earth. Chunks of raw copper are scattered around the ground and large veins of red-orange ore can be seen leading into a cavern. An eagle screeches overhead and lands by the entrance. A large wolf appears from the woods and stands next to the eagle. The eagle has a human voice that sounds like Robert Midew's, and it beckons us to come forward. The sky darkens as the voice warns us of great dangers that lie ahead, and the baleful wail of an unseen creature echoes from within the earth's maw. Instinctively, I know the source of the hideous wail, and my feet are frozen in fear. My family follows the eagle and wolf into the darkness, and I try in vain to stop them. The scene changes again, and we are all inside a great chamber. A glowing, white light shines deep within the cave and illuminates our way. Images of ancient artwork adorn the walls and a vast wealth of gemstones litter the ground. An evil wail echoes within the chamber, and Robert holds his hand up for us to stop walking. A large shadow of an evil being appears on the walls obscuring the cave art. The wail grows louder and morphs into a human-like voice, "I am waiting, and I seek what you hold precious." The voice turns into a haughty laugh, and I awake a moment later still holding my beautiful Maggie, thankful that it was only a passing dream.

Chapter 17

T HE NEXT MORNING arrives with a fresh bright-ness that belies the heartbreaking sadness that occurred in the dining room last evening. I lightly kiss Maggie's lips, and she wakes up giving me a dreamy-eyed smile that expels the remnants of my nightmare. We lie in bed with our arms and legs intertwined, and my world is at peace again. I debate whether to tell her about my dream and decide against it. I mean, why mess with the good karma, right? A few minutes later we get up, and

she texts the others to see if they're awake yet. We all agree to meet for breakfast in an hour.

As Maggie and I enter the lodge's lobby, we're directed to an enclosed porch where breakfast will be served. On the way I look inside the dining room and notice that workmen have already boarded up the destroyed picture window until a new one can be installed. Where we sat another staff member is working on the carpet to remove the blood-stained sections. Yellow crime scene tape cordons off the table. On so many levels the deadly attack has left an indelible stain on a heretofore lovely dining room. I turn to leave and nearly bump into Robert who is standing behind me looking into the dining room.

"I understand a grave tragedy occurred here last evening," he says solemnly.

"You could say that," I reply. "Did you know about this because information has a way of flowing to you?" I ask somewhat sarcastically.

He looks at me sympathetically and dismisses my sarcasm. "Yes, but I also ran into the sheriff on my way in."

"Sorry for my pissy attitude, Robert, but a woman died here last night because of someone's misguided anger." He nods his head in understanding, and we walk toward the porch. When we arrive everyone is seated around a large table, and Grey sits next to Lucretia with his head on her thigh. "Looks like you have a friend, Lucretia," Robert says.

"I think it's only because of the blueberry muffin I just shared with him."

"Well, where we come from, blueberries are magical. Now, you have a friend for life." Robert laughs, but I'm not sure if he isn't telling the truth. Just in case I snag one of the blueberry treats when I sit down. It tastes like any other blueberry muffin to me, and I shrug my skepticism at Robert.

"How's everybody doing this morning?" I ask as our waitress approaches us with two pots of coffee. She fills our cups and waits patiently while we scan the menu and tell her our selections. Each of us looks around the table at the others knowing full well that the last time our waitress delivered our orders, it didn't end well.

"Okay, I slept fairly well all things considered," Tori answers evenly. None of us are feeling enormously ebullient after last night's shooting, but there's not a whole lot we can do about it at this point. We'd cooperated with the sheriff's officers and Lucretia had alerted them about her brother.

"Well, I slept pretty well since I popped a melatonin before I went to bed," Lucretia adds. "When I woke up this morning and opened my door, I found this prince of a beast lying on my doorstep." Grey moans contentedly and Robert gives him a pat of the head.

"I was wondering where you wandered off to last night, Grey." Robert fibs.

"How about you, Mace?"

"Pretty good. I slept with my window open, and every time I heard something outside my juices got flowing, but I eventually drifted off. I like the cool nights up here. Great sleeping weather provided you don't get shot!"

Our server returns and delivers our meals, and our humor improves with a good wholesome breakfast filling our bellies.

"So, Robert, what's the plan today?" I ask between bites of my omelet and another blueberry muffin.

"The plan today is for you to finish your breakfasts, take a few more minutes in your rooms, and then follow me up the road until we come to the grounds of the defunct Brockway Mining Company." A chill shoots through me at the very mention of the mine. Maggie notices me shiver and clasps my hand.

"Sounds good!" I lie. "Mace, will you give me a hand when it's time to haul my lighting and camera gear?"

"Of course, I'm pretty darn excited about what we're going to see."

"Well, Kelli and Rennie are already at the mine straightening up some things for our visit," Robert reports. "I told them to expect us around 10:00 AM."

Several minutes later we finish our breakfasts and agree to meet by our cars in about fifteen minutes. Robert and Grey walk outside and call Rennie and Kelli while they wait for us. "How're you two doing this morning?" Robert asks.

"I suppose you heard about the shooting last night," Kelli asks.

"Yeah, I heard, and a few minutes ago I saw the damage the shooter caused in the dining room. I also ran into the sheriff this morning, and he told me that his men and state police are on alert for anything or anyone looking suspicious, but he didn't sound overly optimistic since they don't even know what the murderer was driving and only have an outdated prison photo of Malcolm Land."

"Malcom Land?!" Rennie cries out nervously. You mean, Lucretia's brother?"

"Yeah, her brother broke out of Joliet prison, and she seems to think he's responsible."

Rennie's heart nearly stops when he thinks back several years ago how Malcolm Land had sent his henchman, Ernst Kline, to kill everyone in his family at the brewery complex. Kline shot Mace in the shoulder when he tried unsuccessfully to get the drop on him, and Rennie was forced to kill him before he murdered the whole family. A shiver goes down Rennie's spine just thinking about it.

"Anyway, just wanted you to know that we'll join you at the mine pretty soon. Anything else going on?"

"Maybe," Kelli offers soberly. "Rennie and I have had a weird feeling ever since we got here this morning. We're hearing sounds we haven't heard before … from within the mine, like deep inside the caverns. It's pretty spooky, Robert."

"We're on our way," he replies. "Why don't you come outside of the mine and meet us, okay? We'll all go back in together."

They agree and hang up. Robert bends down to Grey and gently places the palm of his hand between the large wolf's eyes. The energy from his palm radiates into his animal spirit who absorbs the sensations and stiffens with resolve. "Yeah, my friend, I think we're about to be tested again. Like a phoenix, it seems that the Windigo has risen again. The ancient prophets were right … *evil never truly dies.*"

As we did the whole way up here, Mace and I climb into my truck loaded with my photography gear, and Maggie, Tori, and Lucretia get into Lucretia's car. Robert waits for us to get buckled in and then guides our three-car caravan onto the road toward the Brockway mine. Malcolm watches our entourage go by from a secluded pull-off close to the lodge's entrance. So far, he'd been able to elude the various police cruisers that went sailing past his location looking for the shooter. Malcolm bides his time. He waits some thirty seconds and then pulls onto the road following us.

The view as we ascend Brockway Mountain is twisty and shrouded in a magnificent array of forest greenery and white birch trees. Every few seconds light shadows appear on the road before we dart back under the verdant canopy. I see a road sign that reads *Brockway Mine 2 miles,* and I notice my breathing and heart rate getting more rapid as the stress of returning to this terrifying place changes my whole equilibrium.

"You okay?" Mace asks. "Say something so I know you're in there."

"Something," I say soberly. "This mountain is a very different sort of place, Mace. I know we're going to be seeing and photographing some great paleo art, but it's like the mountain is a yin and yang sort of thing. For all of its magnificent treasures and incredible history, there are evil, deadly forces at play here too. At least that's what we experienced last summer. Hopefully, when Nokomis zapped the Windigo that was the end of it. Regardless, as we get closer to the mine entrance it's still creeping me out. Keep your eyes open and your Weed Killer handy."

We round a bend in the road, and I look over my shoulder at the view of Copper Harbor nestled along the shore of Lake Superior. "Gitche Gumee!" Mace chortles. "What a funny little name for such an immense body of water." A few minutes later Robert turns off the road into the entrance of the defunct and isolated Brockway mine. Lucretia and I pull our cars in behind him, and we park next to Ranger Kelli's vehicle. The sixty-foot tall shaft house looms in front of us in the misty mountain fog. Rennie and Kelli are waiting for us as we get out. I look at the windows at the top of the shaft house and briefly think about how Rex Trammer and his cohort, Digger Finn, closed Robert, Rennie, Kelli, and me inside the mine last summer to die. Rennie and I make eye contact, and we both know what the other is thinking.

"Here," Kelli says as she points to the jackets and helmets we need to wear for the interior of the mine. "Put these on, guys, the fit won't be perfect but at least you'll stay a little cleaner and safer underground." We don the gear and follow her as she leads us to the cog railway that'll take us down to the mine entrance at level seven.

"How deep does this mine go?" Maggie asks.

"Over nine thousand feet," Rennie replies. "In its heyday this mine had ninety-two levels, but these days everything below level seven is flooded with ground water."

Lucretia gulps, "But, that's almost two miles down! Who would want to go down that far?!"

"People trying to make a living," Robert says. "And, it was very dangerous work … cave-ins, poor oxygen and noxious gases, falling rocks, fires, and drill accidents. The immigrants came mostly from Finland and eastern Europe and had a rude awakening when they arrived here looking for the American dream."

"No thank you!" Mace said. "I like being able to see and feel the sun!"

"Ditto!" Tori chimes in. "But, honestly, I like being able to see anything!" She smiles at Robert. We get on the cog railway, and Rennie starts the engine. In the distance we can see Copper Harbor, and Rennie puts the railway in gear, and we begin a slow, steady descent to where we'll enter the mine. As we get closer to the entrance we see a lone figure waiting for us at the bottom of the slope.

"Oh!" Kelli exclaims, "It looks like Thomas Arrowsmith. I wonder what he's doing here."

As we get to the bottom of the slope, Kelli's former park service mentor approaches us.

"Hi Thomas, I'm surprised to see you," Kelli calls out to him.

"Oh, just out for my morning constitutional. Hi Rennie. Hi, Robert, it's been a while."

"It has been," Robert returns evenly.

"Actually, I was hoping to see what you've all been working on."

Kelli introduces Thomas to Maggie, Lucretia, Tori, and me, and then she leads us over to the mine entrance. "Actually, Thomas, we're all here to begin seriously photographing some things, and my boss and Robert have asked that we not have any other visitors until our work is complete."

"Oh, I see," Thomas replies a little miffed. "Can't let the old retired guy get in the way, huh?"

"Now, Thomas, you know how sticky our rules can be. I'm just following instructions. It's good to see you though."

Thomas looks at Robert expecting him to intervene and allow him to enter the caverns, but Robert remains mute. For some unknown reason, it appears that Robert and Thomas never forged a close working relationship when Thomas was with the park service, and even though Kelli likes Thomas, she also has come to trust Robert's intuition. Fortunately for her, she can stick to the *"just following instructions"* response.

"Well, we best get moving along," Robert says as he helps Mace and me with my photo and lighting gear. Just then Thomas walks in front of Lucretia and Maggie when the sound of a large crack echoes off the terrain. A split-second later Thomas Arrowsmith falls to the ground fatally shot. A second crack is heard and Lucretia hears a whiz as another bullet slams into the rock wall behind her. I grab Maggie and Tori's arms and drag them inside the cave entrance. Rennie, Kelli, Mace, and Lucretia dash for the cave as well while Robert and Grey hunker down behind a huge boulder and try to get a glimpse of the shooter. A third shot rings out and Robert ducks back behind the safety of the boulder. "Grey, seek and subdue!" he shouts to his animal spirit, and the great wolf explodes into a gallop toward the sound of the rifle shots.

Through his scope Malcolm sees the wolf beginning to charge his way, and he quickly fires another shot that just barely misses his target. He turns and runs for his car, starts his engine, and begins to drive away as Grey leaps onto the hood of Malcolm's car. Malcolm slams on his brakes and Grey goes flying off to the side. He then floors the accelerator and leaves the wolf in his dust. "Jeezus! That was too close. Never seen a wolf that big before. Wonder who that was that I shot. I swear my sister's got more lives than a cat, but I'm not leaving till I get her even if I have to go into that damn mine to find her!"

Chapter 18

STANDING BESIDE ME Maggie shouts, "What the hell is going on here?! First we get shot at in the restaurant and now this. Two people dead, and it could've been any one of us."

I can't argue with her sentiment, and I put my arm around her for comfort. Waiting for Robert and Grey to join us, we all huddle a few feet inside the mine entrance looking like a motley band of refugees. I see Robert approach, and I help him move Thomas's body to a softer, grassier place. The rifle bullet had torn through his upper chest creating

a large exit wound. It was an ugly way to die. The only positive note was that Thomas Arrowsmith never knew what hit him.

As emotionally strong as both Lucretia and Tori are, they're both shell-shocked by the shooting. Mace has a grim look etched on his face, and I can't say that I'm feeling very chipper either. All I wanted was for this to be an exciting adventure to photograph very rare cave art with Lucretia, Rennie and Robert, and to expose Tori, Maggie, and Mace to the beauty of the Keweenaw Peninsula. I feel Maggie's eyes on me, and I turn and see a sadness that breaks my heart. The very last thing I wanted during this trip was for Maggie and Tori to see what deadly shitstorms I manage to get sucked into. And, as for Kelli, she is deeply saddened that her mentor, a man she considered to be a friend, has been murdered before her very eyes.

Robert calls the sheriff's office to report the murder, and while he's waiting for the cops to show up, Rennie and Kelli somberly lead us inside the mine and load us and my gear into another tram that'll take us to the cave art. Robert and Grey decide to wait outside to meet the police, and Rennie begins our drive forward.

If you've never been inside a mine or a cave, the subterranean world is hard to imagine. Obviously, it's dark, but to experience a realm that is devoid of any light is hard to fathom. I think about the miners who worked underground on the veins of ore and wondered what they did if their candles or carbide lamps went out. They'd be hard pressed to ever find their way out unless they knew the mine's branch system very well. Fortunately, our tram has very bright headlights, and we all watch the changes in rock formations, veins of ore, and high and low ceilings as we move along. After about ten minutes we arrive at a large chamber, and Rennie turns off the engine and the headlights. For a few moments, we're engulfed in total darkness and then Rennie and Kelli turn on their headlamps.

"Just give us a few moments, folks," Kelli says. "Rennie and I want your first exposure to the cave art to be memorable." Kelli and Rennie walk toward a large rock wall. They stand about thirty feet away from each other at opposite sides of the wall. She nods at Rennie, and they both flip the switches on standing light fixtures that illuminate the scene with a warm glowing brightness.

I hear Maggie and Lucretia gasp in wonder at the ancient scenes painted on the wall before us.

"Never in a million years would I ever have guessed that something this magnificent would be hidden away under a mountain in Michigan," Lucretia exclaims. "Not in ten million years!" She walks up to the wall to examine it more closely, her mouth agape. Kelli walks up beside her, and the rest of us join them and spread out to feast our eyes on various scenes of Paleo-Indian life.

"How old do you think these paintings are?" Lucretia asks Kelli.

"Robert would be able to give you a more accurate timeframe, but I recall his saying these paintings and the other artifacts are at least five thousand years old, and possibly as old as ten or fifteen thousand years. Pretty amazing!"

"The colors are still so brilliant!" Lucretia fawns. "The individual figures, the scenes of life, their wigwams, their fields of crops, their clothing. These scenes will totally rewrite what we've thought we've known about ancient Indian life in the Great Lakes region."

"See, Mom!" Rennie says. "Now you know why I'm so excited to be working up here with Kelli and Robert."

"Uh, yeah!" Maggie replies. "You could work on curating a site like this for a very long time, soon-to-be-Dr.-Rennie-Cotton." She beams at him with pride. Mace and Tori are as thunderstruck as the rest of us, and we each take our time in appreciating what we see before us.

"Kelli, you mentioned other artifacts. Are they close by?" Lucretia asks.

"Come with me," she replies, and we form a line and walk some forty feet to the center of this large cave chamber. What we see brings another chorus of praise as we see a series of nine stone benches set in a circle around what appears to be an altar with a niche for something very important. The altar is made of pure copper with bands of silver and gold inlaid into the copper. To adorn it even further magnificent gemstones, including diamonds and semiprecious stones are also set into the copper. When we shine our lights on the altar, it's almost as if it comes alive with color. The vibrance, clarity, and saturation look otherworldly.

"We found this ceremonial site last summer when we were trying to find a way out. Robert told Clay, Rennie, and me that it's the ritual circle where the Midewin healers conducted their mystical healing practices centered on the Megis shell. He said that he was brought here as a young boy to study and learn the secrets of their medicine men, but that he hadn't been back for many years. This niche at the top of the altar held the Megis shell, and Robert moved it after we escaped the mountain last summer fearing that others might stumble upon it. It's hidden in a new location under the mountain, and Robert has spoken very little about it since."

We all walk slowly around and in between the stone benches and the altar. Lucretia lightly touches the altar with her fingertips and swears she feels a surge of something; perhaps energy, perhaps some friction between her fingers and rough stone. "I think it's the most magnificent thing I've ever seen," she declares with unabashed honesty. "With the exception of the ancient Egyptian pharaohs' burial sites, nothing like this is known to exist."

"It's true," Rennie confirms. "We're standing on very holy ground to the Chippewa, and Robert, Grey, and Nokomis are its caretakers."

During our inspection of the altar and wall paintings Tori has been very quiet. We're all feeling humbled by what Kelli and Rennie are showing us, but Tori has been unusually quiet. Several times as she's moved from one viewing spot to another I've noticed her with her eyes closed, not unlike what she would sometimes do when she was blind. It was like her way of focusing on something.

I go over to her and ask if she's okay. Mace joins us. "Yeah, I think I'm okay, but it's weird because I've been having these mental flashbacks to my surprise visit with that old Indian woman, Nokomis, in the shop in Eagle Harbor. I hear her voice … her words. She said that where we're going you all would need my sightless skills. And, when I was close to the altar and wall art, I had sensations like I've never known before."

"What kind of sensations?" Mace asks.

"I don't know quite how to describe them, Mace. It's like I feel like I'm part of something larger, that my life is flowing toward a reckoning of sorts."

Mace and I look at her with a combination of concern and curiosity. "Well, maybe it's just the lack of oxygen down here," Mace offers to help lighten the mood.

"Or, maybe it's as Tori says, Mace. I think you're already beginning to see that there are other realities up here on the Keweenaw." Mace nods his agreement. Kelli and Rennie join them, and I suggest, "While we're waiting for Robert, why don't you guys give me a hand in setting up my studio lighting and getting our power packs connected? Kelli, any particular place you want me to start? I think we should shoot close-up sections across the length of the artwork. That way we can have detailed scenes which I can then stitch together later in Photoshop into panoramas."

"Sounds good," Kelli says. "Why don't you begin here on the left side and work your way to the other end? I appreciate you asking me my druthers, Clay, but you certainly know what you're doing." After we've brought the equipment to the locations I want, Robert and Grey appear out of the dark cavern and join us.

"So, the police came?" I ask.

"Yeah, the same two officers that responded to our call last night at the restaurant. I think they're beginning to wonder if we're like a lightning rod for murder and mayhem."

"Well hell yes, we are!" I reply. I look at Maggie and wince when I see her shaking her head at me.

"The officers loaded up Thomas Arrowsmith's body and took my statement. I told them that we think it's probably the same shooter as last night, Malcolm Land. Unfortunately, I couldn't give them a description of his car from where we were standing. They've got the state boys involved so hopefully they'll nab this guy before anyone else gets hurt."

Robert changes the subject by walking up to Lucretia, Tori, Mace, and Maggie. "So, what do you think of our little treasure trove under the mountain?"

"It's truly remarkable, Robert!" Lucretia gushes. "I feel very honored that our Land Foundation can play a role in sharing the heritage that the Chippewa people hold dear." Grey strides over to Lucretia and affectionately leans against her legs. Mace, Maggie, and Tori each express similar sentiments as Lucretia's, and I can see that Robert feels comfortable with the involvement of my family of friends.

"I think we're in pretty good shape to begin my photography. I just wanted to wait for you to see if you have any thoughts prior to my starting."

The next moment changes our collective mood dramatically when we hear an ungodly howl from something that sends chills down all of our spines. I look in the distance toward the mine entrance where our lights meet the darkness and see the shadow of something demonic that I've never seen before. We suddenly hear the animalistic wail morph into a near-human voice: "Hoo Mans, Hoo Mans! Blood, meat, mine!" And then we hear a haughty laugh before the creature's shadow and voice recede into the void of darkness.

Chapter 19

"WHAT THE FRIGGING hell was that?!" Mace shouts as he feels inside his pocket for his Weed Killer. We all look at Robert for an explanation. Rennie, Kelli, and I are particularly nervous knowing the kind of bloodthirsty creature we encountered here last year.

"It's something that I hadn't expected," Robert confesses. The horrific wail comes from the direction of the mine entrance again followed by the creature's intimidating voice. "Hoo Mans, I am coming for you! I won't rest until I have devoured

every last one of your bones and have found that glowing shell you call Megis."

I look at Robert and say, "Whatever that thing is, we're cut off from the mine entrance. The shadow of the creature appears on the cave walls again. It doesn't look like the shape of the Windigo we encountered last year. That one looked like a cross between a grizzly bear and a giant mole. From what we can discern from this creature's shadow, it's tall and skeletally thin and stands upright on two sinewy legs. It also has long, bony fingers with sharp nails and jagged deer-like antlers. The shadow alone puts the fear of God in us, but seeing its white glowing eyes is truly unnerving. But, the most unsettling feature of all is that it can speak. This is not the same Windigo as last year. This creature has evolved. It's sentient, verbal, and hungry, and that isn't good news for us.

We all huddle behind Robert who hollers at the creature, "You shall not pass! Recede into the darkness from which you've come. We are too many for you. We are too strong for you. We have the light of the Megis shell on our side!" He then dispatches Grey to seek and report. The huge wolf charges forward and a few moments later we hear an awful snarling sound, then a plaintive yelp.

"Grey, return!" Robert shouts and moments later we see the great wolf limp back with a nasty gash on his flank. He leans against Robert's legs in pain.

"Hoo Mans! Is that the best warrior you can send against me?" It erupts with a condescending laugh. "I am coming for you, Hoo Mans!" The shadow on the wall begins to move. Robert picks up Grey and shouts words that I had hoped I'd never hear again. "Run! Our lives depend on it!" And that's what we did. Except in all of the confusion Rennie, Kelli, Maggie, and I dash down one side of the ancient ceremonial room, and Mace, Tori, and Lucretia go in the opposite direction and enter a side cavern closest to them. The beast bellows a blood curdling cry as my greatest nightmare comes to life again. I holler over my shoulder to Robert, "We're cut off from Lucretia, Tori, and Mace. We've got to get back to them."

"We will," he shouts back, "but for now, keep moving!" He carefully sets Grey down and examines his wounds. He reaches in his pocket and retrieves healing herbs. "Keep going, Clay, I'll catch up to you guys. I need to tend to my friend while there's still time."

"But Robert, there are so many side tunnels. How will we know which one to follow?"

"Just get moving, Clay, I'll find you. I promise. That thing will kill us, and Grey will die if I don't tend to his wounds now. So, please, go!" The great wolf lies on the ground panting heavily as Robert kneels beside him. "Hang in there, my friend," he softly soothes the great wolf. "You should feel better soon, and then we need to find our friends."

I hear Robert's words to his animal spirit and pray that they're not the last words I ever hear him say. I take the lead with Maggie jogging beside me and Rennie and Kelli are right on our heels. We enter into the closest of several cave tunnels with only our headlamps to guide our way. I can't believe I'm reliving the most terrifying experience I've ever known, and that I've dragged my family into mortal danger. We hear the evil beast howl again, and we quicken our paces.

Robert continues to render aid to Grey whose breathing is already becoming a little easier. He closes his eyes and strokes the great wolf's side. "Just breathe, my friend, and let the herbs flow within you." Robert looks up and sees the evil Windigo's shadow on the stone walls only thirty feet away. He stands with his feet striding Grey. "You shall not pass, evil one. Return to the depths of the dark and leave us in peace."

At first the the only reply Robert hears is heaving breathing and guttural sounds from the beast. Then, it emerges from the shadows. "Hoo Man, I sense you are not like the others here. I sense that you are from the original people."

Robert is stunned that the creature can form sentences and that its power of intuition is so acute.

"Who are you and where did you come from?" Robert already knows the answers to his questions, but he asks them anyway trying to buy some time for Grey's recovery, and to ascertain the powers of this unexpected enemy.

The Windigo laughs and steps further into the dim light affording Robert a clearer view of his adversary. "You know who I am, Hoo Man, and from whence I come. I am the evil one of your legends … the devourer of Hoo Mans."

Robert is shocked to see how different this creature is from last year. This creature shows no resemblance at all to the huge bear-mole adversary Nokomis vaporized just in time last year. This sinewy demon, standing erect on two muscular legs with craggy antlers and glowing eyes, looks like the pure embodiment of evil. "We killed your spirit and corporeal form last year, and we will do it again. Be gone, you foul-smelling beast!"

The Windigo snarls and replies as it begins to circle Robert and Grey, "Yes, the old woman dispelled my old self, my physical being, but not my spirit. I cannot die. Perhaps your ancient prophets taught you that evil never truly dies. It just rises from its ashes like a phoenix with renewed fury. I am now reborn, and I have evolved. My shape is stronger. My understanding is keener. My ability to communicate is now complete. And, I need to feed!"

"Then know this, vile creature, you cannot defeat us. The magic from the Megis shell will always be superior to any form you take. Leave us! Descend back into your dark hole."

As if trying to comprehend the depth of Robert's words, the Windigo stays silent and briefly stands still. Then, "Ah yes, the Megis shell, your source of power. I shall have it for my own. And, I shall learn the ways of Hoo Mans so that I may defeat you all and feast. I wish to emerge from the depths of this netherworld. I sense there is much to relish outside of this mountain. Yes, Hoo Man?!"

Robert stretches his hand to arm's length and a beam of glowing power erupts toward the beast. "You shall not win. We will not let you pass. You will never know the world beyond this dark, dank realm."

Robert's beam slams into the Windigo which recoils in pain and surprise. "Aaarrrrhhh!" it bellows. "I see I still have much to learn," it snarls back at Robert. "You are strong, but I will eventually learn what you and the Hoo Mans know. I will leave you and your friend for now. I will seek your precious Megis shell and the other Hoo Mans … to torture and to feast. Yes, their fear will yield the knowledge I must know!" And, with that the Windigo recedes back into the darkness, and Robert hears it laughing as it enters the side cavern that Mace, Lucretia, and Tori had used to escape.

After moving at a brisk pace for longer than I thought Maggie and I could, we finally pull up to catch our breath. "I can't keep up like this, Clay," she says. "And do you have any idea where we are and how we get out of here?'"

Rennie and Kelli are winded too and glad that we old folks need to rest. "I know, Maggie, I'm really tired too, but we have to keep moving. Robert needed to tend to Grey's wounds, but he said he would find us."

"Do any of you even know where we are?" she asks again. "It all looks the same to me, and that thing back there … what the hell is that thing!"

My heart sinks as I explain to her that it's the Windigo, or at least a reborn version of the ancient creature that we battled last summer. We thought Nokomis had totally defeated it, but apparently not. I look at Rennie and Kelli to gauge their status and see fear etched on their features. "Some of this looks a little familiar," Kelli offers. "If I'm not mistaken, we'll come to a huge chamber filled with wondrous things before too long, but we can't dawdle there." Rennie nods his agreement. "I think Kelli's right,

Mom. We came this way last year, but with so many side avenues connected to this warren of caves, it's hard to remember exactly which way we went."

"Look!" I say. "Turn off your headlamps, everyone." We all do so, and in the distance we can see a soft shimmer of white light. "I think that light's coming from the Megis shell. Let's follow it and let's only use one of our headlamps so we can conserve our batteries. No telling how long we'll be down here."

I hear Maggie stifle a sob and put my arm around her to offer a little comfort, but she's got every right to be frightened and upset. We all are. Rennie gives his mom a supportive hug too and whispers how sorry he is that she's upset.

"So, this is what you guys experienced last summer, Clay?" she asks plaintively. "And, you still came back here?!"

"Yes," I try to offer calmly, "but we thought Nokomis had killed it. I never would've ventured back here or let Rennie and Kelli work in the caves if I had any inkling of the danger that still exists. I'm sorry, Maggie."

"We need to keep moving, Dad," Rennie insists, "and I think Kelli's right about that large chamber up ahead. And, if I'm not mistaken we then have to slip into that subterranean stream to get to the other side where Robert created that exit for us. The Megis shell's light should guide our way."

We all begin moving quickly ahead with Kelli in front, and the rest of us trying not to stumble on rock rubble strewn along the cave floor. Privately, I pray that Mace, Tori, and Lucretia are safe, and that Robert has been able to revive Grey and come looking for us. The thought of our being lost down here in the dark without Robert's help is not something I wish to even consider, but it's a definite possibility.

Perhaps some ten minutes later our path makes a sharp turn, and we follow the white light toward the large chamber that Kelli had predicted. Even in the dim light we're stopped in our tracks by the scene before us. We each turn on our headlamps to get a better view, and I see Maggie's face fill with awe by the spectacle of raw gemstones imbedded in the chamber's walls and its ceiling composed almost exclusively of copper, silver, and bands of bright gold.

"Oh, my God ..." she utters.

"Now you know why Robert wants us to keep the secrets of Brockway Mountain a secret. If the outside world ever caught wind of the treasures down here, this place would be overrun by greedy opportunists, including our government, and the ancient artifacts of the Chippewa people would be doomed."

"How is this even possible?" Maggie says softly. We walk into the vast chamber, and I see Maggie bend down and pick up a raw diamond the size of a tomato. She then discards it when she stumbles on one the size of a cantaloupe. "Oh, my God!" she says again, and I see a mirthful smile appear on her smudged face.

"C'mon," Kelli exhorts. "We need to keep moving toward the light. No telling when the Windigo will appear again, and none of this treasure belongs to us anyway."

Maggie drops the huge gemstone, and we quicken our pace. I can't help but wonder if we'll ever see our friends again.

Chapter 20

MEANWHILE ABOVE GROUND, Malcolm Land has returned after watching the cops leave with Thomas Arrowsmith's body. He stands by the entrance to the Brockway mine and hides behind a large boulder listening intently for any sound that would indicate where his sister might be. He has a handgun tucked in his belt and carries his assault rifle with several clips loaded with high-powered cartridges. He finds a spare flashlight that Rennie and Kelli had kept around with their other equipment. He listens for a few moments longer and then

steps inside the cave. Footprints in the dusty soil show him which direction his quarry has gone. He takes a snort from his bottle of Jack Daniels and steps further inside the earth's jagged maw.

Mace, Tori, and Lucretia are totally exhausted. They've run as far as they can and finally find themselves standing on a narrow ledge overlooking an underground stream. While Mace and Lucretia huddle together on a boulder, Tori searches in all directions for another way out. The sounds of the evil beast still rings in their ears, and they know that returning in the direction from which they'd come isn't a viable option.

"Just leave me," Lucretia moans. "I don't know what's worse, getting eaten by some nasty, ugly cave creature or getting shot by my nasty, ugly brother, but I just don't think I can go any further." She rests her head against Mace's shoulder and a tear runs down her face. He gently takes her hand and tries to reassure her. "Remember how bleak everything seemed when Malcolm locked us in Samuel Morse's mausoleum? We didn't think we could possibly survive that, but we did, didn't we?"

Lucretia looks into Mace's eyes, and sees a resolve that she knows she can trust. "You really think we're going to get out of here alive, Mace?"

"I don't know, Lucretia, but one thing's for sure. We're not dying here. Not now, not today."

Tori rejoins them. "I can't seem to find another way out other than wading in this stream. It doesn't appear very deep, and it seems to be our only way."

Mace stands and says, "Let's go, Lucretia, we can hang onto each other. Ready for a little swim?" They walk over to the edge of the ledge and look down. The surface of the stream is only about three feet below them and is flowing slowly. "Now that doesn't seem too bad, does it, Lucretia?"

"No, it doesn't," she agrees. "You must think I'm a big baby, Mace."

"Not at all, Lucretia. I'm scared too. How about you, Tori?"

"Shitless!" comes Tori's frank reply. "I'm just glad we've got each other to rely on."

They stand over the stream, and Mace slips into the water. He gets his feet settled on the stone bottom and reaches his arms up for Lucretia. "It's not bad, Lucretia. Just sit down and push off, and I'll catch you, okay?" She nods her understanding and does as Mace suggests. "Oh, the water actually feels pretty good," she says encouragingly. "Thanks, Mace." They wade a little further downstream to give Tori plenty of room to get in."

Tori walks to the edge and prepares to jump in when she raises her head and says, "What is that awful smell?" From out of nowhere the Windigo emerges from the shadows and rushes toward her. She swats away its gnarly hand and leaps for the water. Mace and Lucretia look on with horror as the Windigo thrusts out its other sinewy arm and grabs Tori in midair. It closes its grasp around her waist and drags her back. Tori pounds, scratches, and kicks the evil beast, grabbing onto its antlers and kicking it in the face. It throws her to the ground and holds her in place with its filthy foot. "Hold still, Hoo Man, or I will finish you now." Tori struggles a little longer, but it's clear that this thing has her under its control. She lies still panting for air and totally terrified.

Mace strides against the current and tries to clamber back up the slippery stone to rescue Tori, but the ledge above him is too high and wet, and he can't find a suitable handhold. "I'm coming, Tori!" he hollers, but he just can't find any traction. He reaches for his Weed Killer weapon, but realizes there's no way he can release its lethal force without hitting Tori as well.

"Go away, Hoo Man!" the Windigo snarls at Mace, "I will kill all of you now if you do not leave!" Then, it grabs Tori around the waist and effortlessly hauls her limp form back into the shadows. "This one's mine!" And then the evil man-eating spirit and his captive are gone. The last sound that Tori hears before totally passing out is Mace's voice helplessly calling out her name.

Mace is beyond heartbroken as he wades back downstream and rejoins Lucretia. "I … I just couldn't climb back out to help her. It was too wet and steep. She's gone. It's got her." Lucretia wraps Mace in a sympathetic hug and looks into the big man's eyes. "I … I couldn't reach her," he laments. "We've got to get her back, but I don't know how." For the first time in his eighty-plus years of age Mace feels like and old and broken man.

"I'm so sorry, Mace, there's nothing we can do now though. Let's wade downstream and hopefully we can hook up with Robert or Clay. It seems that if that Windigo thing was going to kill her, it would've done it back there. Let's not give up hope, Mace. Like you said earlier, we've been in dire situations before."

Mace nods his head appreciatively and thanks Lucretia for trying to help him feel better. "She's like a daughter to me, Lucretia. First her brother, Weed, and now Tori." They slowly wade with the gentle flow of the stream, numb with sadness and fear, clinging to each other. About a hundred yards later they reach a gravelly beach and finally emerge to terra firma. A softly shimmering white light illuminates a path and beckons to them in the distance.

"Can you walk now, Grey?" Robert asks his life-long friend. "That damn Windigo took a chunk out of you, didn't it. Next time it's our turn, right big fella?!" Grey stands on his feet and shakes his fur vigorously as if to reestablish his equilibrium. He nuzzles Robert's leg and wags his tail a little. He then barks to let Robert know that he's ready to go. Robert inspects Grey's wound a final time and places a few more herbs on the great wolf's flank. "That should do you for now, my friend," and the two of them set off in the direction that the Windigo went.

With the exception of passing this way last summer, it has been many moons since Robert and Grey have traveled this way. There are many side caverns, and Robert stops every once in a while and closes his eyes as if to divine the right way. They round a corner and come to a shallow pool where they see a lone figure sitting by the silvery water. "Nokomis!" Robert calls out. "You're sure a sight for sore eyes, Grandmother!"

Nokomis turns in her grandson's direction and opens her milky white eyes. "Come sit with me," she directs. "We have much to discuss." Robert and Grey sit by the pool, and several minutes of silence pass before the wizened old woman speaks. "I see that you and your wolf friend have encountered the Windigo, yes?"

"Yes, Grandmother, we have. It nearly killed Grey, and it scattered my friends in various directions in the caverns. I need to find them before the evil one kills them all."

Nokomis stares into the pool and replies, "Yes, I see that they are scattered, and I sense their fear."

"How is it possible, Nokomis? I thought you defeated the evil one last time."

"Yes, I did, indeed, but as our ancient Midewin healers learned eons ago, evil will always haunt us. The legends say that once the Windigo's body is destroyed, its spirit remains in an ethereal state for one year, and then it reemerges as another beast, but with another body form and enhanced abilities. The ancient ones said this has occurred since the beginning of time, and it's the Great Spirit's way to keep our race alert to the evils of the world. The Megis shell is our light in the face of this darkness."

"I was able to stop it temporarily, Nokomis, but I sense that my power is not strong enough to defeat its body again. Will you help me and my friends? Their hearts are good, and they wish to help our Chippewa people."

Nokomis stares into the pool of water again. "Yes, of course, I will help you, but we must move quickly. The Windigo has captured the woman with yellow hair who once was sightless."

"Her name is Tori, Nokomis, and I gave her the ability to see."

"Yes, my grandson, I have met and spoken with her. She does, indeed, have a good heart, and I have told her that her sightless skills will prove helpful to her friends. But, you and Grey must go now and try to free her. If the Windigo does not eat her, he will try to get information from her about the world beyond this dark mountain realm. It is ready to emerge from here and satisfy its blood lust all along the Keweenaw. Go now!" And then Nokomis, grandmother to Robert and the oldest of her line, dissolves into particles of golden light that float momentarily then fall into the placid pool of water.

Robert looks at Grey and says, "Someday I've got to learn how to do that! C'mon, big fella, our friends need our help."

Robert and Grey set off again at a brisker pace now that the great wolf has had a chance to rest a bit more. The light from the Megis shell still glows in the distance, and Robert senses that the Windigo has not killed Tori yet. Hopefully its attention can be distracted between searching for the Megis shell and doing whatever it is it plans with Tori and the others.

Robert and Grey slow their pace as they enter a cavern where they've never been before. It has broad veins of bright copper, gold and silver, but the most compelling feature is another cave mural showing Chippewa life many hundreds of years ago. Robert gasps as he gazes upon the scene and realizes that the images tell of the story of him as a child who has just rediscovered the Megis shell and is presenting it to the chief and the Midewin healers.

"Look at this, Grey, I think this is supposed to be me as a young boy, and here you are too standing near my parents and Nokomis. So many years ago now. It almost seems like a dream." Grey gives a small yelp in acknowledgement. "We'll have to show this to the others at another time, but now we have to try to save Tori and find the others. They take off at a run.

Chapter 21

I HAVE NO IDEA where we're going, but Maggie, Rennie, Kelli, and I keep moving through large caverns and narrow crawl spaces always following the white light that hopefully will be our salvation.

"I'm exhausted, Clay, can we rest for a little bit please?" Rennie comes to provide a shoulder for his mother to lean on. "Sure we can, Maggie, let's just go a little further till we find a stopping place that's more secluded. We don't want to be out in the open if that evil beast returns." About a hundred yards away we find a carved-out niche

behind a boulder and drop down in the dusty soil for a brief respite.

"Any idea where we are, Kelli?" I ask. "Does any of this look familiar to you from last year?"

"Not really, but I'm thinking if we keep going in this direction we're bound to find that underground stream which eventually led us to where we exited the mountain."

"Well, that's at least a little encouraging. I wonder what the hell happened to Mace, Tori, and Lucretia. The last I saw of them they were running in the opposite direction from us toward another cavern."

"And Robert and Grey?" Rennie asks hopefully. "I just pray that they escaped. This new Windigo surprised the crap out of me when it spoke. The one we encountered last year was more like pure dumb brute strength. This one is craftier."

"Well, I sure don't want to meet any of them down here in the dark or anywhere," Maggie asserts.

"Let's go, guys, we need to keep moving toward the light, and hopefully Robert will hook up with us soon."

As we emerge from our hiding place, we step back onto the path and Kelli says, "My God, what is that awful smell?" From some forty yards away we surprise the Windigo as it is striding along, carrying an unconscious Tori. It sees us and bellows a horrific wail in our direction.

"My God!" Maggie blurts out. "It's got Tori!"

I immediately pull my Demon Camera from my pocket and make certain it's set to kill. I charge the beast, and it drops Tori on the ground to repel my charge. It stands and pounds it bony chest. "You cannot have this Hoo Man! It is mine!"

I stop about fifteen feet away from it, and we stare at each other as if to assess weaknesses. Its smell is putrid and toxic in its own right. I notice that Tori is unconscious but breathing. She's alive.

"Leave our friend!" I holler. "And we'll leave you in peace."

It briefly considers my words and then laughs. "Hoo Man, you are small and weak, barely worth my effort, but I will kill you nonetheless. Good meat is hard to find down here!"

"Leave her!" I command again, and this time it begins walking in my direction. I wait for it to approach only another five feet before I unleash the full force of the Demon camera. A blue arc of angry electricity leaps forward and engulfs the Windigo sending it into an angry frenzy. It howls like a wounded banshee and tries to come at me again. I discharge the Demon again with the same electrifying, pain-inducing results. The Windigo reaches down, picks up Tori again in its gnarled, bony hands and runs off into the shadows.

I try to follow, but the beast knows these caves like none other and has speed that I can't match. I return to Maggie, Rennie, and Kelli and see that they're stunned by the violence of what just occurred.

"You did it, Dad! You scared it off!"

"Did what, Rennie?!" I ask with frustration. "That damn thing's got Tori. She may be alive now, but for how long, and they could be anywhere down here. Damnit, I can't believe we're down in this God-forsaken hole again dealing with things that want to kill us. What the hell were we thinking, and where's Robert when we need him?"

"I'm here, Clay," I hear a steady voice say behind me, and we all turn and see Robert and Grey approaching us from the direction we'd come.

Rennie and Kelli go rushing up to him. "Man, are we glad to see you!" Kelli gushes. "We just had a surprise visit from the Windigo."

"Yes, I can still smell the odor of that awful beast, plus some remnants from your special camera, Clay."

"Yeah, my Demon whupped that demon for now, but I've depleted a large amount of power in the process. I'm not sure how many full charges I have left. That damned creature has Tori, Robert. I couldn't get her back."

Robert somberly nods his understanding and asks if everyone else is okay. Maggie replies by asking him if he knows where Lucretia and Mace are.

"I sense that they are near, but we have to find the Windigo before it brutalizes Tori. Come, we must go. Grey, go ahead and scout, but do not engage the Windigo. Come back to me and report. I don't want to risk losing you too." At that the great wolf bounds off into the shadows in the direction that the evil beast fled with Tori.

"So, what the hell are we gonna do?" I beseech Robert. "My family is in mortal danger down here, and we've got Lucretia's nut-job brother outside shooting and killing people."

"We will do the best that we can do, Clay," Robert advises philosophically, "but complaining isn't going to get us anywhere." He turns to follow the Windigo, and we all fall in behind him.

"Sorry, Robert," I say to him. "I've grown to hate this damn cave, and I'm really scared for my loved ones."

"I am too, Clay," he confesses. "This is a different beast than we encountered last year. I'm frankly very surprised that it hasn't killed Tori already. We've got to find it soon though. It needs meat to satisfy its bloodlust. C'mon!" We quicken our pace, and I look to see how well Maggie is holding up. She gives me a weak smile and keeps trudging ahead.

Tori awakens in a confused state. At first she lies still trying to regain full lucidity, and then she bolts upright as she remembers being snatched by the Windigo and hauled off into the darkness. Then, her nostrils fill with a dreadful odor and she glances around in the darkness looking for its source. She sees two glowing eyes staring at her, and she recoils in fear and tries to run away. A large bony hand reaches out and grabs her and holds her until she stops struggling.

"Hoo Man, you are mine. You are not going anywhere, and your friends cannot save you."

"What are you, and why have you taken me? If you're going to kill me, then just get it over with already."

"Yes, I will kill you, but first I want some answers to questions I have."

"What are you?" Tori asks again as she looks around for a possible escape route.

The Windigo laughs. "What am I? I am the evil man-eating spirit that has lived under this mountain for many, many years. I am the living legend that the original people spoke of. I am part physical being and part spirit, and I am hungry not just for flesh but for answers about the outside world that I left centuries ago."

Tori tries to run again, but the Windigo holds her in place. "Well, I'm too puny for you to eat," she insists, "and I'm not telling you anything that will allow you to hurt people."

"Yes, hurt people. Feast on Hoo Mans. Find the Megis shell. Grow. Thrive. And yes, you will answer my questions."

It digs its sharp fingernails into Tori's arm, and she lets out a yelp. She tries to run away again and throws a savage fist into the Windigo's face. It isn't even fazed.

"You want to live, Hoo Man? Then, you must answer my questions. Maybe I'll even let you and the others live."

"What is it you want to know, and how is it even possible that you know our language?"

"Over many years my previous forms have heard Hoo Mans speak. Once there were many Hoo Mans who scratched at these stone walls and hauled away shiny rocks. I have listened to those working in the mines and those that I captured too. You Hoo Mans speak in many tongues, but eventually I learned your tongue. I also learned of a great world out there that I wish to experience. You must tell me about it."

"And, why would I help you? You're just going to kill me and my friends anyway."

"I should eat you now and go get my answers from another Hoo Man. Your kind always squeals when I bite them." The Windigo emits a guttural laugh. "And, I seek the Megis shell, but I do not believe you can show it to me. I have tried to follow the white light, but the Megis remains hidden to me. I sense that only one of the original people, like that Hoo Man with the big wolf, can reveal it to me."

Tori remains silent, not knowing exactly what to say. She lets her eyes adjust to the dim light in the space where the Windigo is keeping her. The only source of light comes from the Windigo's glowing eyes. She notices other bones and bits of cloth she assumes were once someone's clothing.

"So, tell me about the world outside of this mountain. Tell me now. I grow impatient."

"It is large and very different from your dark realm. It has the sun and the moon, trees and rivers, and lakes and different terrains. It has many millions of people, most of whom live in towns and large cities. It has daytime and nighttime."

"What are these towns and cities? I would like to see them and feast as much as I wish."

"Well, I don't think you'd last very long," Tori taunts. "We have police and soldiers, and they would not let you 'feast' as you say. They would hunt you down and kill you."

The Windigo emits a low guttural moan again. "I think not, Hoo Man. I am smart and strong, and you Hoo Mans are frail. I will leave you here while I go in search of the Megis shell again. I will have more questions for you when I return."

"Seriously, you're just going to leave me here and let me wander off to find my friends?"

"Yes. Where will you go in the dark? You will never find your way out, and I can easily find you again." It pinches her thigh and says, "You have good meat. I think I'll eat you when I return. Goodbye for now, Hoo Man, I doubt that you'll go very far." And to emphasize its point, it gives Tori a ferocious slap to her back that sends her sprawling in pain, and then it's gone.

In near total darkness Tori lays facedown in the dusty soil. The Windigo's whack nearly rendered her unconscious, but she's alert. Nonetheless, she lies still, listening for the creature, and doing a mental assessment of her physical condition. A few moments later she decides she needs to get going and escape. It hurts like hell when she starts to get up, but all in all, she's in better condition than she thought she'd be. Now, she finds herself in an oddly familiar state, one that she thought she had left behind forever.

"I'm blind again," she whispers to herself. "The darkness is palpable like it used to be."

She stands very still like she sometimes did when she was blind, using her other senses to supply her with "information" about her surroundings.

Tori's memories of existing in a dark world come flooding back to her. She smells whatever she can, including the vile, putrid stench of the Windigo's nest, but she's smelling the air for other scents as well. She feels a faint breeze coming from what she believes is the entrance to this "nest." She smells the air in that direction and decides she'll give it a try. Of course, her footsteps are practiced and cautious at first. Her fingertips touch the sides of the cavern walls and give her a sense of connection. Step by step she emerges from this place where the Windigo dwells, and she finds herself in a larger cavern. She takes her time trying to assess her surroundings, careful not to stumble on a boulder or fall inside a deep hole. She feels the gentle breeze again blow against her smudged cheek and when she turns in that direction she sees the glow of a faint white light, and her spirits are renewed. "The Megis shell," she whispers to herself. "I can see its brightness." She also notices that the light from the Megis shell is casting a subtle, barely perceptible illumination to a path leading in its direction. Tori feels even more encouraged recognizing that she's not in total darkness. "Just follow the light," she whispers softly to herself. "I can do this, one foot in front of the other."

Meanwhile near the entrance to the mine, Malcolm slaps a full clip into his assault rifle, turns on his flashlight, and begins a slow and steady walk inside the Brockway mine. "Why the heck would anyone want to work in a hellhole like this? I've got to be out of my mind even coming in here by myself."

He takes a few more cautious steps and turns around to look and listen. He can no longer see daylight from the entrance. "Oh well, in for a penny, in for a pound. If I can get a clear shot at Lucretia, I'll take it, then I'll skedaddle as fast as I can."

Malcolm wanders deeper inside the caverns and sees bright flashes of color as the mine's walls reflect veins of copper. Before long he comes to the worksite where Rennie, Kelli, and Robert had been studying the cave drawings. Even as cynical as he is, Malcolm marvels at the ancient artwork. "Now I know why Lucretia's here. She wants all of this for herself. Well, that's not happening. One good shot and she's a goner. The rest of her buddies can deal with her corpse."

Malcolm continues walking further into the cavern and spies large rough gemstones lying around. He picks one up and examines it. "Cool!" I get to kill my sister and get rich at the same time. Maybe this mine's not so bad after all." Then, he hears a sound that sends a chill down his spine. The Windigo's bloodcurdling wail is otherworldly, and Malcolm pats his loaded weapons for reassurance. "What the hell was that!?"

Chapter 22

"MACE, CAN WE PLEASE rest a bit?" Lucretia asks as she plops down onto the sandy soil next to the stream. Mace drops down next to her and stares at the slowly flowing water. "Life," he says softly wondering if Tori's has been snuffed out and if he, Lucretia, and the others will survive the dangers under Brockway Mountain.

Lucretia gives his hand a squeeze as she leans against his side. "Just a few minutes, Mace. I just need to rest for a few more minutes." Mace turns off his headlamp and closes his eyes too. The sounds

of Tori's cry for help are still ringing in his ears. "I failed her," he whispers to himself. Finally, overcome with exertion, fear, and grief, and with the soothing sounds of the gentle stream, they both fall into a deep sleep.

And, Mace dreams … in his dream he's seated at Tori's dining table at home. It's a happy gathering that includes Tori, her late brother, Weed, Maggie, Clay, Rennie, Lex, and Satchmo. In his dream Mace beams with true happiness as he looks at the best and only true family he's ever known. *Me, a little brown boy from the Bahamas, with such a fine family of friends.*

The dream shifts and Weed is gone from the gathering, as is Lex, but now Bodie is among his family. Mace notices how everything and everyone eventually comes and goes. He knows his time will come too. He drifts even deeper into sleep and finds himself under Brockway Mountain, walking cautiously trying to keep harm from befalling Lucretia and Tori. The Windigo invades his dream and attacks. It grabs Tori, and Mace is helpless to help her. He cries out in anguish and awakens to Lucretia gently shaking his arm.

"Are you, okay, Mace? You were having a horrible nightmare."

"Uh, yeah, I'm okay, thanks. No, I'm actually not okay. I'll never forgive myself for allowing Tori to be taken from us. Never!"

"I know, Mace, it's awful. I wish there was something that we could say or do. I know how special she is to you."

Mace stands up and brushes the sand off his pants. He reaches his hand down offering Lucretia assistance in getting up. "No more!" he says. "That damn creature is not taking any more of us. Let's keep going, Lucretia, we'll get out of here, I promise."

The two weary travelers continue walking along the path by the stream and eventually follow the path as it leaves the stream and continues deep inside the mountain revealing sights that no modern human has seen here before. Towering crystal stalactites hang down to them like giant teeth and brightly colored rocks beckon them to admire their magnificence. "Never knew anything like this existed!" Lucretia exclaims. "The sheer wealth on display here is staggering. Every person in the Chippewa nation could live like a king!" she gushes.

"My guess is that Robert is well aware of the vast wealth that their people own, but I think he also knows that such wealth would destroy the spirit of his people and the wisdom of their ancient ways. He knows that true wealth comes from availing oneself to the teachings of the Megis shell, not material wealth."

"Well, as someone born into material wealth, I agree with your assessment, Mace. We have to look no farther than my brother to witness how wealth and greed and lack of empathy for others destroys the fiber of one's soul."

Mace picks up a gorgeous emerald the size of a small chicken egg and gives it to Lucretia. "Here's something to remember me by if I don't make it out of here alive." Lucretia accepts it and looks at Mace to see if he's kidding. He's not.

Tori continues carefully walking through passage-ways that she wouldn't be able to see were it not for the faint illumination from the Megis shell. Even with it she has to judiciously place her footsteps. Fortunately, years of navigating as a blind person have given her a preternatural sense of what to feel for. Regardless, she stumbles a few times and bumps her knees against rocky outcrops, but she feels like she's slowly making progress. Perhaps an hour later she arrives at the place where she, Mace, and Lucretia were trying to enter the stream. She shivers when she recalls how the Windigo had snatched her in midair as she attempted to join Mace and Lucretia in the stream. She's amazed that she's still alive.

This time Tori sits down and pushes off the ledge into slowly moving water. She sips greedily from the water and washes the grime and Windigo scent from herself. She stands very still in the water and closes her eyes. She listens intently for any sound other than that of the water. Moments pass and she feels refreshed. She begins moving slowly with the stream, seeing the faint white light in the ever-distance. A hundred yards later she comes to the gravelly section and exits the stream where Lucretia and Mace had fallen asleep. She notices that the sandy ground is moist and shows signs of being scuffed up from human contact. She quickens her pace in an effort to catch up with her friends before the Windigo reappears.

Soon, she comes to the large cavern with the magnificent crystal stalactites and richly endowed walls. She spies two sets of footprints, one large and one smaller and is tempted to call out to them, but she knows that could prove a death sentence for all of them. She walks through a narrow passageway and turns a bend and sees a sight that brings tears of joy to her eyes. It's Lucretia and Mace sitting on a rock looking into a swirling pool of water that looks like its nestled in an altar of sorts.

Both Lucretia and Mace nearly have heart attacks when all of a sudden they hear a voice say, "Hi guys, remember me!?" Tori runs up to them and engulfs both of them in huge hugs.

"But how did you …?" Mace begins. "Oh Tori, thank goodness you're alive! How did you get away?" Lucretia asks gratefully.

"Let's keep our voices low, okay?" she replies. "The Windigo carried me back to its lair and was more interested in asking me questions about the location of the Megis shell and what the outside world is like. It told me that it was going to search for the Megis shell and then grow powerful enough to dominate the outside world."

"But how is it that you got away?" Lucretia asks again.

"It didn't think that I would get very far in the dark, and that he could find me anytime it wanted. That's why we should keep our voices low. It's hungry and needs to feed."

"Yeah, well let the sonovabitch come this way, and it can feed on my Weed Killer. I couldn't use it when it snatched you because I was afraid of killing you in the process."

"Well, it might've been the humane thing to do, Mace, considering it was probably going to eat me. C'mon guys, let's keep moving toward the light. Hopefully we'll hook back up with the others before Mr. Creepy finds us."

Then, another voice comes to them from the gloom "But, you've found the light," Robert's voice calls out, and Grey comes bounding up to them and buries his face between Lucretia's knees.

"What the …?!" Mace calls back as he sees his family of friends join them around the pool of water.

"Man, are you a sight for sore eyes!" Tori exclaims. "For a while there I was thinking that I'd have to try and lead everyone out of here when our batteries eventually failed."

"You may still need to," Robert replies honestly.

Maggie, Rennie, Kelli, and I join in and give everyone huge hugs. It's hard to keep our voices down considering how relieved we are to see that everyone seems to be all right.

I ask questions in rapid succession: "What do we do now, Robert? Do you know where the Windigo is? Are we close to an exit from this God-forsaken mountain? And, what did you mean that we've found the light?"

Robert walks up to the stone altar containing the pool of water and peers deeply into the liquid. The clear water begins to swirl, slowly at first and then more rapidly until it turns a milky hue and the water begins to rise until all of a sudden a lustrously glowing white shell rises to the top of the water and floats.

"Oh my!" Lucretia exhales in wonder. "That's the most beautiful thing I've ever seen."

We all feast our eyes on the legendary Megis shell, and its energy radiates into each of us giving us a sense of well-being and vitality.

"I agree, Lucretia," Robert says proudly. "To my people, this is the light that shows us the way to lead our lives."

"But why would the Megis shell permit such an evil being as the Windigo to exist in the same realm that it does?" Rennie asks.

"I do not know all of the secrets of the Megis shell, but if Nokomis were here I believe she'd say that humankind can best express its character by how it deals with adversity. The wisdom from the Megis shell has always pointed to the healthiest and most fulfilling ways for us to lead our lives, but it's up to us humans to channel our own destinies."

"So, what do we do now, Robert? Are we near an exit?"

"Yes, it is very near, but first we must protect the Megis shell." The Midewin healer stares at the floating shell then closes his eyes. We all watch as the shell dims a bit and begins slowly dipping back into the pool of water. A few moments later, the shell is fully submerged and the water returns to a clear, still pool. Robert opens his eyes and softly pats Grey on the great wolf's head.

We all begin to murmur among ourselves. We each know that we've witnessed something very humbling and rare indeed. For all of the tribulations we've endured so far, Robert's introducing us to the source of wonder for his people is an honor beyond description.

Tori and Mace approach the pool of water and each privately gives thanks for the life-altering gifts that Robert bestowed on them. Each of us knows that Robert, Nokomis, and Grey are protectors of the Megis shell's essence, and we are blessed to witness just small portions of its wonder.

Robert turns away from the pool of water and stares intensely into the darkness from where we came. "It's approaching," he says lowly but intensely. "The Windigo is here! Move over to that stone wall!"

The next sound we hear is a low, guttural moan that rises in volume to a screeching wail. The sound alone is enough to give you a heart attack, and then we see the evil, man-eating spirit emerge from the darkness. Its white eyes glow with menacing intensity.

"Hoo Mans, I see I have you all together now. How nice. Now, I can kill you all and feast for a long time." It laughs haughtily. "Or, if you prefer, you can tell me the location of the Megis shell, and perhaps I will let you go."

None of us betrays the location of the Megis, and Robert breathes a huge sigh of relief that he'd returned it to its safety in the pool of water before Mr. Ugly showed up. Robert steps forward a few paces, and Grey joins him. Together, they try to assess just how powerful this enemy is. They're not encouraged by what they're sensing. I look over at Mace, and we nod toward each other. I pull out my Demon camera which still has about a half-full charge left, and Mace pulls out his Weed Killer, and we stand alongside of Robert and Grey. I look back at Maggie and see that she's terrified. Frankly, I am too. I give her a little wink to try to reassure her, then turn back to face the Windigo.

"Neither of your choices is acceptable, evil one. You may leave here now in one piece if you choose, or you may face our fury, but you'll never know the location of the Megis shell, and you're not eating any of us."

The Windigo growls and paces from side to side in thought. It's agitated and hungry. It lunges at Robert who parries the assault with a beam of hot, white light that comes out of his outstretched palm. The Windigo recoils in pain and surprise. I look at Mace and indicate for him not to use the Weed Killer. He knows that I want him to keep his weapon prepared for another assault. Robert and I charge at the Windigo and blast it simultaneously while Grey blocks its exit. The Windigo drops to his bony knees briefly, then suddenly rises with a vertical thrust. He knocks me to the ground with a hard thud, and Robert shoots another energy blast from his palm. Mace runs up to me, and seeing that I'm fairly okay, he joins Robert and discharges the full electrical fury of the Weed Killer on the Windigo. I smell burnt tissue and get back up to discharge whatever electricity is left in the Demon camera.

The Windigo sees that Tori is with us and that enrages him even more. "You, Hoo Man!" he directs at Tori. "I did not think that you could find your way out. You have surprised me and cheated me out of a meal." It runs at Tori, and Mace unloads the fury of the Weed Killer on him with effective results. It turns from Tori and lunges at Mace who retreats from the Windigo's attack and stumbles over a rock as he discharges the Weed Killer. His weapon's burst goes wide and explodes against the cavern's stone wall. Had it hit the Windigo, it it probably would've dealt it a death blow. Instead, the discharge blasted a large hole in the rock wall exposing something we didn't expect to see, daylight! We're all totally surprised, including the Windigo who takes the opportunity to evade our weapons. It runs for the hole in the wall and bellows in triumph! "Hoo Mans! At last I am free!" It shows us a ghoulish grin. "Now, I will feast!" And then it's gone!

Robert and Grey chase after the vile beast and return a few moments later with Robert shaking his head negatively. "It got away. We need to leave the mountain now and notify the authorities. The thought of the Windigo running amok in the general population is a terrifying thought. It will ravage mercilessly. We need to somehow subdue it, and either kill it again or return it to this underground realm."

We all step outside and breathe in the fresh warm air. I put my arm around Maggie and tell her that we're safe now. She looks at me skeptically and buries her face in my chest. Lucretia is in a near state of shock and leans against Mace for support. Rennie and Kelli are virtually speechless. We know how lucky we all are to be alive. Robert calls his contacts with the Michigan State Police and various law enforcement authorities along the Keweenaw Peninsula. He scratches Grey behind his ear and says aloud, "They have no idea what's coming for them."

Chapter 23

As THEY DO MOST DAYS when weather permits, Imogene and Ed Hansen walk along a woodland path near their home just outside of Copper Harbor. It's a glorious day to be taking their usual constitutional near the shore of Lake Superior. The sun is shining brightly and the leaves from the overhanging trees cast dappled shadows along the path. They see the great lake shimmering and watch as fishermen guide their boats over the steel-gray water.

Now, in their early seventies, they're both retired from their careers and have made a commitment to staying healthy and fit. They figure that a five-mile hike a day will keep the doctor away.

"Uh, I think my meal and all of this hiking is catching up with me, dear," Ed comments to his bride of fifty years. "I think I'll need to stop at that port-o-let just up ahead." They quicken their pace because they don't want to have any unpleasant accidents.

"Doesn't it seem like the birds and squirrels are unusually noisy today? It's like something has them a little agitated," Imogene remarks. "I thought I saw some deer antlers rising above the bushes a moment ago, but I doubt they'd spook the rest of the woodland creatures."

"Oh, you know it could be anything," Ed adds as he sees the port-o-let and makes a mad dash for the rustic rest stop. "I'll just be a minute, Imogene." A few minutes later she hears a horrible racket coming from inside the outdoor commode.

"My goodness, Edwin, what is all of that racket about?" She approaches the front door and recoils at the smell of something truly disgusting. "Land sakes, Ed, I can't believe that horrible smell coming from in there." She hears a few muffled sounds and tries to open the front door to make sure her hubby is okay. The door is locked and so she decides to go around to the back to see if the rear entrance is open. "Ed!" she calls out. "Are you okay?" And then she sees that the rear door has been ripped off its hinges and she peers inside. The sight of the vile Windigo chomping on her husband's neck renders her speechless and causes her bladder to empty. She tries to run but is frozen with fear and can only moan. The Windigo sees her and reaches its bony hand out and grabs the hapless spouse and drags her inside the port-o-let. The sounds of it cracking bones and sucking on flesh now has all of the woodland creatures atwitter. The Windigo steps outside a few minutes later with what looks like a shredded thigh hanging from its blood-red maw. "Good meat! Want more!" It sees the town of Copper Harbor in the near distance and begins walking along the path in its direction.

The town of Copper Harbor, Michigan, is quaint and charming. Despite claiming to be an all-season resort town, it gets about three hundred inches of snow annually which makes you question the "all-season" part of the advertising. It only has a population of about one hundred people which means everyone basically knows everything about you. In truth, there's not really much to see in Copper Harbor, except Lake Superior and a few modest motels, restaurants, and curiosity shops, plus a whole lot of trees. Located near the very tip of the Keweenaw Peninsula, it's generally a very quiet part of the world.

Wanda Crisp steers her open Jeep along Highway 26 from her home near Agate Harbor. She's running a little late for her evening work shift at Zak's Diner and tries to make up time. As she enters Copper Harbor she sees a figure ahead that's just ambling down the middle of the road. She slows so she doesn't hit it, but she sees that it has no intentions of getting out of the way. She approaches to within twenty yards and rubs her eyes when she sees antlers on the figure. "C'mon you dumb ass deer." she hollers. "Get the hell out of the road!" She briefly looks at her watch to check if she's late for work and has to slam on her brakes to avoid hitting the pedestrian. She honks her horn again at this skinny dumb ass wearing a wonky-looking, two-legged deer outfit. That was a move she came to regret.

There's no clear area to pass this figure, so Wanda pulls her Jeep to within a couple of feet and comes to a stop and lays on her horn. The Windigo is annoyed by the intrusion to his enjoying the last tasty bites of a Hoo Man thigh, and it turns in Wanda's direction. She instantly sees that this is not your typical deer, or for that matter, not your typical anything. She crams her Jeep into reverse and begins to haul ass out of the town's main drag, but a moment later she sees, and smells, the Windigo as it leaps onto the front hood of her Jeep. The Windigo launches a terrifying wail at her and reaches over the windshield and grabs Wanda by her hair and begins clubbing her with the last remnant of either Imogene or Ed's leg bone. The Jeep rolls to the side of the road and comes to rest against a stone wall. The Windigo drags her lifeless body from the vehicle and crosses into a nearby park to inspect his trophy. Two tourists from Duluth witness the Windigo's arrival and decide to take a few pics of the indigenous wildlife. When the Windigo flashes his blood-red teeth and antlers at them, they decide it's time to head for home. Fortunately for them the Windigo is full, and it wanders down to the lakefront for water to wash down its meal. After drinking, it belches and lofts Wanda's slack body onto an overhanging tree limb to save it for a later meal. It looks up ahead toward the middle of town and hears music and laughter coming from a large wooden building. It heads in that direction.

Officer Rory Lathrop arrives in Copper Harbor to do his appointed rounds along the town's main drag and at the marina. All appears quiet with the exception of a barking dog and the screeching calls of a few lake birds. Officer Lathrop pulls into the waterfront park and slowly drives through its parking lot. He gets out of his cruiser to relieve himself and then starts back to his car when his head bumps into something hanging down from a tree. He looks up and sees a human leg wearing ripped jeans and a sandal.

"What the …?" he stammers as he looks more closely and sees that the leg is attached to a body whose head is battered and bloody beyond recognition. He stumbles at the sight of this corpse hanging in a tree and calls for backup. He looks around for any other evidence or for any witnesses to what had occurred. At this point the two tourists from Duluth are long gone. The officer's radio chirps and he retrieves a message from the command center confirming that backup is on the way. It also issues a message to be on the lookout for a "creature" that Robert Midew from the Keweenaw Bay Indian Council has advised is on the loose and very dangerous. Officer Lathrop gulps as he reads that message wondering what the hell kind of creature it could be referring to. He looks up again at the human figure hanging from the tree, and he instinctively touches the handle of his firearm for reassurance. A few minutes later two other officers arrive in the parking lot, and while one of them remains at that site awaiting an EMT team to transport Wanda

Crisp's body to the morgue, Rory Lathrop and his new partner, Tyler Johnson, decide to drive into town looking for the culprit.

Meanwhile the Windigo has arrived outside at Zak's Diner and sees patrons sitting at tables through the large picture window. "Hoo Mans!" it mumbles to itself. "Not hungry now but want to kill!" It enters the diner through a rear door and the carnage begins. A moment later 911 calls start coming into the local command center with reports of a demonic creature killing people in Copper Harbor. The two police officers arrive on the scene shortly thereafter and can't believe the number of bodies they see scattered on the floor and across dining tables. Nearly everyone is dead, and they recognize several of the ravaged bodies as people they know.

Officer Lathrop radios his command center again and anxiously reports, "We've got a mass murderer on the loose in Copper Harbor. Send all available help ASAP!" He and Officer Johnson spy a trail of blood on the floor and see that it leads outside through the diner's rear door. They exit and see the Windigo searching the interior of a dumpster looking for additional treats to eat although at this point it isn't very hungry anymore, just mean-spirited.

The two officers pull out their handguns and Lathrop screams, "Hey you! On the ground now!" The Windigo looks at them and smiles a demonic grin and shakes its antlers in defiance. "Hoo Mans! You will all die!" It begins walking at them quickly. Both officers order for it to stop and then begin firing their weapons when it doesn't heed their command. The Windigo leaps at Lathrop and lands on his chest knocking him unconscious. Tyler Johnson crams another clip in his handgun and begins firing at the Windigo from point-blank range. The evil one howls in pain as the bullets rip into its skeletal body. It makes a slashing motion toward the officer with its sharp claws and severs Johnson's head from its shoulders with one swift motion. Rory Lathrop regains consciousness a few moments later and sees his decapitated partner, but the Windigo is gone. He radios to his headquarters, "Officer down! Multiple casualties at Zak's Diner. Where the hell's that backup! We need the friggin' National Guard up here pronto!"

Chapter 24

ONCE WE'RE ALL outside of Brockway Mountain, Robert brings us together to give us his blunt assessment of the situation. "Well, we've obviously got a serious situation on our hands, and I'm afraid it's about to get even more serious for a lot of unsuspecting people."

"Isn't there something that you and your grandmother and Grey can do to get that damn creature under control?" Lucretia asks hopefully.

"We're going to do everything we can, but this evil Windigo is different from the one we encountered last year."

"I'll say," Rennie adds. "Never knew it could speak ... and that horrible laugh."

"I always knew it was clever, but when Nokomis supposedly killed it last year, its evil spirit came back reincarnated into a different body and with increased cognitive abilities."

"How is that even possible?" Tori asks.

"Good question. But it's possible for the very same reason we were able to give you sight and Mace his infusion of vitality. All of us, even you, have certain supernatural abilities that you're not aware of. We Midewin healers have a far greater mastery over supernatural forces because we've devoted ourselves to the Megis shell and have studied and learned. Although the Windigo doesn't possess the knowledge of the Megis shell, if you live alone in the dark for the number of centuries this creature has you begin to focus your attention on otherworldly skills. Somehow this Windigo has mastered speech, but it hasn't outgrown its need for blood and meat and dominance. If it ever learned the source of the Megis shell's power, I doubt that we'd ever be able to defeat it. That's why we either have to kill it again or contain it, but it can never possess the Megis shell."

"So, what do we do now?" I ask. "I doubt that anyone's really in the mood now to go back inside and photograph the cave art."

"Uh, not today, honey," Maggie chimes in, and all of the others either nod or mumble their agreement.

"Tomorrow's another day, Clay" Mace advises. "Robert, what can we do to help?"

"Not much right now. I suggest that you return to the Evergreen Point Lodge and rest up. I'll come and see you after I meet with the police and we implement a strategy. That path over there will take you back to the parking lot. It's only about a ten minute walk." He and Grey turn to leave us when all of a sudden a rifle shot rings out, and the dirt by Lucretia's feet explodes upon impact. We all duck behind a large boulder, and Mace and I pull out our weapons. Unfortunately my Demon camera is in serious need of recharging, but Mace's Weed Killer is still lethal. Robert and I look at Mace who motions for us to stay put.

Malcolm fires another rifle shot in our direction to make sure we know he's still around. "C'mon out Lucretia!" he hollers from just inside the cave opening. "C'mon out and I'll let the others go!"

"She's not going anywhere!" I shout back at him and another rifle shot slams into the boulder.

"Cut it out, Malcolm!" Lucretia hurls at him. "Haven't you caused enough damage for one lifetime. I'm sure mother and father would be really proud of you."

"Yeah well, lucky for me they're not around, huh?!" he replies adolescently. He fires off another shot at us as if to clarify that he really doesn't care what anyone thinks.

Mace looks at Robert and says, "I've got this." He carefully slides his head and hand around the side of the boulder so he can see his target. He sees Malcolm putting another clip in his rifle and then presses the discharge button on the Weed Killer. Its angry bolt of harmonic power slams into the side of the mountain just above the opening and sends a huge amount of rock and rubble cascading down the mountainside. In moments the cave opening is sealed with Malcolm Land trapped inside Brockway Mountain.

"Oh man, Mace! You did it!" Rennie erupts, and Robert slaps Mace on the back with appreciation. "Heck, you don't need a Megis shell when you've got Mace Davis on the job!" he jests.

"Good riddance to bad rubbish!" Lucretia adds. "At least we don't have to worry about my crazy brother now … I hope."

With Malcolm now securely enclosed inside the mountain, Robert and Grey take off for Copper Harbor to help the authorities find the Windigo. Kelli and Rennie take the lead on the path as we weary older adults trail along behind them. Almost ten minutes later we reach our cars.

"Well guys," I say sarcastically. "How's everyone enjoying their summer vacation so far?" Needless to say, my attempt at humor falls on deaf ears.

"Which part?" Maggie asks sarcastically. "The part where we've been shot at multiple times, or perhaps that two people were murdered that were standing right next to us, or perhaps wandering around aimlessly for hours in a dark cave, or maybe getting chased by an evil man-eating spirit that you thought was dead but now's back even stronger than ever … and did I mention it wants to eat us?! Gee Clay, I'd say our summer vacay is just going swimmingly. What do the rest of you think?"

Fortunately for me, the others don't pile in on me for trying to add a little levity to an absolutely terrifying stream of events. They know that I'm just as upset as they are, so they cut me some slack. I just pray that Robert and the cops can get this Windigo under control as soon as possible.

When Robert and Grey arrive in Copper Harbor, they immediately see that the town is being treated like one huge crime scene. A handful of police officers and volunteer firemen from surrounding municipalities have just arrived and are cordoning off the waterfront park and Zak's Diner. Robert identifies himself to a young officer and asks who's in charge and where he can find him.

"It's Chief Ray Muldoon from Calumet, and you can find him in the diner although I understand it's a pretty bloody place."

"Thanks, I know Ray well. C'mon Grey."

As they enter the front of the diner, they see the unspeakable carnage that the Windigo unleashed on the unsuspecting guests. There's a lot of blood and medical technicians are in the process of identifying the victims and putting their corpses in body bags. Robert sees Chief Muldoon speaking with one of the medical personnel, and he and Grey walk over to him.

"Hey, Robert, good to see you. I understand you're the man who knows who and what we're dealing with here. Wanna fill me in more?"

"Sure, Ray." And, over the next couple of minutes Robert gives the police chief a complete description of the Windigo and his assessment of what it's capable of. "And, Ray, this is just the beginning. This thing is evil, it's cunning, and it's very powerful."

"So, what do you recommend, Robert? What would you do if you were in my shoes?"

"First thing, you're going to need a lot more personnel up here armed with military-grade weapons. Definitely bring in the national guard and probably seasoned military. Next, I would deploy your men so that the Windigo can't get any further down the peninsula to more heavily populated areas. Third, let Grey and me see what we can do with this vile thing. We've spoken with it, and it'll remember me. Now that it's killed and eaten, maybe it'll be more likely to communicate. Any idea where it is now?"

"We keep getting reports from residents saying they think they've seen it, but nothing definitive yet. One person even claims it's twenty feet tall and can fly." Just then an officer comes rushing up to us and reports that there's been a confirmed sighting near Fort Wilkins. Robert and Chief Muldoon look at each other and nod. "Looks like we may be catching a break. Better to have that thing at an old abandoned fort at the tip of the peninsula rather than in our towns."

"I agree," Robert adds. "Any idea how many people work at the fort and when we can expect more personnel, Chief?"

"I've been told that the national guard is mobilizing and Airborne troops are being deployed. I suspect we could have several hundred men and women up here in a couple of hours. I understand there's only one caretaker manning the fort."

"Couple of hours will be too late for anyone who comes into contact with the Windigo." They quickly look at a map together and Robert points to the narrowest portion of the peninsula. "Here, Chief!

Position your people across this stretch of land. If we can contain it here, we'll definitely mitigate our losses." The chief nods his agreement, and Robert and Grey take off for Fort Wilkins.

Chapter 25

ORT WILKINS IS AN anachronism. Built in 1844, it was the northernmost outpost for the nation's perimeter defense. It was established originally to help local law enforcement along the Keweenaw, and to defend the copper miners from aggressive raids by Chippewa Indians. The fort was abandoned in 1870 but some twenty buildings still remain in its present historic park. They're mostly barracks, mess halls, stables and storage sheds, plus a lumber mill and large enclosures to store timber for construction and firewood … lots of firewood. Muggs

Larsen serves as its lone caretaker, and he enjoys the solitude of the park after all of the visitors have left for the day. He feels a special kinship with those soldiers who were posted here long ago.

Muggs knows the history of the fort very well, including the service that its troops provided during our war with Mexico and our own War Between the States. One thing's for sure, it's definitely a remote outpost. Another thing is just how long and brutal the winters on the tip of the Keweenaw Peninsula can be. Those are just some of the reasons why desertion was so rife among the troops. When the United States entered the war with Mexico, no doubt there were many soldiers eager to live in a much warmer clime even if it meant getting shot at.

Every morning and every evening Muggs takes a stroll among the buildings enclosing the fort's parade ground. He circles each building looking for timbers that may need repair or another coat of paint. Each day he waters his modest vegetable garden and tends to his small flock of seven chickens. It's a good life. A little lonely sometimes, but his cat, Sven, keeps him company and has proven to be an effective mouser. And of course, there are woodland animals that come to visit frequently … deer, raccoons, skunks, possums, groundhogs, badgers, bobcats, and the occasional hungry bear or wolf. Muggs puts a mineral block out for the animals and gives them ample room to roam around.

As Muggs approaches the chicken coop, he hears an unusual amount of squawking and the sounds of birds flapping their wings. He notices that the door to the henhouse has been ripped off its hinges and tossed haphazardly on the ground.

"What the …?" he starts to say as he sees what looks like deer antlers inside the coop. "Hey, you get out of there!" he shouts at what he thinks is a large buck. "Go on now! Get out of there!"

Then the Windigo turns and snarls at the hapless caretaker. "Well, what in the hell are you?" he mumbles at the intruder.

"Well, what in the hell are you?" the Windigo repeats in heavily broken English. Muggs can't believe what he's seeing and hearing and turns to run.

"Hoo Man!" the Windigo calls after him. "I will find you later, Hoo Man, after I finish off these fat birds. Run and hide. It will be fun to hunt you."

Muggs Larsen has seen a lot of things in his life, but nothing like this weird deer-like creature standing on two legs that can speak. He runs all the way back to his cabin, locks the doors and windows and calls the state police.

"I don't know what the frick this thing is up here, but I need help, and I mean pronto. It's eating my chickens, and it says it's coming for me next." Muggs listens for a few moments as an officer explains what's been going on in Copper Harbor and that they believe Muggs has just encountered the culprit. The officer suggests that Muggs might want to just sit tight and wait for backup to arrive.

"Yeah, well, you ain't seen this thing, and there's no way I'm sitting tight. I'm out of here!" He drops the phone on the floor, grabs his cat, Sven, throws him in a crate, and takes off for his car. As he begins to pull away he feels and hears a loud thud and sees the Windigo in his rearview mirror eating a chicken and grabbing the car's rear bumper. He stomps on the accelerator and after a few immobile seconds, he finally feels his car lurch free from the grip of the evil one. About a mile from the fort Muggs sees a small convoy of four police vehicles approach carrying eight uniformed officers. He stops to inform them what he's encountered and tells them they're gonna need a lot more men.

A cocky, young Lieutenant Williams tells Muggs not to worry and that he's confident they can take care of it. "Don't worry, old timer, me and my men saw what this thing did in Copper Harbor, and we aim to settle the score. I mean, we're heavily armed and just how bad can this thing really be?"

"Well, sonny, it's pretty bad, and good luck with that numbskull attitude. Like I said, you're gonna need a lot more men!" And then Muggs's tires spray a rooster-tail of gravel on the road as he speeds away toward Copper Harbor. Lieutenant Williams watches Muggs Larsen's rapid departure and mumbles, "Crazy old coot."

Robert and Grey run like the wind from Copper Harbor toward Fort Wilkins. They know that time is of the essence when it comes to the level of carnage the Windigo is capable of delivering. They see a car speeding toward them and get it to stop briefly. It's Muggs Larsen, and it's clear that Muggs isn't in the mood for idle chitchat. "Those dumb-ass cops have no idea what they're running into," he blurts out. "I ain't never seen anything like that creature before, and it killed all of my lovely hens. It almost got me and Sven too!" And then he floors his accelerator before Robert can ask him any more questions.

When he and Grey arrive at the entrance to Fort Wilkins, it's eerily quiet, too quiet. He sees the four police cruisers, but no cops are around. He closes his eyes and tries to sense what lies ahead for them. "Not good, Grey, I'm not sensing much." They enter the fort's parade ground and see Muggs's chicken coop all torn apart with a few chicken feathers wafting lazily in the air. They approach the henhouse and peer inside. Grey sniffs the ground near a large, overturned bucket and is surprised by a flurry of wings as a sole surviving hen tries to escape. Robert manages to gently pick up the terrified bird up and places it in a nesting box. He closes his eyes as he gently strokes the poor bird, and it settles into a more relaxed state. "C'mon, Grey, let's see if anyone or anything else is still alive in the fort."

They exit the henhouse and begin exploring one building after another. It's still very quiet, and Robert is beginning to wonder if the Windigo has already left the fort. Robert asks Grey to scout the remaining buildings but not to engage the Windigo if he spots it. Grey understands and quietly heads off alone. Robert reaches for his cell phone and calls Chief Muldoon in Copper Harbor. He keeps his voice very low.

"What do you have to report, Robert?" the chief asks.

"We're at the fort, and we haven't spotted anything yet except for a beat-up, old chicken coop. We ran into the caretaker about a mile from the fort, and he wasn't in the mood for conversation. He's heading your way."

"What about my police officers? Have you seen them? I tried to reach them on the radio, but I'm not getting a response."

"I saw your officers' cruisers, but none of your men so far." Just then Grey returns and yelps at

Robert to follow him. "I've gotta go, Chief, I'll get back to you when I know more." They end their call.

Robert follows Grey's lead as they stay close to the long shadows of the old, white buildings. They pass the fort's mess hall and a latrine, and Grey comes to a stop as they approach a large barracks where the enlisted men once bunked. Grey emits a low growl, and the two of them stealthily approach the wooden frame structure. Robert sneaks up to a window and looks inside. What he sees shakes him to his core. All of the officers lie dead, scattered around in pools of blood and gore. Robert pulls out his phone again and ever so quietly calls the chief.

"They're all dead, Chief, not one man left alive. We haven't spotted the Windigo yet, but I sense it's very near."

There's dead silence on the phone. "Chief, are you still there?"

"Jesus," comes the chief's plaintive reply. "I knew all of those men well. I'll have to personally tell their families. We'll be attending a lot of funerals. Look Robert, we just had about two hundred men from our national guard arrive. They're well armed, and we're heading your way. Be there in fifteen minutes. Oh sweet Jesus!" Then, the chief hangs up.

"Any idea where it is, Grey?" The great wolf emits a low growl and begins walking toward a building that once served as the officers' living quarters. Grey stops as they approach the entrance to the structure, and the two of them close their eyes to sense the Windigo's exact location. A moment later Robert and his spirit wolf step onto the porch and look inside the front door. They spot the Windigo stretched out on a cot, snoring away as if it doesn't have a care in the world; just one, sweet, man-eating spirit taking a nap. On the floor by its cot lies a horribly mangled officer, quite dead. It's the body of Lieutenant Williams. A look of utter shock is etched on what is still recognizable in the young officer's face.

The only question in Robert's mind is do I kill it now while it sleeps, or is there another way to end this horrific carnage? His instinct is to attack with as much ferocity as he and Grey can muster, but then the unexpected happens again, and he spies a twinkling of familiar golden light and Nokomis appears at their side.

"It cannot hear us now," Robert's wise grandmother communicates to them telepathically, "but soon the Windigo will awake, and we must be ready."

"Why not just kill it now, Nokomis, and avoid any of us getting hurt, or worse?"

The ancient Midewin healer turns to face her grandson. Her milky white eyes peer into Robert's, and she gently strokes the top of Grey's head. "Yes, what to do is the question, indeed. Yes, we can kill it, but we both know it will return, probably even wiser and more confident from his experiences outside of the mountain. Thankfully, it does not possess the Megis shell, but even so, each time it's killed, it comes back with even more fearsome abilities than before. We must find a way to manage the Windigo because we can never permanently overcome the evil in the world."

"What then do you have in mind, Grandmother? Your words speak truth and wisdom, but many people have died and many more will also unless we act. This thing cannot be trusted!"

"Trusted?!" Nokomis telepaths. "No, of course not, but that is our strength too. We know we cannot trust this beast, but it is also learning to respect our resolve. If necessary, yes, we can kill its corporeal form, but remember there will be a price that we will ultimately pay … in just a year when it is reborn, yes, Grandson?"

It's a surreal scene, to say the least. An ancient Chippewa medicine woman, a huge wolf, and wise Robert Midew staring at a slumbering evil, man-eating spirit snoring away on a nineteenth-century army cot.

Robert feels his cell phone vibrate in his pocket and quietly steals a glance at it. "It's Chief Muldoon," he whispers. "He says he's at the main entrance to the fort with about two hundred men. He wants to know where to deploy them."

Robert texts him back and asks him to position his men on the parade ground, very quietly. Robert watches as Chief Muldoon quickly follows his advice.

"Awake the beast," Nokomis says to Robert, "and be prepared for it to react violently."

Robert strides up toward the slumbering Windigo and steps over the ravaged body of Lieutenant Williams. He reaches his hand out and shakes one of the evil one's antlers. "Time to wake up, sleepyhead!" Then he leaps back a step and extends the palm of his hand at the Windigo. Its eyes flash open revealing glowing white orbs, and it bellows when it sees Robert. It immediately lashes out at the Midewin healer but is stopped dead in its tracks by energy bursts coming from both Nokomis and Robert.

"You shall do no more harm!" Nokomis hurls at the Windigo as it recoils in pain. "You shall return to your home under the mountain."

"You have injured me! You will soon pay with your lives!" it snarls back at them as it leaps up and crashes out an adjacent window. It immediately sees the large gathering of armed men standing stoically awaiting instructions. It wails at them menacingly, and they hold their positions. Robert, Nokomis, and Grey follow after the Windigo and see that it is assessing its options in the face of such a large enemy.

"Cease your violence!" Nokomis hollers at the enraged beast."

"We can make a deal!" Robert tries.

"Deal! No deal! Only death to Hoo Mans!" It begins aggressively striding toward the officers and guardsmen, and Chief Muldoon gives the command to fire. The onslaught of their firepower is awesome, and the beast tears into the men, slashing flesh and crunching bones as it goes. Nearly thirty men lie in scattered heaps, but the Windigo has taken its share of bullets and is beginning to tire. It raises its head and roars in anger and pain, and then it runs off into forest to nurse its wounds.

Robert approaches Chief Muldoon. "We've got to go after it. We must press this fight before it regains it strength." They lead a battered troop of some ninety men after the beast and occasionally hear a man cry out in pain as the Windigo kills one after another. Finally they have it cornered next to a great rock wall. Nokomis and Grey appear and the three of them stand with the chief and his men for a final assault.

Robert tries again, "Deal. We can make a deal, if you're willing, but we will never let you leave this place alive if you refuse. And know this, there are thousands upon thousands of other Hoo Mans that will come to defeat you if necessary. You will be constantly hunted. We will never give up."

The Windigo is enraged from his battle wounds, but it senses that what this Hoo Man says is true.

"Deal?! What deal?" it snarls at the Midewin healer and his grandmother. "Too many Hoo Mans. Make them go away, and maybe we can … deal."

Robert looks at Chief Muldoon who nods his understanding. Both of them know that the Windigo is not to be trusted. Regardless, the chief risks giving the order for the majority of them to pull back to the parade ground and await further instructions. A small contingent of ten men remains with their automatic weapons poised.

It's clear that the Windigo has been hurt. It leans against the stone wall and pants heavily. Nokomis steps forward and addresses it. "My grandson, his wolf, and I descend from the Anishinaabe, the Original People. You are legendary to our people as the evil, man-eating spirit. I destroyed your form twelve moons ago, and you have returned. I can destroy you again, or as my grandson says, we can make a deal that satisfies you and us."

"Meat! I must have meat!"

"We can provide you with meat, but you can no longer kill Hoo Mans!" Robert declares. "And, you must return under the mountain and never enter the outside world again."

The Windigo remains highly agitated as it considers the words. "When I emerged from under the mountain and came into the light of day, I remembered what it was like for me once a long, long time ago. It was wild and lush with earth, trees, water, and sky; not so many Hoo Mans. Now it is different. The stench of this world is noxious to me now. Too many Hoo Mans. Too much sound and too many lights at night. I prefer the quiet and the darkness."

"So, do we have a deal if we promise to bring you food?" Robert asks.

"Hmmm, I will think on it," it replies evasively. "But, I need purpose in my life too. Need meat and a reason to exist."

"Windigo, we are very different, but we share a common history. You have been a part of our Chippewa lore since the beginning of time. Alas, always in a fearsome way. Your time in the outside world has come and gone. Now only to my Chippewa people are you known. 'Purpose,' you say. Perhaps we ancient Hoo Mans and you can craft a mutual purpose."

"What is 'mutual purpose'?" it asks. "How can I trust you to honor my existence and my history? I need meat, but meat can only sustain my body. I need purpose to sustain my spirit!"

"If you return with us now under the mountain, we will show you what I mean, and I promise you that we will respect your wishes provided you cease your savage attacks on our people. No more death. No more destruction. Peace for you and for us. Yes?!"

The Windigo looks at the Hoo Mans with their firesticks pointed at it. It feels the pain from where their little bits of metal ripped into its body like angry bees. It sees the resolve on the faces of the men, and it considers Robert and Nokomis's offer.

"Do you really think you can trust this thing?" Chief Muldoon asks Robert. "It's probably killed over fifty people in less than twenty-four hours, many of whom were people that I knew."

"No, of course I don't trust the Windigo, but one thing's for sure, we just can't let this thing run rampant along the Keweenaw Peninsula. Can you imagine the damage it would do in a larger popu-lated area? We need to try a different approach."

"You seem to know this vile creature, Robert, what do you suggest?"

"Have your men stand down, Chief, and let's see if it's honestly willing to come with us back to its realm under Brockway Mountain. But, be prepared to attack if it's being disingenuous with us."

The chief looks at the Windigo and then orders his men to stand at ease. He radios his other men and orders them to begin gathering their fallen comrades. The Windigo watches as his adversaries fall back.

"We are dealing with you in good faith," Nokomis says to the Windigo. "My grandson and I will lead you back to your home, but do not view our willingness to help you as weakness. We are not to be toyed with, and many more Hoo Mans will come and destroy you, and we will help them if you do not comply. Deal?!"

The Windigo shows agitation at being told what to do. It shifts its weight from one sinewy leg to another. It stares at the remaining cops and guardsmen and then into Nokomis's intense, milky white eyes. "Deal," the Windigo repeats, "but only if I have meat and purpose."

Chapter 26

EANWHILE TWO MILES away at Evergreen Point Lodge, Maggie and I are seated at a rustic wooden table on the lodge's cozy screened porch. The view is lush with deep greenery as we face the forest leading up to summit of Brockway Mountain. Crows call out as they glide on warm air currents, and seagulls intersect their flight patterns with their own. If it weren't for all of the turmoil we've endured, it would be an idyllic setting.

Mace, Lucretia, Tori, Rennie, and Kelli are seated with us which is a blessing in itself given the violence we've faced. The fact that Tori is even with us at all is beyond miraculous. We'd all attempted to take naps in our rooms when we returned, but the sounds of sirens and gunfire in the distance made that impossible. Instead of going back to their apartments in Calumet, Rennie and Kelli chose to stay with us and await further word from Robert. We're all pretty whipped from a long, arduous day, but it's the emotional stress that we suffered under the dark mountain, and from being stalked by Malcolm Land, that actually has us more exhausted than the physical exertion. Smartly, Mace and I took the opportunity to recharge our weapons so we'll be prepared if we have to face the Windigo or crazy Malcolm again. So now, we sit here in relative safety, reflecting, and waiting to hear from Robert.

"Next time I say we just stick with shopping on the Magnificent Mile. How about you guys?" Lucretia directs at Maggie and Tori.

"Amen to that," Tori says matter of factly. "On the other hand when was the last time you got chased by a demonic creature in a cave featuring wonderful artwork and precious gems? Sure will be something we remember. Actually, screw that, Lucretia, I'm with you. Next time we'll shop till we drop rather than running in terror till we drop."

"Well, count me in, ladies," Maggie adds. "And now I know the kind of insanity that my husband and sons get into when I'm not around to supervise."

I know that anything I try to say in the way of defense will not work to my benefit, so why even go there?

"And you, Mace Davis, I had no idea that you're the mastermind behind these lethal weapons that you and Clay carry around."

Again, I remain silent, but Mace tries to offer some clarity to the conversation. "Uh, it was actually Weed who came up the first designs, I just ..."

"Silence, sir!" she levels at Mace, and then gives him a weary smile. "Do I want to even know what kind of 'episodes' you guys have been involved in over the years?" Maggie asks rhetorically.

I finally break my silence and utter, "Uh, no." She gives me the look, and not the *come hither* look that I prefer.

"You guys have actually been great," Tori offers. "And, Mace's Weed Killer blaster-thing got us out of the mountain, and Clay stung that Windigo's ass pretty good ... and here we all are ... beat-up but alive."

The fact of the matter is that we're so relieved that our family of friends is still intact. Maggie leans over to Mace to give him a warm hug and Lucretia joins her from the other side. As for me, I just sit here quietly taking in the scene. I look up and Rennie's eyes meet mine, and he has a warm smile on his face. "Thanks, Dad," he mouths, and a tear comes to my eye in gratitude for all of us.

A few moments later my phone vibrates, and I see that it's Robert calling. I immediately answer it and put the phone on speaker so everyone can hear the conversation. "Where are you?" I ask him. "We heard a lot of sirens and shooting toward the end of the peninsula."

"Yeah, Chief Muldoon brought a healthy contingent of cops and guardsmen out to Fort Wilkins, and we've got the Windigo."

"What do you mean 'you got the Windigo?' Is it dead?"

"No, I mean we've got it here with us, and Nokomis, Grey, and I are going to escort it back inside Brockway Mountain."

"You're shittin' me, right?! And, I don't think now is a good time to be kidding around, Robert," I admonish.

"Clay, have you ever known me to kid around especially when it comes to something like the Windigo?"

"Uh, no, so what the hell are you talking about?"

"We, along with about two hundred of the chief's men cornered the evil one and were blasting the crap out of it. We were preparing for a final assault which no doubt would've killed the creature, but Nokomis advised against it. Basically, we struck a deal with the devil. I can explain more to you later, Clay, but for now I want to see if we can truly manage to get the Windigo back inside Brockway Mountain. Nokomis has dematerialized and gone off somewhere, and Grey and I are moving quickly overland with the Windigo back toward the cave's main entrance. We should arrive around in about ten minutes. Why don't you and Mace join us up here, and I'll make a formal introduction for you to the bane of our existence."

"Lovely," I reply sarcastically. "Mace, Rennie, and I will meet you there, but we're going to leave everyone else here, okay?"

"The hell you will!" Maggie interrupts, and she asks Robert, "Do you really think that beast can be controlled?"

"We're about to find out," he replies.

Maggie sees Kelli, Tori, and Lucretia nodding affirmatively, and she says, "Great, we're coming too."

I try to argue against their plan to join us, but I know that I've probably already pushed the male-chauvinist-pig-thing a little too far already, though my intentions were pure.

"I guess we're all heading your way, Robert."

"Okay then," he replies, "and if we're not there when you arrive, well maybe Mr. Ugly has had a change of heart and eaten us. If so, just run like hell. Just saying."

We end the call and all get up from the table and head for the parking lot. I look at Mace and see that he's shaking his head in disbelief. "Here we go again!" he says, and we each pat our jacket pockets for the reassuring feel of my Demon camera and Mace's Weed Killer.

———

Deep inside the mountain Malcolm Land has managed to retrace his steps with the faint light from his flashlight. His poor-me attitude makes him even angrier with his sister as he vows again to get her if it's the last thing he ever does. He stumbles on rock rubble and finds that they're actually large diamonds and other precious gems. "Unbelievable! I've gotta get out of here so I can come back with a truck and haul all of it away." He puts a few especially attractive pieces in his pocket and keeps moving in the the direction of the main entrance. "Unbelievable!"

———

When all of us arrive at the entrance to the Brockway mine, we see a scene that makes us very anxious, actually scared to death. Just inside the entrance

Robert and Grey stand about ten feet away from our nemesis, the Windigo. There appears to be no tension among them. The Windigo stands somewhat erect, but it's clear that it suffered some physical damage in his encounter with Robert, Nokomis, and Chief Muldoon's men. Grey's eyes haven't left the creature, nor will they until Robert bids him otherwise. Robert sees us approach.

"I suggest that you all stay about twenty feet away, Clay. Our new ally here, the Windigo, has made a deal with us to return to his home under the mountain, but as you know, trust is something that is earned, not given freely." My friends and I do as Robert instructs, and we stand stone-still staring at the malevolent beast.

"Deal," it says aloud in guttural tones. "Trust. Not given freely. Earned!" it says aloud to no one in particular, almost like it's practicing its speaking skills.

All of us find it very unnerving that a creature that lives inside a dark mountain can communicate at all. Mace and I look at each other and nod knowingly. We have our hands in our pockets with a grip on our weapons. To his credit, Robert is attempting to be as nonconfrontational as possible to give this detente with the Windigo a chance to take root.

A moment later we see something else that reminds us that we mere mortals don't know everything about our world. Nokomis materializes out of sparkles of golden light and stands next to Grey.

"Ah, Grandmother!" Robert effuses. "So good of you to join us! I was wondering if you would be joining us."

"Of course, my grandson. Today is a momentous day, and I'm pleased to see that your friends are with us as well."

At this point each member of my family of friends has had personal encounters with the wise old Chippewa healer. "Hello, Nokomis," we say in unison almost as is we are greeting a teacher on the first day of school.

"Hello," she replies, "and how is our new friend, Mr. Windigo, doing today?"

I almost laugh out loud at the absurdity of calling the evil, man-eating spirit 'our friend,' but we go along. The Windigo stares at the old woman, which he knows has special powers, and grunts at her deferentially. She approaches the beast and fixes her milky white eyes on the creature's cloudy orbs and says with authority. "We are pleased that you have agreed to our deal to return to your home here. We will uphold our part of the bargain."

"Deal. Bargain. Uphold," it echoes her words. "Meat and purpose, yes?! You promised!"

"Yes, I did, and you shall have meat on a regular basis," Nokomis replies and then she vanishes.

A moment later she returns with two fat rabbits, and throws them toward the Windigo's feet. It immediately picks up one of the rabbits and begins devouring it with relish. "Hmmm, good meat! Want more!"

"You shall have more in a little bit, but first we want you to come inside with us, so we can discuss your 'purpose' that we talked about with you earlier."

"Yes, meat and purpose! Deal!"

Nokomis leads our entourage inside, and we begin the trek to the site where Rennie and Kelli are cataloging the magnificent ancient cave art with Robert. It's still a totally surreal experience that we're doing anything civil with the Windigo, but my mortal fears are assuaged knowing that Mace and I are armed and that we have Robert and his grandmother with us. We arrive at the site a few minutes later, and Rennie and Kelli turn on the lights to illuminate the project.

"Hmmm," the Windigo exhales. "Old pictures from the beginning of time."

We're all surprised that the creature has a genetic memory that allows it to recall things that occurred to its predecessors over many hundreds of years. We all stare at the cave paintings with reverence and see the Windigo react similarly.

"Hoo Mans and my earlier forms," it says aloud. "Meat then, not now. Deal!"

Robert, Grey, and Nokomis stand together, and the old woman addresses the Windigo as Lucretia, Mace, Maggie, and I stand behind them. Rennie and Kelli flank all of us and adjust the direction of the lighting.

"In some ways, Windigo, you are very similar to my grandson, his wolf-spirit, and me. We come from a very different time, and we view the world in different ways from the modern Hoo Mans. We respect nature, and we have learned the secrets of healing and longevity from the Megis shell."

"Yes, Megis shell," it repeats longingly. "Is Megis shell part of deal?"

"No!" Nokomis replies unequivocally. "The Megis shell will never belong to you as it was a gift given to our Original People, the Anishinaabe. It is not ours to give, nor is it yours to ever receive."

The Windigo grows agitated briefly but calms itself as Nokomis sends a beam of warming light to the creature. "We face a serious dilemma, Windigo, one that we're hopeful that you'll help us with. This is the purpose of which I speak."

"What is dilemma? How is dilemma my purpose?"

Robert takes over for Nokomis at this point. "When you left the mountain and reigned terror on the outside world, you not only savagely murdered scores of people, which would ordinarily be reason enough to end your existence, but you also let the outside world know of your existence and some of the powers that my grandmother and I possess. Soon stories about you and our ways will become common knowledge and people will want to descend on this mountain to hunt you and steal whatever treasures they think you possess."

"I will kill all who come for me!" it says savagely.

Robert disregards its braggadocio and continues, "It is our history written in the cave art and the gems and minerals that belong under the mountain that we need to protect. The sparkling stones and bright metals inside the cave are nothing special to you, but to many Hoo Mans they're worth killing for. This we cannot allow, and we must keep them hidden from those who would steal it. It is not just our wish, it is a basic tenet in the teachings of the Megis shell."

"I do not see anything special about sparkling rocks, but I understand that others would try to invade my realm and even kill me for them. Purpose! My purpose is to protect our ancient paintings and gems, the record of our ancient ways and our wealth, yes?!"

"Yes!" Nokomis replies. "In exchange for meat and peace, we want you to be a guardian for all that is sacred to you and our people under this mountain.

"Hmm, guardian! Yes … purpose … guardian of history … under the mountain. Meat. Deal!"

For the first time each of us is beginning to think that there's a real chance that Nokomis and Robert's gamble to trust the Windigo may actually pay off. I look at Mace, and we nod again knowing that we're not going to be duped into letting our guard down with this creature. Regardless, we're beginning to feel some encouragement. Nokomis tosses the Windigo the other rabbit as a token of positive reinforcement for its understanding our dilemma … and our offer of a noble purpose.

Chapter 27

WHAT HAPPENED NEXT shook all of us to our core. The bullet from Malcolm Land's handgun shatters the stillness of the cave and ricochets off the stone walls. We look and see Malcolm standing some thirty feet away on the other side of a deep chasm.

"Well, isn't this a nice little party?!" Malcolm shouts sarcastically. Grey begins striding toward him, but Robert tells it to stay. All of us are really scared to death, and the Windigo is becoming extremely

agitated. "Hoo Man!" it bellows at Malcolm. "Leave us! Leave my realm!"

"Oh, I plan to leave alright, but only so I can come back with a truck and take more of these." He reaches inside his pocket and pulls out one of the large diamonds he'd taken earlier. The Windigo hisses its disdain.

"And now, dear sister, it's time for us to have our final reckoning. I've waited a long time for this, and hell, nobody'll have to bury you because you'll already be more than six feet underground." He laughs adolescently at his own humor.

"All right, Malcolm, you've been a royal pain-in-the-ass all of my life," she hurls defiantly at her wacko brother. "You've chased me around the country for years tying to kill me, and you're so pathetic you've never been able to get that right. Have you? Let's see if you've got the balls to finish this finally. Just let everyone else go!"

"No can do, Lucretia! You know the old saying, 'dead men tell no tales,' and this is what you get for calling me pathetic!" He points his gun at Lucretia and pulls the trigger.

I see the muzzle flash as Malcolm makes good on his threat. Sadly, I also see another flash of motion as my closest friend, Mace Davis, dives in front of Lucretia offering his protection. Malcolm's bullet pierces Mace's back and instantly explodes his heart. He slumps against Lucretia and then falls to the ground … dead.

I scream as I've never screamed before and pull my Demon camera out and begin discharging its lethal electricity at Malcolm. I'm so enraged and despondent by what he did to Mace I can't get a decent shot off at him in time, and that sonovabitch, Malcolm, runs into the shadows on the other side of the chasm. I immediately run to Mace to render whatever aid I can and fall to the ground next to Lucretia who is already there with Mace's head cradled in her lap. "Is he?" I begin, and Lucretia's eyes fill with tears. "He's gone," she whispers to me. Maggie wraps her arms around me as we both sob from the depths of our souls.

"Robert! Nokomis! Please help my friend. You can bring him back. Please. Robert, you gave him renewed vitality a year ago. You can do it again! Please!"

Robert kneels down in the dirt with Lucretia and me and Maggie. "I'm sorry, my friend, but there is nothing that we can do." Rennie and Kelli join us, as we form a circle around our fallen loved one. The Windigo stands apart and watches a spectacle of human interaction unlike anything it's ever seen before.

"Oh, Mace! Please God, no!" My tears are profuse but none more than anyone else in our family of friends. Tori is beyond despondent as she had known and been great friends with Mace since we bought the brewery complex twenty-plus years ago. She and Weed and Mace were often inseparable. Family!

But, it's Rennie that I'm most concerned about. He and Mace had lived together in our power-plant for years. It was Mace who was with me when we found Rennie as a young, homeless street urchin in Indianapolis and brought him home with us to the brewery complex. It was Mace who he lived with at our home. Mace was like the father Rennie never knew, and Rennie was the son Mace never had. And it was perfect that two black men, one old and one young, could learn and grow alongside the other. But now, I'm really worried about Rennie. I don't see tears streaming down his face like the rest of us. The shock of Mace's murder has him virtually catatonic. He just stands there, staring at us, staring at Mace with the most forlorn look I've ever seen on anyone's face. Kelli gently takes his hand, and he finally breaks down into a torrent of tears and rage. "Mace!" he screams at the top of his lungs, and the sound of his wail echoes off the cave's walls and careens from one subterranean chamber to another, far into the distance. Maggie and I go to our adopted son and envelop him with our arms. All of us are sobbing.

Robert approaches the Windigo. "So, you see, we Hoo Mans can be wondrous beings like these, and we can also be evil ones like that Hoo Man that did this to our friend. You see how much damage evil can do! You know this because you have done evil yourself. It is your nature, but with the Megis shell and our guidance, we offer you a separate way. Join us! Respect our deal, and we will respect our part of the agreement as promised."

The Windigo looks at the faces of the Hoo Mans and nods. "Deal. Meat. Purpose. Protect."

Robert runs like the wind back to the mine's entrance where he can get a signal and calls Chief Muldoon. He explains what's been transpiring with the Windigo and of Malcolm's murdering Mace. He runs back to join us, and says "The chief is bringing an EMT transport vehicle and should arrive in several minutes. I suggest that Rennie and you others go meet him. C'mon, Clay, let's go hunt that bastard down! Grey, seek!" Robert commands.

"I'm coming too!" Rennie declares, and he reaches inside Mace's pocket and retrieves his Weed Killer device. "Ready when you are, but how do we get across this chasm?"

"Follow me," comes the voice from an unexpected source, and we fall in line behind the Windigo as it starts walking quickly toward the entrance to another cavern.

After we leave, Maggie, Tori, Lucretia, and Kelli try to console each other over Mace's death. "I hate seeing him lying on the ground like this," Lucretia laments. "He was so good to me. He protected me from harm on several occasions. He did it all from the goodness of his heart and never expected anything in return except respect. And now he's gone because of me and my jerk brother."

"We all loved him, Lucretia," Maggie offers sympathetically. "He was there for all of us, right Tori?!"

"First Weed and now Mace. I don't know how my life can ever be the same without them. Oh, Mace, you were the best of the best." Her tears flow like a river. A few minutes go by, and Maggie notices that her flashlight is beginning to lose it power. She also notices that she's the only one with a light. "I think we have another problem. We're about to run out of juice, and we need to find our way back to the entrance to show the EMT guys where to go." They all get up and begin walking in the direction of the entrance when Maggie's light fails, and they are cast into total darkness.

"Shit!" she says as their world goes dark. "Anyone else have a light?" "No!" comes their collective reply. "Well, I guess we'll just have to hoof it in the dark. Can't be any more than a half mile."

"C'mon everyone. I'll lead the way," Tori says trying to sound confident. "I know a thing or two about navigating in darkness. Grab the belt or the shirt of the person in front of you, and we'll take our time till we find our way out. I sure hate leaving Mace here alone like this though." They take a moment to queue up and grab a handhold on the person in front. Tori starts taking measured steps as she did when she was blind, and slowly but surely they move forward.

The first hundred yards they walk are awkward at best highlighted by some nervous chirps of laughter as they try to overcome their fear of the dark. "Listen up, guys," Tori advises. "I need for all of us to remain very quiet so I can try to hear what's coming up. When I was blind I'd developed a very keen sense of hearing to make up for my lack of sight. There could be some nasty holes and drop-offs that I might be able to discern, but we need to remain silent to help me locate them."

The thought of holes and drop-offs gets everyone's attention, and they immediately clam up. During the course of the next quarter mile the sounds of ground water dripping off the cavern walls into puddles punctuates what Tori was talking about. At one point she stumbles in a shallow pool of water but recovers quickly and alerts everyone behind her what is coming up. In the distance they hear the sounds of Grey howling and the Windigo wailing announcing that they are hunting for Malcolm.

"If those sounds don't scare the bejesus out of Malcolm, I don't know what will," Lucretia says. "They scare me and I'm one of the good guys."

Again Tori advises everyone to remain silent, this time the admonition is a little late as Tori takes a step and falls ass-over-elbows down a steep grade. Kelli had been holding on to her belt and comes cascading down the fifteen-foot slope with her. They land together in a heap but are unhurt.

"Hey, where are you guys?" Maggie calls out. "Are you all right?"

"Yeah, I think we're fine," Tori replies. "Sit down on your butts and gently move down this slope. We're only about a dozen or so feet away from you. Just take your time. One by one Maggie and Lucretia do as she says, and they all meet at the bottom and reform their single file line. After carefully walking another several yards the ground begins to form another slope upward and before too long they're all out of the shallow pit and walking on level ground again.

"You're doing great, Tori!" Lucretia exclaims. "I don't know what we'd do without your sharp senses, and the thought of hanging back there in the dark with poor Mace waiting for someone to show up is not a pleasant thought."

"Happy to be of service," Tori tries to say brightly and right at that moment she stumbles again over something low and hard. "Hey, I just found a pair of steel rails. The miners probably ran their ore cars along these. I'm pretty sure if we follow them, they'll lead us to the mine's entrance. Just in case, though, let's continue walking as we have. No telling what other surprises we might bump into."

Again they walk in silence allowing Tori's sense of hearing to be their guide. They round a bend, and Tori calls out words that brighten everyone's spirits, "Daylight! I see daylight." Two hundred yards later they exit the mine and are greeted by Chief Muldoon with a contingent of his men.

"Boy, are we glad to see you!" the chief calls out. "We got here about thirty minutes ago and weren't quite sure where you were."

"Yeah, we're darn glad to be out of that hole in the mountain," Lucretia replies, "and thrilled to see you. Honestly, if it weren't for Tori leading the way, no telling where we'd be now." Lucretia, Kelli, and Maggie hug Tori and thank her for bringing them back out into the light of day. A guardsman approaches and offers them bottles of water which they happily accept.

"Where are Robert and Clay and that Windigo thing? I sure hope they've got it under control because I don't relish the thought of bringing my men into its dark home territory to try and kill it."

The four women take quick turns filling in details about the Windigo appearing to behave itself so far, and about Malcolm Land's murdering Mace as he took a bullet meant for Lucretia. "It was the bravest thing I've ever seen anyone do," she manages to say with a catch in her voice. "Clay, Rennie, Robert, and Grey are hunting for Malcolm now. I swear it was the damndest thing I ever saw: The Windigo leading the four of them off into the darkness to get my brother. Never thought I'd see the day when an evil, man-eating spirit shows more character than my goddamn brother."

"I'm very sorry about your loss," the chief says. "Seems like I've been saying that a lot these last couple of days. Heck, we thought the shooting of that young server at the lodge, and then Thomas Arrowsmith was bad enough, but then all of those folks in Copper Harbor and our men at Fort Wilkins. I've got a lot of men that just want to hunt your brother and that damn creature, regardless of whatever deal Robert says he's struck with it. And frankly, I'm inclined to let them."

"Chief, believe me, we all sympathize," Kelli says, "but one thing I've learned is to trust Robert

Midew's advice. I definitely do, and you would do well to heed what he says. He's got a knowledge and wisdom that's most unusual … and always accurate."

"Yeah, I know that Ranger Katterman," he acknowledges. "I understand that he's got very special talents, but still …" He just let those words hang in the air. He then instructs his men to grab their infrared head gear and weapons, and to follow our lead to where we left Mace's body.

Chapter 28

MALCOLM LAND HUDDLES behind a large boulder and curses to himself as he realizes that once again he's failed to kill his sister. "I swear that dang woman has more lives than a cat. At least I knocked off that old black man so that's one less person I have to worry about."

He feels the large gemstones in his pocket and mumbles, "I think it's time for me to get the hell out of here and cut my losses before that thing and Lucretia's pals catch up with me." He comes out of hiding and walks close to the edge of the chasm.

"Well, I'm sure as hell not getting across here." He turns around and retraces his steps in the direction from which he'd come.

The Windigo leads us on a swift jaunt from one cavern to another. Rennie and I do our best to keep up with Robert and Grey who are just a few paces behind the evil one. We go from one cavern to another trying to catch up with Malcolm, and along the way we see new wonders that Brockway Mountain has held secret for centuries. Veins of copper, silver, and gold attract our attention as our headlamps and flashlights reveal their bounty.

"Hey, hold up a second, will ya?!" I holler to Robert. "I'm not in as good of shape as you guys are." "Me neither!" Rennie confesses. I hear Robert ask the Windigo to slow down, but it keeps forging ahead without us.

"Deal! Protect!" it hurls back at Robert as he and Grey slow down to join us. The Windigo continues on, and Robert surmises, "It'll find us when it's located Malcolm, or he may just change his mind and eat us," he jests, but Rennie and I aren't laughing at that thought. Grey nuzzles my knees as if to infer that Robert is just teasing. In the near-distance we hear the Windigo's wail echo off the cavern walls. "I hope that wail is meant to rattle Malcolm because it sure as hell spooks the crap out of me." Rennie nods his agreement.

"I've never ventured into this part of the cave system," Robert confesses. "No telling what kind of surprises we're likely to encounter."

"Gee, swell! Surprises! That'll be fun," I blurt out sarcastically.

"C'mon!" Robert exhorts us. "We've got to catch up or the Windigo may, indeed, change its mind about helping us."

"Swell!" I sarcastically reply again.

We forge ahead with Grey leading the way and finally come to a grotto that Robert finds very interesting. "Look here at these cave paintings. They're very different from what we've seen before. I believe these paintings show our Anishinaabe ancestors camped by the great salt sea in what we believe are the Canadian maritime provinces." Robert inspects the cave paintings closely and says, "This portion depicts the origin of the Megis shell as a gift to our original people." We examine the painting and recognize the white glow coming from the shell and the exaltation of the native villagers. We look in the soil in front of the paintings and see the Windigo's large footprints.

"The evil one will always pine for the power of the Megis shell, but it's something it will never possess." We see its footprints lead off into another dark cavern and follow after Robert and Grey. Before long we finally catch up to the Windigo which is waiting for us. "Bad Hoo Man is just up ahead. I can smell it. Meat! Want meat!" it snarls salaciously.

"We need to do this our way," Robert says to the Windigo. "We need to try and capture him and bring him to justice outside of the mountain."

"Justice? What is justice without a full belly? Meat! I kill him now!"

"You have honored your pledge to us so far, Windigo, now we Hoo Mans must try to stop one of our own." The Windigo snorts its dismay but complies.

We all quietly move forward looking to surprise Malcolm. Grey takes the lead, then Robert, with Rennie and me tagging along behind. The Windigo goes in another direction so we can cut off any exits to this persistent assassin.

"I really want to kill him," Rennie says to me uncharacteristically. As his father I don't like hearing the bloodlust in his voice, but I feel exactly the same way. Mace was a great anchor to our lives, a touchstone for all things good and right. And now, he's gone because this pimple of a human being is pissed off at his sister. "We'll get him," I say to Rennie. "But, we need to let justice prevail. Your mom, Tori, and Lucretia are going to show Chief Muldoon and his men where Mace's body is."

And, a few moments later, we see flashes of light and the sounds of footsteps as they appear out of the gloomy dark and settle around Mace. We're tempted to holler over to them but don't want to give our location away to Malcolm. That proves to be a mistake as the sound of a gunshot echoes loudly off the cavern walls and one of Chief Muldoon's men goes down. The men and ladies immediately scatter for the protection of large rocks, and I hear Robert say to Grey, "Attack but do not kill!" The great wolf springs off into the dark and the next thing we hear is a whole lot of snarling and another gunshot. We run up to a spot near the edge of the chasm and see Grey standing menacingly over a sobbing Malcolm Land with the Windigo watching the spectacle from a few away. "Meat!" it drools.

"Finally, at long last, Mr. Land, we meet again," I say evenly. Grey continues to keep our assassin pinned on the ground, and Robert collects his handgun and rifle which he gives to me and Rennie. We're more than happy to keep the guns trained on Malcolm. My only concern is that Rennie chooses to blow the bastard's head off. I look over at my son who has anger etched on his face and we make eye contact. He knows what I'm thinking. "Don't worry, I won't do it, Dad, unless he tries to make a run for it."

"Get it off of me!" Malcolm screams, referring to Grey who isn't giving him any room to move. We all know that Malcolm isn't going anywhere since we have him totally surrounded. Robert instructs Grey to release Malcolm who slowly staggers to his feet with contempt written on his features. Robert calls out to the ladies and Chief Muldoon, "We've got him. You can come out now."

Maggie, Tori, and Lucretia are deeply saddened by seeing our beloved Mace loaded into a body bag and the slain officer laid into another. I don't know how I'll ever be able to help Rennie, Tori, and Maggie deal with this loss, and a torrent of tears quietly cascades down my face as I wonder how I'll ever be able to deal with his being gone too. Sensing my sorrow, Robert walks up to me and places his forehead on mine. Instantly, I feel a surge of loving energy and see Mace's smiling face coming to me from somewhere beyond. The message is that he's at peace, and that provides me with some solace. "Thanks," I say to Robert. "He was like my true north star." Robert nods his head affirmatively, and we then turn our attention to Malcolm.

"Ready to go back to prison, Malcolm," I say say to him.

"No prison will ever hold me," he taunts back at me, and something inside of me says he's probably right. Robert calls back to the chief saying we'll catch up with everyone at the mine entrance, and Rennie pushes Malcolm forward with the muzzle of the Malcolm's rifle. The Windigo watches this Hoo Man spectacle with hungry interest. Some thirty minutes later we've traversed the caverns the Windigo had lead us through earlier and finally reach the others at the entrance to the cave. Lucretia walks up to Robert and slaps him hard across his face. "The thought that any member of the Land Family would behave like you have is like an indelible stain that will never go away. You're a disgrace to our parents' memories!"

Malcolm looks at her while rubbing his face where Lucretia had slapped him, and he utters an obscenity. Grey growls at him, and Robert and the chief discuss transporting the bodies to the morgue and Malcolm to jail in Calumet. At the mention of that, Malcolm swings around and grabs the rifle out of Rennie's hand and points it at us.

"I'm not going anywhere with you!" he taunts. He points the rifle at Lucretia and begins slowly backing out of the mine entrance. "And now, dear sister, I do need to be leaving you now." He begins to pull the trigger when a large bony hand reaches out, grabs him by the neck, and lifts him off the ground. A rifle shot rings out but harmlessly hits the cavern's ceiling. The Windigo holds his prize up for all to see. "Hoo Man! Mine!"

Robert, the chief, and I look at each other. Despite our respect for the rule of law, the three of us talk about our options. Lucretia joins us and says one word, "Justice!" and we all know what she means.

The four of us are joined by Rennie as we approach Malcolm who is hopelessly held in the Windigo's grasp. "Windigo," Robert says, "You remember our deal, yes?"

"Deal, meat, protect mountain's secrets! Yes, I remember deal."

"Good," Robert says, "and we're counting on you to keep it from this point forward, yes?"

"Deal," it affirms. "I do this for you and the Anishinaabe, the original people."

Robert looks to the chief and says, "It's your call, Chief, what form of 'justice' do you want?" The chief considers Malcolm Land's history of violence and the expense and nuisance of keeping Malcolm in the correctional system. He looks to his men who are angry at the death of another one of their own. His second-in-command looks at him and says, "We all vote to end it here, Chief!" Chief Muldoon and Robert look at Lucretia who nods her understanding, and then Robert approaches the Windigo and Malcolm. "We've made a deal with you, Windigo, and this Hoo Man is yours. Take him as our first offering of meat. Take him, consume him, and spread his bones in the darkest recesses of your home."

The Windigo replies with a resonant laugh as he grasps Malcolm's neck even tighter. Malcolm tries to resist, but the Windigo erupts in a victorious wail and walks off into the direction of its lair. Malcolm tries to scream a final plea for mercy, but the sound of his gurgling voice is cut off midscream, followed by the sounds of bones crunching … then silence.

Chapter 29

W E ALL EMERGE FROM the darkness of Brockway Mountain into the brightness of a lovely Keweenaw Peninsula day. Despite our living another day, none of us is ebullient. Yes, Malcolm Land is finally and thankfully dead, and the Windigo has pledged to keep his promise to remain under the mountain and not feed on Hoo Mans, but there's not much else to feel happy about.

Mace's death will haunt each of us for the remainder of our days. I see Rennie and Ranger Kelli holding hands which makes me feel a little

less concerned about my son's emotional well-being. Tori joins Maggie and me as we prepare to take the cog railway up to the parking lot. Robert and Grey join us also as we watch Chief Muldoon and his contingent of men take the bodies of Mace and the fallen officer to the morgue. I've given the chief my contact information so we can talk about where to send Mace's body after the legal forensic work is done. We all want to properly bury our friend back home in Indiana.

Robert and I agree that we should all take time to heal, and I've assured him that I'll return in a couple of weeks to finish the photography assignment with Rennie and Kelli. Lucretia says she remains committed for the Land Foundation to curate images of the cave paintings for worldwide distribution, and Tori says she'd like to stay here with Rennie until I return and then see how she feels afterward. And for now, I just want to help Lucretia return to Chicago, and for Maggie and me to get home to the friendly confines of our home in the brewery complex. I sure don't relish the thought of telling Bodie that Uncle Mace is gone.

We thank Chief Muldoon for his bravery and offer our deep condolences on the death of so many innocent people. We say goodbye to Robert and Grey for now, arrive at our cars in the parking lot, and drive the few miles down the mountain to the Evergreen Point Lodge. We've only been gone from home for about a week, but it seems like an eternity.

When we get to the lodge, Lucretia and Tori retire to their rooms, and we all agree to meet for dinner in about two hours. Maggie holds lovingly onto my arm as we walk down the corridor and into our room. Words fail us as we sit on the bed and look into each other's eyes. "I love you," I say. "I'm so sorry for exposing you to all of this heartache. I never would've dreamed anything like this could happen up here." And then I think about Mace and how sad I am that he's gone. My eyes fill with tears, and Maggie holds me close. We lie down, holding each other, and eventually fall asleep.

Tori enters her room and goes to the bathroom sink to freshen up, and to try to wash some of the sad memories of the last few days away. She's exhausted, both emotionally and physically. The sadness of Mace's death hangs on her like a funeral shroud, and she weeps for an important person in her life who is now gone forever. She kicks her shoes off but is too weary to even undress. She just plops down on the bed and listens to the wind and birds outside of her open window. "Life goes on," she whispers to herself, and she softly hums a melody that was always one of Mace's favorites. She closes her eyes and drifts off to sleep.

Several minutes later there is a knock on her door. It rouses Tori from a deep sleep, but she's uncertain of the nature of the sound. There's another knock on her door. and this time she realizes that someone is outside her room.

"One second," she says as she tries to wipe away the last vestiges of her truncated sleep. "What is it?" she says as she opens the door and is totally befuddled by who she sees standing in the doorway. It's her therapist, Dr. Adrian Dale.

"Adrian?! What are you doing here? How did you find me?"

"Hello Tori, it's good to see you. You told me where you would be staying up here, remember? May I please come in?"

"Look Adrian, I don't know why you've traveled all the way up here, but this is not a good time for me. I'm very tired and really need to get some rest. Perhaps we can talk when I get home, but this is not a good time."

She begins to lead him out of the room, but Dr. Dale pushes the door closed and locks it.

"What are you doing? Get out of my room. I told you this is not a good time for me. Please go now!"

"Oh, I've really missed you, Tori, in fact I've been thinking about you quite a lot. I thought I could meet you up here, and we could go away together for a few days, just the two of us. How's that sound?"

Tori is very alarmed by the unannounced presence of her therapist who she was already beginning to suspect is more than a little creepy. "That's not happening, Dr. Dale, and I find your presence and suggestion to be totally unprofessional and unwanted. I told you I've been through a lot and I need some rest. I want you to leave now or I'll have to call for security."

"Now, now, Tori that won't be necessary, and I've got something to help you rest," and at that, he pulls a syringe from his jacket pocket and stabs it into Tori's upper arm. She lets out a yelp and reaches for her phone. In seconds the drug courses through Tori's bloodstream and she falls to the floor unconscious.

Dr. Adrian Dale lifts up her lifeless body and drops her onto the bed. He turns out the light and stands over her greedily admiring her beautiful face, her golden hair, and her trim, athletic body. He places his hand on her breast and closes his eyes in delight. He goes off to the bathroom to pee and returns totally naked and aroused. He begins unbuttoning her shirt and marvels at the pretty lace trim on her amply filled bra. He begins to unbuckle her belt and slides onto the bed next to her. He slides her pants off and is about to have his way with Tori when out of nowhere he notices a golden light shimmering throughout the darkened room. He turns to look for the source of the unusual light, but seeing nothing, he casts his gaze back at his unconscious, delicious-looking prize. That's when he sees an ancient-looking Indian woman with milky white eyes sitting on the edge of the bed.

"What the???" Adrian says. "Who are you, and how'd you get in here?"

Nokomis casts her stare into the therapist's eyes, and he recoils in sharp pain. "Aaarrrggghhh! Stop it!" he commands imperiously. "Who are you and what do you want?"

Nokomis stares at Dr. Dale, and says,"Who I am is the person who will prevent you from harming this woman. She is special to us!"

"Get out now, old woman, or I'll throw you out!" Adrian demands. Nokomis looks at his now flaccid "manliness," then points and giggles like an adolescent girl. "I don't think so," she replies.

"Why, I never …" Adrian begins as he reaches for the old healer's arm. Nokomis deflects his aggressive reach and surrounds him in her golden aura. The hapless therapist is unable break free. "What are you doing to me?" he cries out.

"Oh, something that should've happened long ago when you began abusing your female clients."

"But how could a dried up old Indian hag know anything about me?" he protests.

She looks at him unsympathetically and evenly replies, "Oh, information has a way of flowing to me. C'mon, let's go, Dr. Adrian Dale. Your therapy session is up!"

"But where are you taking me, and I need my clothes!" he weakly protests.

"There's something I want you to meet, something that lives under the great mountain that I've made a deal with, and oh, you won't be needing your clothing."

A moment later both Nokomis and Dr. Dale twinkle amid golden photons of light, and then they're gone. Two seconds later the doctor's clothes disappear as well, and Tori rests peacefully, fully clothed again, safe and secure inside her room.

About two hours later Maggie and I walk into the lodge's dining room and see Lucretia already seated at our table. She has a cocktail in her hand and raises her glass to us as we approach. "Greetings!" she says warmly.

"Greetings!" Maggie and I reply in unison. "Were you able to catch a few winks?" Maggie asks. "Maybe a few," Lucretia replies. "I just have so many emotions whirling around in my brain now," Lucretia admits. "I never would've guessed our trip would turn out as it has in a million years." I give her shoulder a gentle squeeze. "I know, Lucretia, none of us could've. Not even Robert or Nokomis."

"So, should we think about returning home soon?" Maggie asks.

"I think so," I reply. "I want to talk with Robert, Rennie, and Kelli to see about rescheduling my return to photograph the cave art, but I'm ready to return home."

"Oh yeah! Photographing cave art! That's the reason we came up here. Now I remember," Maggie jests. "Do you really want to go back inside that mountain again, Clay?"

"Not really. Two summers of death and turmoil is enough for a lifetime, but I've made a promise to do the project, and I know how important it is to Robert and his people."

Just then Tori joins us wiping the last remnants of sleep from her eyes. She yawns and gives us a small smile. "Hi guys," she manages. "Don't mind me, I'm still waking up."

"Did you get a good nap?" Lucretia asks her.

"I'm not sure," comes her frank reply. "I must've really needed it because I feel drugged, and I had the weirdest dream."

"Well, being up here in the land of ancient Indians and sorcerers will do that to you," I offer.

"No, I mean this dream felt so real. I dreamt that my therapist, Adrian Dale, came to my room and was pressuring me to go away with him."

"That is weird," Maggie says, "but from what you've told us about him, I guess I'm not surprised."

"But it felt so real, Maggie. Like he was standing in my room."

"I guess the trauma of what we've experienced is enough to give all of us nightmares for a lifetime," Lucretia offers. Maggie and I nod our heads in agreement.

"I suppose," Tori concedes, "but it felt so real ..."

After dinner Maggie, Lucretia, and I spend the rest of the evening just lounging around the lodge's grounds. None of us feel very keen about doing much of anything. Kelli and Rennie call to say their goodbyes for now and agree to stow my photography gear for my return in a few weeks. Robert also texts me to say that he's busy with the authorities trying to tie up legal ends. He informs me that he and Chief Muldoon have agreed that they'd say that the Windigo was killed under the mountain and would never bother Hoo Mans again. No sense in keeping folks scared to death or wanting to explore the mountain looking for stuff they have no business looking for. I just pray that plan works, but up here in the Keweenaw Peninsula, one never knows for sure. We decide to turn in and get an early start in the morning.

The next morning feels rather anticlimatic. The ladies and I enjoy a leisurely breakfast and pack our vehicles for the drive south to Chicago and then back home to Indiana. Maggie and Lucretia climb into Lucretia's car, and I get in my truck for a long solitary drive with lots of time to think about the meaning of life. I look over at my empty passenger seat that Mace had occupied and realize that the older generation of our family is now gone for good, and that my time will come someday too.

As we pull our vehicles away from our parking spots, I look in the rearview mirror at Tori who's waving goodbye to us. I see Grey emerge from the trees and saunter up to her. A moment later Nokomis materializes as well. I wave to all of them until they're out of view.

"Carpe diem," I murmur aloud to myself, and for the first time ever I truly understand that, despite the magic of life, everything and everyone eventually comes and goes.

~ The End ~

About the Author
Stuart Fabe

'M A VERY FORTUNATE MAN! Marla and I live in the bucolic countryside near Greencastle, Indiana, and it's from here that many of my creative impulses spring. Yes, it's true that I was a "suit" for many years in Cincinnati, Ohio, but even during those years, I always kept a wet darkroom where I created fine photographic prints. It was how I maintained the soul of an artist while striving to make a living in the corporate world.

Since retiring from that life several years ago, I've directed my creative energies to writing suspense novels, mastering night sky photography, illustrating whimsical scenes, and weaving on hardshell gourds. Over the last four decades, I've also published six fine art photography books and exhibited my artwork, photographs, and books at numerous art shows, galleries, and libraries. Along

the way, I've made good friends, and I'm proud that many pieces of my art grace homes across the country.

Evening Intrigue is my seventh novel and the sixth story in my Clay Arnold series. I write purely for entertainment and enjoy crafting page-turning plots with fascinating characters. I hope you enjoy!